I0606637

Julia had only one chance to escape, and she prayed her magic would work...

Listrel was smaller than he appeared on the stoop, not much taller than she, but he had probably a hundred pounds on her. He was dressed in dirty jeans and a shirt that may have once been white but now was an indiscernible color of filth. He smiled at her, revealing a mouth half filled with teeth.

"I asked you where you thought you were going?"

Julia stood to her full height, though that did little to make her intimidating. Quickly she scanned the emergency escape ladders overhead until her eyes rested on an object. She breathed a sigh of relief.

"Something funny, girlie?" Listrel asked, anger flashing in his voice for the first time.

"I suggest you go back the way you came," she said in a voice that sounded foreign to her.

He chuckled. "I don't think I want to do that. Not without you at least."

One more step. One more second. Now!

There was a loud crash, and the man was slumped on the ground twenty or so feet in front of her. Julia tried to catch her breath. Thankfully one of the tenants above was an avid gardener. The large planters, probably in violation of fire codes, lay in pieces at her feet, their former occupants scattered along the street. Blood mixed with the dirt and terra cotta surrounding the man. Julia could make out the faintest movement from him. He appeared to be breathing but was not moving. She kept her eyes on the stilled figure as she gave him a wide berth and began to walk back out of the alley.

"So, what have we here?" a new voice said behind her.

A rough hand trapped the scream in Julia's mouth.

In the final book of the Four Corners Trilogy, Levi, Aura, Julia, and the rest of our group are split up and scattered across two worlds, but their goal remains the same: defeat Lady Grustmiener and secure the peaceful future of Earth. As they race to be reunited, new forces, both for and against them, come into play. Will they find each other in time, or will evil triumph once and for all?

KUDOS for *One Earth*

In *One Earth* by Kristin Durfee, Levi Roberts is once again fighting for Esotera, only this time, his own world is also in peril. The evil and power-hungry Lady Grustmiener is still trying to take over both worlds, and thinking she has finally killed Levi—the Missing Link—she is more determined than ever to see her evil plan succeed. But she has underestimated not only the people of the Four Corners world, but the people of Earth as well. If she wants to rule the worlds, she is going to have to fight for it against people equally determined to see her fail. But Levi, Queen Aura, and the rest of the gang from Esotera will have their hands full stopping her in time. As delightful as the first two books, this one is charming, intriguing, and full of twists and turns—an adventure you won't want to end. ~ *Taylor Jones, The Review Team of Taylor Jones & Regan Murphy*

One Earth by Kristen Durfee is the third and final book in her Four Corners trilogy. This time, the evil would-be ruler Lady Grustmiener stabs Levi during a battle in Esotera, and thinking she has killed him, hurries through a portal to Earth to claim her prize—the rule and dominion of both the Four Corners world and Earth. But it's not quite as simple as she seems to think. Although mortally wounded, Levi was healed and survived, and he and Queen Aura refuse to allow this evil witch to rule their land. But wars are full of surprises, and this one is no different. Julia follows Lady Grustmiener to Earth, trying to keep tabs on her, while the rest of the gang tries to quell the fighting in the Four Corners world. But prophesies of an even larger battle are foretold by an animal that can see the future, and the defenders fear the war will soon engulf Levi's home world as well. *One Earth* is a worthy addition to the series, and as much as I enjoyed it, I am almost sad to see the story end. Well written, fast paced, and enchanting, this is a story you'll enjoy reading over and over again. *~ Regan Murphy, The Review Team of Taylor Jones & Regan Murphy*

ACKNOWLEDGMENTS

So much of the early writing process involves the author alone. Sometimes with music, sometimes with the din of a coffee shop or other public place, but the method is a simplistic one: sit and write.

But then once the story is complete, the writer has to let go a bit. Let the work out into the world so others can look at it and help make it better. To get it as polished and perfect as possible so when the reader holds it, they are able to delve right in without interruption. This process, when done well, isn't noticeable. It's an incredible amount of work to get to that place.

I learned so much during the four-year journey of publishing this trilogy, and I am eternally grateful to those in my life who helped me along.

Lauri, Faith, Arwen, Jack, and the entire Black Opal Books team: you held my hand in various aspects in bringing these books to the public. It wasn't easy, but I've emerged as a better and stronger writer because of all of your help.

Jessie, Erin, and Amy: your early reading of drafts was instrumental in making this book happen. Thanks for giving me hours of your time over the years. These books are what they are because of you all.

Matt C: I am so proud to have your beautiful artwork on my covers. Your talent is incredible, and I'm blessed that you shared it with me.

To my friends and family for your continued interest and excitement. It's been a wild ride, and I'm glad you've all been on it with me.

And finally, to Matt: for the times you "kicked me out" to go write and the support you've given me to follow my dreams, I couldn't have done this without you.

One Earth

Kristin Durfee

A Black Opal Books Publication

DEDICATION

*To Levi and Aura, for showing me
the magic of your world.
And to The Three Bears,
for showing me the magic of my own.*

in absentia luci, tenebrae vincunt
(in the absence of light, darkness prevails)

Chapter 1

Sweat began to gather under Julia's arm pits and behind her knees. The cacophony of the noises that surrounded her made her ears ache. The battle had been loud, but it was nowhere near the din that bombarded her now. How was it possible that just moments before she had been in a magical land and now was walking on a busy street in her world?

The fighting she had left felt like a lifetime ago. She'd forgotten what her world felt like and wondered how long it had been since she'd left it—since the woman named Theirra came and took her away. Took her to the other place with magic and dragons. A place where she was not alone in her powers.

She turned her concentration and energy on gathering as many images as she could in her sight line. She could feel the coolness surrounding her brain that indicated Jada, one of the other kids that Theirra recruited to come back with her, was reading her thoughts and trying to figure out where she was. Julia didn't know how much time she had, and she was desperate to relay where she was. She willed the woman in front of her to turn around, even just partially, for just a second so Jada could see who it was.

Lady Grustmiener knocked on a door.

"Who is there?" a deep voice asked.

"She is waiting for me," she answered.

"Who is there?" the voice repeated.

"Oh, let her in, she has come from far away and worked hard enough to get here, Listrel." The woman's voice from inside sounded old, or possibly far away. Julia strained to hear.

Thankfully, just before she entered the building, Lady Grustmiener turned and her reflection caught in a mirror. Like a jolt, Julia felt her mind snap back to normal temperature, and she began to pant slightly at the sudden abandonment. The shock of seeing her must have done something to Julia's mind and enabled her to break the connection with Jada. She'd never been able to beat him before. In all the times they practiced together, Jada was always able to break through. This time when Julia felt the coolness creep back in, she was able to push him away. She needed to concentrate now and didn't have time for someone else to share her thoughts.

Sitting back against the brick wall, she tried to catch her breath and ignore the trash smell wafting from the can next to her. The last few hours had been a whirlwind. She'd followed Levi through the woods as soon as the battle had begun. While Julia knew that she should stay to help watch over the castle, she was tired of standing around and wanted to see some action. The fighting hadn't come close to where she was stationed, and she suspected that her and Levi's post there was more to keep them out of danger than the building itself.

She left some protections behind and rigged a sort of

an alarm system to alert her if someone tried to cross into the castle grounds. She told herself that she would only follow Levi a short way and would return at the first sign of trouble but soon found herself walking farther and farther away from the place she was supposed to protect.

She hid behind trees and boulders, watching in horror, as person after person came at Levi. Several times when it looked like his foe had the upper hand, Julia lifted a branch or shifted the person's weapon, so Levi was able to prevail. She was so absorbed in watching him battle a man and trying to figure out how she could help, she almost didn't notice Lady Grustmiener in the distance.

Something caused Julia's eye to shift, and she saw the woman standing a few yards away with burning hatred visible even from the distance they stood apart. Julia wasn't proud of what she did next. She wheeled around and ran toward the castle, but after about fifty feet, she stopped and turned back. Levi was still fighting. He still had not seen what was approaching him. Julia tried to concentrate and push Lady Grustmiener back, but she was unable to even move a hair on the woman's head. The power within the woman scared Julia even more. It was a resistance that she'd never felt before.

Afraid that if she yelled she would get Levi killed by a momentary distraction, she began to affect the people and animals that stood between the two of them, slowly brushing them away. It was exhausting work, a long way from the branches that Tab had her lift and lower in their training, but she got into a rhythm and ignored the ache in her mind from the effort. The path that was created gave Levi a direct line of sight to Lady Grustmiener, but he still did not see her. Unable to take it anymore, Julia summoned all the strength she had left and caused a root to reach up and grab the ankles of the man he was fighting, sending him backward. The man lost his balance, fell upon a rock, and did not get up. The path she'd created seemed to work, because, as soon as Levi looked up, he stiffened. It was clear he spotted Lady Grustmiener at once.

Julia began to back away quietly, unsure if she could watch the battle commence between the two, but was soon drawn to inch forward, unable to look away. She covered her mouth with her hands, not trusting herself not to yell out. She was terrified of breaking Levi's concentration. She felt the tug of her defenses at the castle and wondered if it was from a friend or foe, but she didn't dare return and leave her vantage point. Something in her told her that no matter what, this was where she was supposed to be.

Fear coursed through her. She felt a connection to Levi as soon as they'd met. He shared a lot of her insecurities and helped her in her training and confidence. As scared as Julia was, it seemed Levi was well equipped to fight the powerful woman. For a brief moment, Julia was sure that he was going to win. He'd borne down on her, even cutting her arm. Julia was just breathing a sigh of relief when the air around her seemed to shift. As if the world had slowed down and a wave of fury seemed to build in Lady Grustmiener. Before Julia could comprehend what was happening, the crazed woman began to advance with renewed fervor. In an instant, it all fell apart.

Levi's attention was drawn to his left, so he didn't see the spear as it moved directly toward his chest. Her hands still over her mouth, the air caught in Julia's throat, and she forgot how to do anything, even to breathe or call to him. Before she had time to float a leaf into Lady Grustmiener's eyes, only the hilt appeared outside of his body. A scream filled the woods, and for a second Julia checked that her hands still covered her lips, afraid it was unwittingly coming from her, but she made no sound. Lady Grustmiener pulled the weapon from Levi's chest, and he fell in an instant. She began laughing as she retreated through the trees.

Without thinking, without waiting to confirm that Levi was truly dead, Julia followed the wretched woman. As she got closer, she could hear more laughter emanating from her. A sudden urge to wrap her hands around the woman's throat made her fingers tremble, but Julia fought the impulse. She knew she couldn't kill her, both physically and mentally. No matter how the ache of Levi's loss punctured her, she had to admit to herself that her weakness overshadowed any thoughts of revenge. She felt slightly sickened to realize that she would not be able to avenge any of them. All she could do was follow and hope to trap his killer until someone else could come and finish her off.

Soundlessly, Julia followed as they moved into a part of the woods void of fighters. The quiet felt strange as the noises of the battle melted away from them. Several times she had to freeze and jump behind a tree or bush as Lady Grustmiener looked around. It was one of these times, perched behind a strange looking tree that resembled an evergreen but with a twinkling blue light, that another person came out to join them. Julia held her breath to better hear and, hopefully, not be heard.

"My lady," the woman said. She was small, maybe only four feet tall, but it was obvious that power surrounded her, like waves of heat rising off asphalt in the summer.

"Have you done it?"

"I have. The portal will be open for only a few moments, then it will close again."

"And where will I be once I go through?"

"In the place you described," the woman continued. "I went through earlier today to ensure that the location was correct. Are you sure you do not want me to accompany you?"

"Travel with me?" Lady Grustmiener laughed. "What makes you think I have any continued use for you?"

"I can stay here then, wait for your return." The woman seemed stung at the lady's ungratefulness.

"Oh, no. No, my dear witch. I cannot have you telling others where I have gone or risk them being able to find me. No, that will not do."

The witch—Julia *knew* there was something strange about her—cowered back a half step, but she was too late. Lady Grustmiener moved her arm in a sweeping motion, and the woman fell. Her blood, mixed with what still clung of Levi's, covered the spear. Without looking back, Lady Grustmiener stepped through a shimmering spot a few feet to her right and disappeared.

Julia didn't hesitate. She ran forward, and before she could fully think, before she could second guess herself or make a pro and con list about what she was doing, she flung herself through the same spot.

Sunlight blazed in her eyes and the honk of horns filled her ears.

Chapter 2

Next

S he's in Philadelphia."

The words rang in Levi's ears. How was this possible? How did the portals open, much less bring the two of them through? Were they still open? Was there still time to go and get them and bring them back? A strong pull to protect little Julia tugged him in a painful way. He needed to save her.

The events of the last few hours swirled around him. He'd been killed. Lady Grustmiener had stabbed him, but then Emily and Adam found him and rushed him back to the castle with Kalan, the kid who could turn invisible. Adam used every ounce of power he had to bring Levi back to life and sacrificed his own to do it. Theirra, too, had not made it through the fighting. Her blood still covering Aura's hands and tear-stained face. And now Julia was gone? Missing in his world following that dangerous woman? It was too much, it was all too much.

"I do not understand," Aura said with frustration in her voice. "Levi? Levi, explain."

From the expression on her face, she had obviously been trying to figure out what this information meant. The group from his world looked back and forth between each other, too stunned to speak.

"Levi," she repeated in a pleading voice.

"She's in Philadelphia," Jada repeated.

Levi looked over at Emily. Even in the dim light, he could see the fear in her eyes.

"I do not understand," Aura said. "Where is this place?"

"Wait, like our Philadelphia? Like Pennsylvania?" Tab asked.

"Please, someone, explain," Aura repeated, worry increasing in her voice.

"In my world. Somehow, somehow Lady Grustmiener got through," Levi said. "She must have gone through a portal."

"It's strange," Jada continued. "For a flash, it looked like Julia was showing me the same portal we went through. It was like she was trying to tell me something. Maybe how to follow her?"

"If the portals are open," Levi said, trying to figure it out, "I wonder if whatever shut them could have scrambled them."

"Scrambled?" Aura looked confused.

"Yeah, switched them around, moved them. Ours was from Dallas. That's how we got here."

"And Dallas is not in Philadelphia?" Milskar asked.

"No," Raigan said slowly. "It's about fifteen-hundred miles apart."

"Maybe whatever she did to open them, or whatever magic was used to close them, moved them around. Maybe they don't come in and out at the same places anymore. Have you ever heard of something like that happening?"

"The portals do not move," Calanthe said in her calm, commanding voice. "They have stood for hundreds of years. They are not moving things."

"Well, maybe this one is," Jada said defensively.

"You must be mistaken," Calanthe said again.

"Well, I'm not," he said.

"All right, for the moment who cares if the portals have changed locations—" Levi started.

"The portals—" Calanthe tried to interrupt.

"Yes, we know, they don't move," Levi cut her off. "Let's just forget that for right now. Maybe the more important thing is that they are open."

"You were right," Aura said in a hollow voice. "You said that she would not stop with our world. I did not believe you. You knew she would try to cross over."

"I had a hunch, yeah, but it's not like we would have been able to stop her. I mean, she killed me, so that's one thing that would have prevented me." The look on Aura's face reminded Levi that she didn't know how close to losing each other they had come.

"They are in our world, in my world." He knew it was his voice speaking the words, but they sounded a million miles away.

"I do not understand." She looked over at Jada. "The portals are closed. How did they get through?"

"I—I don't know. I just see her there."

"And you are completely sure that's where she is?" Levi asked. He didn't want to challenge Jada, but the kid had just recently improved his powers from seeing ideas and intentions inside a person's mind to a so-called "live feed."

"She knew I was looking in," Jada said. "She made a point to look around the city and at signs so I could tell."

A silent hum fell over them. The darkness was beginning to make it difficult to continue the conversation where they were as they could hardly see one another. Levi's body had begun to sag under the weight and stress of the day. His mind was buzzing, but the only thing he wanted to do was lay down.

"We should go inside," he suggested to the group.

"What about the war?" Galina asked. Even in the dark, an intensity could be seen in her eyes. A chill went through Levi that had nothing to do with the cooling air.

"I imagine that it will be over now, at least here," Milskar said.

"Do you think everyone will just stop fighting?" Kalan asked.

"There is no one left to fight for," Aura said.

"Like hell, there isn't!" Galina said. "Do you think I am just going to let them kill Adam and get away with it? Do you think I am not going to hunt down and kill every last one of them?"

"Galina, I know you are upset—" Aura began but was swiftly cut off.

"You have no idea," Galina seethed.

"I have more of an idea than you will ever know," Aura said with venom in her voice. "But these people were fighting for someone, not necessarily for themselves. Some were kidnapped from their homes and forced to bear arms for that terrible woman. She put her drive for power and revenge above all else. If they are willing to surrender, I believe we should let them. In the morning, I will send word to King Theaus of Lady Grustmiener's betrayal and will offer him an end to this fighting."

"And if he won't take it?" Levi asked.

"Then we will have to battle on two fronts. Right now, our priority needs to be sleep. Once our affairs are in order here, we will travel to your world."

As the group walked toward the castle, Levi pulled Aura aside. Milskar and Calanthe stayed back as well.

"Do you think we will be able to get through?" Levi asked.

"I hope so." The exhaustion was palpable in Aura's voice.

"And if not? And if the East and North do not want to surrender, what then?" Calanthe challenged.

"I do not know."

"That does not sound very convincing."

"Calanthe," Milskar warned.

"It is all right," Aura said, pinching the bridge of her nose. "She is right. I do not know what we are going to do. There is a half-fought battle going on around us that I have no idea if it will continue and, somehow, I need to figure out how to get to your world through portals we do not know are still open. If we do get through a portal, we do not know if it will be the same one they went through, and even if it is, we have no idea how to find them, or what to do with them when we do. Can we really bring a war to the other world too? Especially if one is still going on here? Am I to abandon my people to be slaughtered while I go after one individual?"

They looked at one another for a long time before Aura left them to enter the castle.

"Not very convincing at all," Calanthe said.

Levi was afraid that he agreed.

Chapter 3

King Theaus

It felt wonderful to Aura to sleep in her bed again, instead of the forest floor like the past few nights. For a moment, as the last dregs of sleep were wearing off, she was almost able to forget the events of the last few days. Heck, she was almost able to forget the events of the last few *years*. With her eyes still shut, she pretended that she was fifteen again. Her biggest care in the world was what part of the kingdom to ride Serenity, her beloved mare, through. Her father would have been asleep across the hall, and the entirety of the kingdom and its inhabitants would be his responsibility. The thought tasted delicious in her mouth, but just as the day dream enveloped her, something brushed against her leg and gave her a start, her senses on high alert again.

It brushed against her again, and she had to stifle a scream as she processed what was happening. It all came flooding back to her. The battle. Theirra. Almost losing everyone. Lady Grustmiener somehow escaping to the other world. Retreating to the castle in the night with Milskar, Calanthe, The Kids, and Levi. Levi!

She rolled over and faced his sleeping form in her bed. *In her bed.* More images flooded through her, like she was watching the previous few hours in a flash back. Going up to her room and not wanting to be alone. It had only been a few nights, but she had gotten used to him by her side while they slept under the stars and she didn't want him to go. The two of them crawling into her bed and her falling asleep as he held her tight. Emotions swirled around her, making her head spin slightly for each one that vied for her attention.

As if sensing her watching him, Levi awoke and rolled to face her. He took one look at her and burst into laughter. "Well, it's nice to see you too," he said.

"I—I—" she stammered.

"Aura, you don't have to look so horrified. How many nights have we slept next to one another?"

Before she could respond a quick knock came at her door and Milskar walked in, trailed by Calanthe. The look on their faces made Levi choke down even more giggles. Aura wanted to crawl into a dark space and never emerge. Thankfully, the two did recover quickly though.

"My queen, should we come back?" Milskar said, avoiding Aura's gaze as she scrambled out of bed.

"No—no, of course not. Milskar," she stammered and proceeded to turn bright red.

"I think it is about time," Calanthe said in her thick accent. Aura's mouth fell open.

"All right, all right. Milskar, Calanthe, good morning," Levi said. Aura was grateful that he was able to speak and put an end to the awkwardness. She still hadn't found her voice. "Aura didn't want to sleep alone, so I offered to keep watch in case someone decided to enter the castle. Nothing is going on."

Calanthe smiled but did not seem too convinced as Aura gave him an appreciative look.

"Like I was saying, my queen." Milskar was clearly trying desperately to stay composed. "The sun will be rising any moment, I think we need to get back to the battle sides and inform everyone what has happened. We should send a jadwiga to King Theaus letting him know what has occurred and asking him to meet with us. Hopefully, at that point, we can reach a resolution. He may even offer to help in the capture of Lady Grustmiener." She knew the messenger bird would be able to find the king more quickly than they could. Time was of the essence.

"Do you think so?" Levi asked, a skeptical tone to his voice.

"Why would he not want to help us now?" Calanthe asked. "That wretched woman talked him into fighting for her and then abandoned him the moment she got what she wanted. If he has any semblance of intelligence, he will seek revenge on her and will want to become an ally with any and all who are against her."

"Unless his goal was the same as hers," Levi said quietly.

"Levi?" Aura asked, finally able to look him in the eye.

"I mean, if I was fighting with someone, I probably already had my own reasons. I doubt he was doing it out of love for Lady Grustmiener, right? So, if he had a reason, what makes you think that her absence changes that? It might be the exact opposite. He may be happy that he got rid of her and can continue this fight on his own, hopefully against what he imagines is a weakened opposition."

"Do you think he will want to keep fighting?" Aura asked Milskar.

"Levi brings up a good point, but I think we still need to know for sure. Until then, I say we have our army stand down at the moment until we can figure out what our next move should be."

"Please send the bird immediately. We can meet in a neutral place away from the battle if he wants something more private. Let me know the moment his response arrives."

"Of course, my queen," Milskar said as he and Calanthe turned to leave. Right before he walked out the door, he paused for a moment and turned back to face Aura. "And, my queen?"

"Yes?"

"In the future, if you need protection, or if you are in any kind of fear, I would be honored to keep guard for you during the night." These last words were spoken directly to Levi.

Now it was Levi's turn to blush.

Chapter 4

Lookout

Julia's mind whirled as she tried to slow down her breathing. She mentally went through her calming techniques that a psychologist taught her years ago to calm herself down and get her bearings.

Her name was Julia Jones. She was fourteen years old. Her parents died eight years ago—how had eight years passed so quickly?—and she was left an orphan. Then one day a few weeks ago, a woman came to the orphanage and took her away. She went to another world. There were dragons. There were others like her. She was able to use her powers for the first time without fear. Then war broke out. Fighting. Death. And Lady Grustmiener. And now she was here, in Philadelphia.

Julia tried to figure out what part of that was the strangest. Each statement was, in equal parts, unbelievable. She wished desperately, just as she did any time she was faced with anything overwhelming in her life, that her parents were still alive. But what if they were? Would she even have met Theirra, gone to Esotera, known that she wasn't an abnormality but that there were others like her? Would her parents had been accepting of her abilities? She liked to think they would have.

Her breathing returned to slow and even intervals as she tried to figure out what do to next. She knew she'd shown enough to Jada for him to figure out where she was. She made a point to look at as many landmarks as she could and kept her eyes on the *Welcome to Philadelphia* sign for long enough for him to read it. Any moment now, the rest of them would be breaking through and would help her. She was sure of it. Any moment now.

It began to get dark out, and Julia started to worry. Could the portals have closed behind her? She heard Levi talk about how time worked differently, could she have been catapulted into the future? Or was it the past? Was she beyond their reach? The panic began to bubble and left a metallic taste at the back of her throat.

A noise down the alley refocused her attention. She peered around the trash cans she was still hiding behind and was just able to make out the door. The burly man named Listrel who had been guarding it stepped outside and lit a cigarette, closing the door behind him.

Julia felt a sudden urge to run. She needed to tell someone what was going on. Part of her felt like she should walk up to the door and try to sneak inside, perhaps the element of surprise would give her the advantage? Maybe she could just kill Lady Grustmiener without anyone knowing it was her and then flee back to Esotera. If she was able to get back. She pushed the thought out of her head.

It was strange. She hadn't spent that much time in the other world, but it already felt more like home than any other place she had been since her parents were still alive. Somehow it felt like none of it had actually happened. Had she honestly just been in a place with dragons—dragons!—just hours before? The noise of the streets around her felt completely foreign after listening to the sounds of battle the last few days. Battle.

The image of Levi, dead and laying on the forest floor, filled her mind's eye. She felt a connection to him that lasted even past his own life. He had looked at her in such a way that she felt visible for the first time in…she didn't even know how long. Part of her wished Jada would enter her head just so she could feel some small connection back to that place. She said a silent prayer that she would find herself there again, but not before she could avenge Levi's death.

Julia was so lost in thought, it surprised her to look up and see the man from the steps no longer standing outside. She looked around her, frightened that maybe he noticed her watching him and had come to confront her. It was difficult for her eyes to adjust as the sun was slipping quickly below the horizon. Only peaks of burnt orange made their way through the buildings surrounding her. She stood, deciding she needed to find a place to sleep for the night, when a voice called out from directly behind her.

"Now, what do we have here?" The voice was rough and low and sent an immediate chill through Julia. She closed her eyes and willed the person to leave. Was it the man from the stoop? Had he circled around her?

"Hello my, darling," the deep voice continued. She refused to turn around even though she could feel his presence close to her. "Are you lost, little girl?"

She heard another noise but did not turn to investigate its source either. She began walking, though quickly realized due to her position, the only place to go was deeper down the alley. She knew it was the wrong move as soon as she had made it. Why hadn't she turned and ran the way she'd come? There was a busy street behind her, surely someone would see her and help or call the police. Now she was trapped.

"Where do you think you're going?"

Julia heard movement above her, but it sounded strange and hollow. She looked up but was unable to see. The street lights were out on more than half of the poles. Maybe the darkness could hide her. Maybe her plan wasn't as foolish as she thought.

She passed the faded blue door that held her enemy and kept walking. Julia had misjudged the alley, thinking that it was longer and maybe emptied into another side street, but too quickly she found herself approaching a brick wall. There was nowhere to go. Resolved, she turned to face her pursuer.

Listrel was smaller than he appeared on the stoop, not much taller than she, but he had probably a hundred pounds on her. He was dressed in dirty jeans and a shirt that may have once been white but now was an indiscernible color of filth. He smiled at her, revealing a mouth half filled with teeth.

"I asked you where you thought you were going?"

Julia stood to her full height, though that did little to make her intimidating. Quickly she scanned the emergency escape ladders overhead until her eyes rested on an object. She breathed a sigh of relief.

"Something funny, girlie?" Listrel asked, anger flashing in his voice for the first time.

"I suggest you go back the way you came," she said in a voice that sounded foreign to her.

He chuckled. "I don't think I want to do that. Not without you at least."

One more step. One more second. Now!

There was a loud crash, and the man was slumped on the ground twenty or so feet in front of her. Julia tried to catch her breath. Thankfully one of the tenants above was an avid gardener. The large planters, probably in violation of fire codes, lay in pieces at her feet, their former occupants scattered along the street. Blood mixed with the dirt and terra cotta surrounding the man. Julia could make out the faintest movement from him. He appeared to be breathing but was not moving. She kept her eyes on the stilled figure as she gave him a wide berth and began to walk back out of the alley.

"So, what have we here?" a new voice said behind her.

A rough hand trapped the scream in Julia's mouth.

Chapter 5

Dreams and Nightmares

Aura could hear her heart and blood pulsing in her ears as she ran. Cool air passed in and out of her lungs in painful, burning gasps. Fear spurred her on. A feeling in the depth of her stomach pulled her forward.

She was sure she was making a huge amount of noise as she crashed through the woods, but no one seemed to hear her. She turned to steady her breathing and whirling mind as she took in the sight in front of her. The images were sluggish in her brain. They came to her in pieces.

A hand tangled in brown hair. Legs pressed together. Lips touching.

Aura cleared her throat in a desperate attempt to announce her presence, but neither Levi nor Amaline stopped to look at her. If anything, Aura's arrival seemed to make them kiss more passionately. It felt as if her world was breaking apart. She closed her eyes, unable to look at the two any longer.

Amaline, who had betrayed him. Who, years ago, had a hand in Lady Grustmiener's kidnapping of Levi and had set off the course of events they were currently in. Yes, she had apologized, made up for her mistakes and then some. Yes, she and Levi had worked through their differences, but to this extent? To the point where they would be caught kissing deep in a secret corner of the woods.

"I never really loved you," Levi's voice said, his breath hot on her ear.

Aura's eyes flew open but were met by darkness. The woods and daylight had been replaced by the pale shapes in her room. An arm tightened around her waist.

"I love you," Levi whispered in her ear. Her heart pounded as she tried to sort out which of the two phrases he'd spoken to her was actually the truth.

She extracted herself from the bed and began getting ready. He didn't stir at her movement. She hadn't realized that they had fallen back asleep once Milskar and Calanthe had left. They'd laughed nervously in the dark, and Aura spoke of how she was trying to find the words to address the other armies. But the late hour, exhaustion, and blackness of the room must have pulled them back into sleep.

As her eyes adjusted, she could see light peaking over the horizon. It was a start of a new day. She hoped it would be a successful one.

Now fully dressed and awake, Aura descended the stairs to meet the others. "Is everyone assembled?" Aura asked.

"Yes, my queen, everyone that we could get. There are still some farther out. I've sent scouts to get them," Milskar answered.

Aura nodded and exited the castle flanked by Calanthe, Levi, and Tab, who insisted on accompanying them.

The rest of The Kids that Theirra had assembled, what felt like a lifetime ago, stayed behind. Theirra. The image of her friend, covered in blood and not moving tried to fill every inch of Aura's thoughts, but she pushed it away. She couldn't allow her mind to travel to such dark places, not yet, not now. There was too much left to be done, and she knew if she gave herself over to the grief, she'd never be able to pull herself out of it again.

Her initial embarrassment had eased now that she was properly dressed and looked more authoritative than she had that morning. While she knew she had done nothing wrong, she could tell by the way Milskar kept looking at her he did not agree. Surprisingly though, the events seemed to improve her stock with Calanthe, who kept smiling at her reassuringly and giving dirty looks at Milskar any time he seemed to be about to say something disapproving. Aura was not sure what exactly Calanthe thought had happened, but her father often complained about their southern neighbors being "unconcerned with morals." Aura was starting to figure out what he'd meant and felt herself blush all over again before quickly regaining her composure.

She also tried to push the dream from her memory. She knew how Levi felt about her, and while he had become closer to Amaline, it was ridiculous to think that anything was going on between them. The thought still twisted at her stomach, but she tried to ignore it.

There were still several fires burning as she met the bulk of her army. They had fought hard for several days, not allowing the Omaner and rouge Lady Grustmiener soldiers to gain any ground. Many had died, but not in as great a number as The Great Battle from seven years ago. To think of all that she and her people had gone through. She felt guilty for sleeping in the castle and getting properly cleaned and dressed for the first time in days.

Those around her were caked with dirt and blood. She cursed her stupidity and vanity, hoping the near darkness of the morning would hide her appearance.

"My dear, brave Esoterans," she said, raising her voice to carry through the masses. "I have received information that Lady Grustmiener has abandoned her army."

Murmurs erupted from the crowd. People instantly broke off into groups to discuss the news. There were cries of joy and others of anger, wishing revenge on those who had fought against them.

"Please, please," Aura said, raising her hands and voice to regain order. It took several minutes and shouts by Milskar and Calanthe to get everyone to quiet down. "I know this sounds like exciting news, but we do not know exactly what it means yet. Still, I wanted each of you to be informed of what was going on. For the time being, we are at rest. I implore you to lay down your arms until I can speak with King Theaus and we see where we stand."

"Are they still going to fight us?" a woman called out.

"That I do not know. I do not know if he is aware of Lady Grustmiener's departure."

"She surrendered?" a man asked.

"Not exactly, we think she left the battle to travel—" Aura paused and looked over at Milskar, who nodded solemnly. "—to the other world."

Her words were met with complete silence. She stood, unsure of what to say next.

"She has convinced others to fight for her to create a diversion for her true goal," Levi broke in. Part of Aura acknowledged that she should have been furious at him for speaking out of turn and for her, but she had no words and appreciated the help he was offering. "She has traveled to the other world. We have someone following her, so you do not need to worry. We know exactly where she is, and we are working on apprehending her and bringing her back."

This last part was only partially true, but Aura did not think it needed correcting. She wished she had Jada's abilities and could see exactly where Lady Grustmiener was. But even without that talent, she knew there was no way she would let Lady Grustmiener walk into her world ever again. It was true that they knew where she was, and it was true that they were going to get her, but for Aura the end result of the mission was one thing only, to kill.

"So, the war is over?" someone else called in a soft voice.

"I do hope so," Aura said, finding her voice again. "I hope we can unite and fight for this one cause, this most important cause of stopping this terrible woman."

"So, we are going to cross over and fight there?" A boy of only twelve asked fearfully.

"We know nothing yet, so it is not worth your energy fretting over. I will speak with King Theaus. I am confident that we will come to a resolution. Until then, rest, please. Take this time to begin the healing process. You will be kept abreast of my every action."

She turned and walked back toward the castle.

"Do you think he is going to surrender that easily?" Levi asked again as he jogged to catch up with her.

"What is left in all of this is hope and fear. I choose hope."

Chapter 6

Doyenne Cecily

Sitting around here is doing nothing for me," Lady Grustmiener said with impatience in her voice.

"It is what needs to be done," the woman responded without looking up. In her hands were several documents that were covered in symbols.

Lady Grustmiener strained her eyes but was unable to decipher what any of them meant. "I do not understand," she started but was promptly cut off.

"Yes, that much is evident. You do not understand." The woman looked up at her. She was much older than Lady Grustmiener, but there was a strength that brimmed under the surface. "Did you think you could just waltz in here, and…what, take over?" The woman paused and then laughed lightly.

"I was under the impression that if I got rid of the boy, there would be some reward for such an act."

"Yes, I do appreciate that. I only wish Lady Amadea could have still been alive to see it."

"That brings me to my next point. With Lady Amadea's passing, who is now in charge?" Lady Grustmiener asked, trying to sound casually interested. But her senses were on full alert.

When she'd arrived in this place hours before, she was unsure of who would be greeting her. The previous rulers of the non-magical and magical worlds, Lady Amadea and Lord Vertrous, had both moved on to the next life. Lady Amadea recently and Lord Vertrous hundreds of years prior. Before his death, he had split his lands into the Four Corners, and her late husband's family had inherited a portion of it.

Now with Levi dead, Lady Grustmiener had been convinced that she would be able to take over at least some of the other world in addition to capturing her lands back along with Omaner, Vertronum, and Esotera. While she was not there to witness the end of the battle, she was confident that Lieal would continue the fight without her so when she returned after securing this land, she could openly rule the majority of the world. In her mind's eye, she could see him leading her army to victory as Queen Aura sobbed over her losses.

Lady Grustmiener was a little disappointed that she would be unable to see it in person, but she'd needed to start the second phase of her plan immediately.

This woman sitting in front of her had brought that to a screeching halt. "Why are the people in your world so concerned with whom rules whom?" the woman said, again returning her attention to the papers in front of her.

Lady Grustmiener laughed. "And you are not? I hardly believe that."

"Ah, here it is," the woman said, not responding to taunts thrown at her. She removed one of the papers and smoothed its edges. It looked vaguely transparent and incredibly old.

It was clear that the paper held some sort of lineage tracker, but Lady Grustmiener had never seen one set up quite the same way. Pages were attached at strange angles, and once fully opened, filled most of the space on the table. Lines jutted out and abruptly ended while others seemed to trace throughout the entire document. There was one word that was much darker than the others and extremely clear. It hung off the end of a short page attached to the bottom of an even shorter line, but it was obviously the freshest entry: Levi Roberts. The woman leaned over, and with a flourish of her wrist, the birth and death brackets under the boy's name were closed. 1994-2018. A smile tugged at Lady Grustmiener's lips.

"Now what do we do?" she asked.

"We?" the woman said. "Haven't you done enough?" The woman was now studying the chart and hadn't even looked up while speaking.

Lady Grustmiener's hands balled into fists. "Yes, *we.*"

"Well, I suppose if you are that invested in what happens, you may stay. Respin," she called.

The man who showed Lady Grustmiener into the room stepped forward. "Yes, Doyenne Cecily."

"Go check on Listrel. Where is he?" She looked up. "He let her in and then disappeared? Always such a nuisance. I wonder sometimes why I keep him around."

Lady Grustmiener was frustrated yet pleased that she was being included in whatever this endeavor was. Maybe they would eventually end up back in the other world so she could be properly appointed as the ruler. Or maybe there were affairs to get in order here first. She knew better than to ask, though it was hard for her to take a back seat after working so hard for so many years to be back in power. *Patience,* she told herself. *Just a little while long-*

er. She heard the door shut and hurried footsteps come back toward them.

Just as Lady Grustmiener stood and sent the chair she was in to crash into the floor, the door to the room burst open. Respin looked around the room as if he was expecting an army to greet him. He began to close the blinds and draw the curtains until all the light that was left was from dim lamps scattered throughout the room. The effect was disconcerting, making Lady Grustmiener feel even more on edge.

"What do you think you are doing?" she asked in a commanding voice. The woman across from her didn't even seem to notice the commotion happening around her.

"Keep your voice down," he hissed. Lady Grustmiener didn't appreciate his tone with her, but she sensed his urgency and decided to stay silent.

Once the room was completely quiet, he shut and locked the door, and sat down at the table. He waited patiently for several moments before the anticipation got the better of him and he addressed Cecily directly.

"My lady," he said.

Lady Grustmiener perked up, wondering what could be happening to cause him to fortress them into the room.

"Can you not see that I am in the middle of something, Respin?" Cecily answered without looking up.

"I know, and I apologize, but something rather important has happened, and I think you may be in danger. We may want to move locations."

"Oh?" She sighed. "I was rather getting used to this place. I do hate having to pack up my things." Cecily looked over at Lady Grustmiener, reluctantly including her in the conversation. "One always ends of misplacing something that is of great importance. Things are never quite right once they have been deconstructed. They never go back exactly the same way again."

"Why do we need to leave?" Lady Grustmiener asked.

"Oh, yes, please do tell us, Respin."

"Listrel has been killed. I found him at the end of the alley with an array of flower pots surrounding his head."

"Oh, Listrel," Cecily tisk tisked. "What mess has he gotten himself into?"

"Well, that's it, my lady," Respin continued. "I think someone did it to him. From the position he was in, I don't think he would have gone that far down the street unless he was following someone."

"And you do not think that these flower pots fell on their own accord?" she asked, returning her gaze to her previous work.

"I don't," he said firmly. "The woman who lives in that apartment takes great care with those flowers. I see her all the time working with them." He paused, blushing slightly in the dim light. "She makes sure they will not tip or blow over with any storms. I am sure that someone did it. I think they were brought down from below," he added quickly at the end.

This seemed to trigger something in Cecily, and her eyes flew up. Respin nodded. Next, her gaze turned on Lady Grustmiener, and her expression was fierce. "Were you followed?" she demanded.

"No."

"How can you be sure?" Respin asked.

"The portal was closed before, and it reclosed after I passed through. No other portals were opened."

"Are you sure of this?" Cecily asked her, raising from her seat and taking deliberate steps forward.

"I am positive. No one followed me through. This must just be an unfortunate coincidence. Nothing more."

Her voice sounded firm, but inside her mind was whirling.

Of course, she was not going to mention that the portals did not close the *second* she passed. They needed to remain open to allow her to go through without risk, but she knew she wasn't followed. No one came through after her. The witch had performed some magic to reseal them, but Lady Grustmiener also knew that had to have happened, or the whole army of the Four Corners would have come after her. No, she was sure. There was no way.

"To be safe, I still think we should relocate," Respin said.

"I should have known that you would bring more trouble that you were worth. Oh, all right, make sure everything is packed. It is your head if anything goes missing," Cecily said as she walked out of the room and down the darkened hallway.

Lady Grustmiener watched as Respin gathered various, seemingly random-looking items from the table and room.

Fifteen minutes later, then were rumbling along in a moving box with wheels. A cart with no horse pulling it, bouncing down the road as Lady Grustmiener's fingers turned white with how hard she gripped the door.

Chapter 7

Revenge

Luther found himself wandering around the woods in a sort of lost stupor. As soon as the battle had begun, he disappeared among the masses. He kept trying to find a place for himself, a way to use his powers, but had so far been unable to figure one out.

When he was first brought here, Lady Grustmiener gave him such hope. He'd never felt like he'd belonged before, but now, now he had a reason for his powers. Could put a name to why he could control the dead, that it was magic, not evil that coursed through his veins. She'd made him promises, said she could give him everything he wanted if he just helped her. His thoughts filled with Unna.

She'd come along with him to this world. They were different, sure, but also the same. She couldn't raise the dead—no, he alone held that terrible power—but she could shift and become anyone. He fell in love with her as quickly as walking off a cliff and plummeting. Lady Grustmiener promised not only glory but that Unna would love him back. If he could prove himself, prove his worth, she would be unable to resist him.

But it had not turned out that way.

At the end of the first night, Unna was electric with excitement. She told him how her powers were getting stronger the more she was using them, and she was going to try to get as close to the enemy queen as she could the following day. Luther was frightened for her, but also jealous of her success. He tried to play off that he'd had some success that day as well, but luckily in her enthusiasm, she barely registered anything he was saying, much less if there was any truth in it.

After several people came up to her to congratulate her, the site around them began to settle down for the night, but she was still abuzz. One particularly impressive-looking man had just shaken her hand before walking away, and Unna turned to face Luther with a huge smile on her face. She ran to him, and he automatically took her in his arms.

"I've never been good at something before," she said, pulling back from him slightly so they were eye to eye.

"I doubt that," he responded, without thinking, and immediately could feel his cheeks flush. She laughed and kissed him full on the mouth. He was so shocked it took him a second to kiss her back, which he then did enthusiastically. After what felt like a blissful eternity, she pulled back again, gave him a quick peck on his cheek, and slipped out of his arms.

"You get some rest," she said. "I'm too amped up to sleep." And with that, she disappeared into the growing darkness.

Luther could still feel her lips and body pressed against him. Maybe this was the beginning of the change he wished for. He gave himself into the fantasy, of being successful in battle and living the rest of his days in this magical place with Unna by his side.

A bit of worry had crept through him though when he awoke the next morning. She hadn't come back to the camp site the previous night. He'd asked around, and no one reported seeing her. Could she have made it through the other side? Could she be held captive by the other army? Knowing her, though, she would have slaughtered them all and was now sitting on the queen's throne. He would somehow find himself in the other castle, and she would be in there laughing and gesturing around as if to say, *See what I did while you were tramping around the woods*?

The light was beginning to stream in larger strands through the trees. Luther knew the days fighting would commence soon, but something propelled him forward. He wasn't sure what he would do if he came across another fighter. Would he just run? He had no weapon to speak of and saw no bodies directly around him. He suddenly felt very vulnerable. He was just about to turn around and call it quits when a shimmer of yellow caught his eye. To his left, he could just make out a soft mound on top of the forest floor. Fear turned the blood in his veins to ice.

He inched his way forward, already knowing the truth but needing to see all the same. The ground around her was in disarray. Clearly, something big had happened here, but only one body was on the ground. Only one body.

Only Unna.

Even in the bright sunlight, Luther's vision turned a deep crimson. The anger and pain that built in him were unbearable. He fell to his knees beside her and stared down at her face. Her eyes were wide open, and her mouth was frozen in a perpetual "O." Her weapon was yards from her, Luther hadn't even noticed that he'd almost stepped on it to reach her. What had happened here? Had she lain her sword down and was killed anyway? He tried closing her eyes, but it was too late. They were doomed to stare blankly into the heavens. His kissed her forehead and rose, wiping tears from his cheeks.

"It was the wretched queen who did it," a voice spoke behind him. He jumped and stood.

"W—Who?" Luther stammered.

"The queen, Queen Aura." The man spoke in a sneering tone as if using the word "queen" along with the woman's name tasted bitter in his mouth.

Luther was confused. "From Esotera?"

"She killed this girl. I saw it. Stabbed her in the chest and then walked away like nothing had happened. Dragged another body away, but clearly didn't care about this one. Did you know her?"

"Yeah," Luther said, "sort of, I guess." And that really was the truth. He didn't *know* Unna. He wished he had, imagined he had, but they'd known each other for mere weeks. He loved her, though, that he knew. He loved her and was going to avenge her death.

"There are bodies all over," the man said.

Luther stared at him, recognizing him from when he and Unna first came to this place. An image of the man with a woman in shackles was brought up by his memory, but he couldn't remember the man's name. Something that started with an A, he thought. The man was old but had a spryness about him that didn't seem to match his age. Luther wondered how old the man really was. Ninety? A hundred and ninety?

"Seems like a waste," he continued.

"Unna, yes, a waste," Luther agreed. *Abaddon.* It finally came to him.

"Oh, no, no the bodies. All those bodies. Wasted just lying on the ground." Abaddon stepped back as he talked and began mumbling to himself as he turned and slipped back into the woods. Luther looked around. Had that just happened? Had his mind materialized the man to speak what he was already thinking?

The ideas were forming in his head faster than he could sort them out. Would it work? He had trained, sure, but not like this. Not prepared for this.

He looked down at Unna one last time before walking, not back the way he came, but forward, toward what he knew was the enemy side. They would pay for what they did to her. He may not have been truly vested in this battle before, but now all he wanted to do was destroy every last one of them. He would not be satisfied until this whole place was reduced to a burning pile of ashes, people included.

Chapter 8

Help

Julia had gone completely still. She knew it was futile to try to break the man's grasp. She cursed herself for getting into this situation, and her thoughts whirled with trying to figure out how to get out of it. Of course, the house would be heavily guarded. It was clear that someone very important lived there. Did she think that she could just sneak outside the place and not be noticed?

"I'm going to remove my hand," the man's voice said in her ear. "I need you to not scream, or you are going to alert them inside."

Confusion more than anything kept her quiet as the grip on her mouth rescinded. Why would he not want to alert the people inside?

"Toli, we have to get out of here," a woman's voice said.

Julia turned around slowly. It was difficult to make out the two figures in the poor lighting. The woman reached forward and grabbed the back of Julia's arm.

"Come *on*. We have to get out of here."

She marched forward, dragging Julia along as the man named Toli followed. They reached her old hiding place and quickly looked both ways before crossing the street. Julia took one look back at the dark mound at the end of the alley. It didn't appear to be making any attempts to get up.

"Where are we going?" Julia stammered.

"Away from that place. What were you thinking, hanging around there for that long?"

"Deserae, I doubt she knew," Toli said.

Toli. Deserae. Julia repeated the names five times in her head to set them to memory.

"Doesn't matter," Deserae responded. "We still gotta get some distance before they find him and investigate what happened."

"Who are you people, where are you taking me?" Julia began to slow down, but the grip on her was painfully tightened. The few people who shared the sidewalk with them began to stare.

"Missed her curfew again," Deserae growled at them. "Going to have to lock her up until she's eighteen."

For some reason, this seemed to appease the people they passed. Part of Julia was tempted to yell out for help, but she had a sneaking suspicion that was already what she was getting.

They turned down several more side streets until Julia was thoroughly confused at what was happening. She shut her eyes and prayed that someone would come to save her soon. How would they ever find her if she didn't even know exactly where she was?

They abruptly stopped in front of what looked like an abandoned set of row homes. Toli looked around them before moving a piece of graffiti covered particle board away from a door frame. It was the only house on the block that didn't appear to have been ravaged by fire at some point during its existence.

Deserae pushed her through before finally, mercifully, letting go of her arm. Julia rubbed the sore place for several seconds before turning to look at her surroundings. What appeared on the outside to be an abandoned property was surprisingly well-appointed. There were several couches and, while mismatched, they appeared clean.

A mattress in the far corner and a table with several chairs rounded out the first floor. There were stairs to the right of her, but so many of the slats were missing, Julia wondered if the second floor was even accessible. From the items scattered around it appeared as though the first floor was the only one in use.

"Where am I?" she asked.

"A safe house. I almost forgot where exactly it was, but luckily no one else is using it at the moment. We will stay here until morning and figure out where to go from there. We were staying at a much nicer one," Deserae continued, glaring at Julia, "but I doubt we can go back there now."

"I don't know why," Julia said with a hint of bitterness in her voice. "I am the one who attacked that man. I heard you above me, though you didn't seem too keen to help then."

"We didn't want to alert him to our presence," Toli said, putting a quieting hand on Deserae. "If we did, there was a chance he would have called out and others would have arrived. I was about to jump down on the man, but then you made those potters fall."

Fear coursed through Julia again. Had they seen all of it? She was hoping that, in the dim light, they wouldn't have been able to make out everything that had happened.

"I don't know what you are talking about," she said

elusively. "You must have knocked them as you were descending the fire escape."

"Nice try, but we were on the other side of the alley. I know you moved them."

"I don't know what you are talking about," she repeated.

"Oh, give it up. It doesn't matter. Do you think we would have saved you if we didn't know what you were? What we are?" Deserae said while inspecting her cuticles.

"I'm sorry?" Julia tried to look innocent, but she knew her face must have been displaying all of her emotions.

"This is tiresome," Deserae said. "I'm going to lay down."

"Come, sit," Toli gestured to the table and chairs. "Are you hungry, thirsty?"

The adrenaline that had been coursing through her had made her momentarily forget how famished she was. She honestly could not remember the last time she had had food or a drink.

"Both, actually."

She smiled appreciatively when five minutes later Toli placed a cup of hot tea and a sandwich in front of her. She dug in ravenously and did not look up again until both were finished.

"I guess you were." He laughed quietly, looking over at the now-sleeping form on the bed. "Don't mind her. We were doing some recon, and it was not going well. She is just taking her frustration out on you."

"Recon?"

"On that house you were scoping out. Guessing someone sent you as well. We received information that someone high ranking was there, but only saw that one woman go in and that guard. Doesn't seem to be a lot of activity to speak of."

"I know who that woman is."

"Excuse me?" Toli said, taking the seat across from her and staring pointedly into her eyes.

"The woman. I was following her. I don't know anything about that house in general. She brought me there."

"You were following her? Why? Who is she?"

"It's a complicated story," Julia said. While she felt like these people were trying to help her, and, obviously, either had some powers themselves or worked for people who did, she was still not totally sure if she should trust them.

"I'm a quick learner," he said. Suddenly, Deserae was sitting at the table with them. Apparently, she was not as asleep as Julia had thought.

"Her name is Lady Grustmiener," Julia continued.

The two sitting across from her looked pointedly at one another, eyes wide.

"Do you know who that is?" Julia asked.

"It's impossible," Deserae said. "She's dead. That can't possibly be her."

"It is."

"How can you be sure?" Toli said, ignoring his counterpart's protests.

"Because I followed her here from the other world. There is a war going on, and I think whoever lives in that house has now brought it to your doorstep."

Chapter 9

No Surrender

Aura had just turned to say something to Levi when a giant white bird flew low toward them. It landed heavily on Milskar's outstretched arm, clutching a letter in its curved beak.

He grabbed it and gave the bird a soft push as it took off back into the air. He handed the thick, creamy paper to her.

She broke the blue seal and scanned the document. It was only two lines long.

We will never surrender. Battle will continue at dawn.

Aura handed the paper to Levi who also quickly read it and passed it along to Calanthe and Milskar.

"I guess it was too much to ask," Aura said. As if on cue, a large boom was heard in the distance.

"We must hurry and get our troops assembled," Calanthe said. "They are not ready for this."

"Are any of us?" Aura said, dejected.

Levi smiled weakly at her and kissed her cheek. The

images in her dream fought to press into her mind, but she pushed them away.

"We will get through this," he said. "We will tell the army to inform anyone they come across of Lady Grustmiener's abandonment. If he will not surrender, perhaps his people will."

"I will pass along the word and get ready to fight," Milskar said, leaving them.

"Theirra," Aura said weakly.

"There will be time to grieve for her, but that time is not now." She nodded at him and fell into his chest for several breaths before composing herself.

"The castle," she stammered.

"It will be fine. I am not leaving your side."

"I cannot lose you, too."

"And you won't," he said flatly.

"The Kids."

As if the words had summoned them, they appeared around the tree line. Galina looked ready to either explode or implode, Aura was not sure which. Possibly the girl wasn't sure either.

"I do not want to risk your lives…" Aura said, her voice trailing off.

"Too late for that, boss lady," Galina said. "I am going to kill every last one I can get my hands on." Thunder rumbled in the distance as she ran off toward the sounds of fighting.

"Jada," Levi said, stopping him as he walked by. "How is Julia doing?"

Jada had a forlorn expression as he watched Kiya and Kalan walk away, but he didn't ask them to wait for him. He turned back toward Aura as his eyes became unfocused. Moments later they seemed to snap back.

"She's in a room with two people."

"People," Aura said. "Is she hurt, is she okay?"

"Yes, they are helping her. They are like us too," Jada continued, his brows furrowed in concentration as Julia came in and out focus. "She's writing something on a piece of paper. 'Help me.'"

Jada looked up at Levi and Aura's worried faces.

"We will, Jada. We will do everything we can," Levi assured him. "Maybe you should stay back at the castle." He interrupted the boy's protests. "You are very valuable. I know everyone here is, but if we lose you—" Levi paused. "—we can't lose you."

Jada looked hopefully over to Aura, who just shook her head. "Fine," he said before storming back up to the castle.

"If we lose him, we lose Julia, too," Levi said, justifying his actions.

"I know." Aura placed a hand on Levi's shoulder. "Come, the day is starting without us."

Chapter 10

Connection

Julia was getting a little anxious. She was still trying to figure out how these two could possibly know Lady Grustmiener's name, but each time she asked them, they ignored her. Toli and Deserae had their heads close to touching, and they were in a deep and animated conversation. Julia could tell they were trying to be quiet, but every now and then Deserae's voice would rise.

"Yes, we *know* that," she snapped.

"I don't understand how you expect to do that."

"Well, now you are the one being impossible."

Julia was unable to hear Toli's response each time, and for a few more moments they would be quiet again before another outburst.

"Well she's here now," Deserae said, finally turning to face Julia.

"I—I—" Julia stammered, frozen by the look the woman was giving her.

"Des, please relax. We need to get all the information we can, and then we can proceed," Toli said in a calm voice. "Let's start with something easy, what's your name."

"Julia. Julia Jones."

"Hi, Julia. So how did you end up having this information?"

"How do you know—" Julia started, but Toli raised a hand.

"I promise we will answer your questions, but we just need you to answer a few first."

"Could she be a spy?" Deserae said, looking stricken with panic.

Julia found this so ridiculous. A spy? Who *were* these people? Part of her was screaming to leave, to run away from them, but where would she go? She didn't know a single person. She barely knew any people in the entire world, but not a single one in this one. If she did run away, how long would it be for someone to find her? Surely the man outside the house would be found, and, at the very least, the police would be on the hunt. Or if Lady Grustmiener found the man first, she and some henchman would be on her track. Even if Julia did get away from all of that, what did she have? A few gold coins rattled in her pocket that she sheepishly picked up from the forest floor the previous day. Some fallen solider probably dropped them. At first, she was going to hand them over to Levi or Theirra, but she wanted to keep them. She wanted some proof that she had really been in that other place if it suddenly disappeared.

She was glad she'd held on to them. But even if she did get away and somehow exchanged the gold for money, where would she go? Back to the orphanage? Would she call them and have them send someone to get her, and what were her prospects there? She had disappeared for however long she'd been gone. Had they been trying to check in on her and found the woman who took her had disappeared as well? Was her face showing up on milk cartons?

Part of her was even more terrified to discover if the answer was no. Would no one have noticed she was gone? Did no one out there care, even a little bit, for her? Here she was in some house in a city she had never been before, and all she wanted to do was cry. She took a deep breath to steady herself. Maybe it was for the best to just tell them the truth and see where that left her.

"I was found by a woman named Theirra. She came to me from the kingdom of Esotera, asking for my help. I traveled to the Four Corners with her when a war broke out. There were several of us who went, and—and I don't know how many more of them are alive, but Levi—" Her voice caught. "—Levi is dead."

"Levi Roberts?" Deserae said, her face draining of some color in the dim light.

"Do you know him?"

"Every hybrid knows him, Julia," she said with a bite.

"Des," Toli warned. "There are several of us in this world, probably more than any of us are aware of, that have traveled back and forth between the worlds. When Mr. Roberts's book came out, we knew the truth that was in it. We were frightened that we would be found out and persecuted."

"Persecuted?" Julia asked fearfully.

"People have been slaughtered for less," Deserae said.

"Not that we thought that would happen," he said pointedly to her. "We just knew we would have to be more vigilant. Then a few days ago, the portals seemed to be closed."

"Lady Grustmiener closed them," Julia said.

"But I guess they are open now," Toli said.

"I don't know. I think if they were still open, my friends would have come here by now. Unless—" She paused in thought. "—does the time change thing affect that? If they came right after me, would they not actually show up for a week?"

"No," Toli said. Desi looked like she was about to say something, too, but closed her mouth and let her counterpart speak. "It's true that time works different in both worlds, but it takes a while for it to make a real difference," he continued.

"How much time?" Julia asked

"Quite a lot. I don't think you need to worry." Toli spoke the words with finality.

Relief temporarily washed over Julia. They could find her. She could go back. But if they could, why hadn't they yet? The fear started to simmer again. Was Levi the only one who truly cared for her and, now with him dead—she tried to not even register that fact—was her only link gone? Was she trapped or just simply unwanted?

Chapter 11

A New Depth

Aura couldn't remember being more exhausted in her life than she was now. Each time she was sure she'd reached the bottom of her reserves, she had to find it in herself to keep going. Her fingers ached, and she found it difficult to even hold on to her sword, much less raise it up and down. Her voice was becoming raw from yelling to her counter parts.

"Stop fighting!" she called. "Lady Grustmiener has left you. She abandoned you. You do not need to fight anymore. I will offer to protection." Crash. "You do not need to worry!" Crash. "We will defeat her." Crash. "And you." Crash. "Will be safe!" Crash.

Finally, the person would fall under a fatal blow of her sword. She didn't want to do it. She didn't want to fight anymore, but she was terrified that if she didn't, if they laid down their weapons in the hopes that the others would too, King Theaus would take that as a surrender and annihilate all of them. So, she continued to fight as the soreness in her body became overwhelming.

In a brief moment of respite, Levi and Omire walked toward her. Omire was sporting a deep cut on his left arm that was bleeding freely, and Levi looked a little worse for wear, but both men were standing upright and breathing.

"This cannot continue," Aura said. "We have to find a way to get them to stop that does not involve killing them all."

"Is there a stopping point that does not end there?" Omire asked. "I think I would like to see that."

"I am serious," she said.

"I am afraid I am as well."

Aura noticed a far-away look in his eyes.

They stood for several seconds, constantly looking around them. The fighting was still going on, but it appeared as some change was happening around them. Aura couldn't quite figure out what it was. It was as if the air itself had shifted. Maybe it had something to do with the closed portals. She had just turned to Levi to ask him his thoughts, when she caught the look on his face. Pure terror had washed over him. She wheeled around.

Blackened bodies were moving through the trees. At first, Aura thought they were making some horrible noise, but she realized that it was the people around her. Their cries sounded wretched and guttural. The bodies continued to move in a broken line and pushed everyone back toward her. Fighting stopped as both sides began a strange retreat. Aura's mind couldn't process what was happening fast enough, and she was rooted in place.

They ticked into focus like the second hand on a watch. Levi reached for her hand at the same moment she reached for his.

"Oh, my," Omire said in a whisper, as if that was all he could manage.

Several dozen corpses moved toward them as if what

was left of their bodies didn't work the same way they previously had. Like they were rooted to the ground more strongly than before. Their eyes were either closed or frozen open, their faces in the same distorted position as when they had died. They shuffled forward, some on clearly broken limbs. Every hair on Aura's body stood up, and her flesh crawled with fear.

Some even appeared to be the bodies that had dropped from the sky and with even more horror, she realized that King Piester, or what was left of him, crown still sitting precariously on his head, lead the procession.

Aura took several steps back before Levi held her.

"They are dead. They can't hurt us, they are just meant to scare us," he said, but he couldn't hide the shaking from his voice.

"What magic is this?" she whispered.

"We need to find the person who is doing this. We need to stop this," he said calmly and looked straight into her eyes. She nodded, a new adrenaline-filled energy coursing through her. She barely felt the pain in her hands as she grasped her sword.

The two of them began moving forward, followed by Omire. Without speaking, Levi reached the first body. He reached his hand out to move it, but the woman—if you could still call her that—reached out and grabbed his arm with such force, he stumbled backward.

"Levi!" Aura called.

Omire rushed forward, pushed the body back, and pressed his sword through its head.

Aura was terrified as Levi moved to stand slightly in front of her, and the swarm of bodies descended upon them. She quickly stepped up into position and helped him and Omire. They walked in a jagged line as they cut down those that walked toward them.

It was terrible work, but they soon got into a rhythm. Aura tried not looking at any of them and methodically moved her arm back and forth, catching legs and necks of whatever body walked toward her. One of the figures got close to her and was just about to wrap its hands around her neck when Levi sliced through its middle, breaking it cleanly in half.

"Help us," Levi called back over his shoulder to the masses behind them. Suddenly men and women stood beside them. She didn't recognize them all and slowly figured out they were from each of the armies, all working together to defeat this terrible attack.

It seemed like for each new body that fell, two more took its place. Aura looked around wildly, but she was unable to see the source that was controlling them. Could it be something else then maybe? Could it be some type of magic or spell? She had heard the witches and sorcerers were on Lady Grustmiener's side, but she had never heard of a curse that raised the dead.

In the distance, she was able to make out a figure that was clearly a living, breathing human. He looked young, yet the rage in him was palpable. Aura grabbed Levi's shoulder and pointed.

"There, I think that is the person doing this."

They began to pick their way in an arc toward the boy. His face was smooth in concentration, and his eyes appeared glassed over.

"Do you think he can see us?" Levi whispered. Aura shook her head. "Be quiet, though, so we do not break his concentration."

They snuck up behind him, but at the last minute, Levi stepped on a dry branch. The crack it made seemed to be a sonic boom. The boy whirled around and the sound of crashing bodies reverberated around them.

"You," he said to Aura. The hatred in his voice startled her.

"I—I do not know who you are," she stammered.

"You killed her," he boomed and rushed toward her.

The movement took Aura by such surprise, that even though her sword was raised, she did not react quickly enough to bring it down. He crashed into her and began punching and scratching every square inch he could get his hands on. Thankfully, Levi was there, and after what felt like an eternity the boy was pulled off of her. She panted and tried to catch her breath as she heard the struggle between the two and then silence. She sat up in fear but was relieved to see Levi sitting up. The boy was nowhere to be seen.

"What the hell was that?" he asked her.

She shrugged and fell back against the earth, chest still heaving.

Chapter 12

Move

Lady Grustmiener tapped her nails on the counter in rhythmic succession. She was feeling stir crazy, and it hadn't even been two whole days that she'd been here, but her blood was still pumping with the adrenaline of the battle. She felt edgy and needed to expel the energy coursing through her. She needed to fight something, kill something, *do* something. She had spent too many years hiding. Too many years lying low. If she had to spend one more second in this place, she was going to lose her mind.

They'd traveled in the *car* contraption since they'd left Doyenne Cecily's home. It took a long time for Lady Grustmiener to relax enough to let go of the door handle, but she still wasn't used to how fast the things moved by. If she didn't stare straight ahead, she found that she got a little nauseous. It was a feeling unbefitting of a ruler, but she still mentally begged Respin to slow down and let her get her bearings.

Mercifully, when they reached some invisible distance from where they'd come from, the car seemed to slow. She was able to look around and noticed the buildings thinning and the trees getting thicker and thicker. For a moment, she wondered if they were going to drive this thing back to the other world, but they turned into a long road which held a house at the end.

While it wasn't as grand as the castles that she was used to, it was a vast improvement to the small house Cecily was previously in. The walls were so dark, they blended into the colors of the surrounding trees and was only truly visible once you were practically upon it.

Respin parked the car and ran to open the door for Cecily. Lady Grustmiener sat where she was until he did the same for her under the guise that she, too, was royalty, but mainly because she had no idea how to exit the contraption.

It felt wonderful to stretch her legs. She was glad to be out of the city and back in the woods. Being so far from nature had unnerved her. Here the air smelled sharp and earthy, but not entirely like her home. Something was a little off about it, but she couldn't put her finger on what it was.

Cecily moved toward the structure. The other two followed obediently into whatever this next chapter of their adventure would bring.

Chapter 13

Joining Forces

Aura finally stood with the help of Levi's outstretched hand. He brought her up and immediately pulled her toward him. She trembled slightly from the excursion her already exhausted muscles had just endured, and she took a few shaky breaths before she felt a bit more like herself. She pulled away slightly and kissed him lightly on the mouth.

"Thanks," she said.

"Aren't you glad you didn't leave me at the castle today?"

She laughed quietly and broke away from him. As she turned, she stared at what was in front of her. Dozens of men and woman in a half-moon shaped line around her and Levi and the bodies that littered the forest floor.

Instinctually, she felt the urge to put her hands in the air but fought against it. Sometimes she still had to remind herself that she was the one in power and shouldn't show any signs of weakness. Had they seen her trembling as she fought for air? She hoped not.

The figures in front of her were still. Some she recognized, but most seemed to be from the opposing armies. None held their weapons out at the ready.

Aura looked around her for the boy who seemed to be controlling the dead only moments before. He was nowhere. She also couldn't locate Omire. Her heart beat ferociously in her chest, still not recovered from her ordeal. "Where did the boy go?" she asked.

Levi was turning as well. "I don't know."

"You stopped him," a man said.

Aura faced him. "Dark magic has no place here." She tried to make her voice sound firmer than it felt. Her throat still ached, and it was somewhat difficult to speak at a loud volume.

"She made him do it," a woman said. "Lady Grustmiener made him do it as we marched here."

"I'm sure she did," Levi said.

"It is done now," Aura continued. "Do you see? Do you see the things she will do to try to gain power? These terrible things. These things she is making us do? She left. She left each and every one of you, yet she still expects you to fight for her name. And what has she done for you? She has stolen you, killed those you loved, and raised the dead against you. Is that who you want leading you? Is that really who you want to fight for?"

The crowd was quiet. The members of her army were imperceptibly moving toward her. Their movement was so slow, it was as if they were afraid of spooking the others.

"What options do we have?" someone asked.

"How will you protect us?"

"What will we do?" another called out.

Aura raised her hands and gestured for the crowd to quiet. She noticed more faces pressing in. Again, there was an even mixture from both sides. None appeared to have weapons at the ready. She could feel their want like a pulse through the Earth. They longed for peace. They wanted a leader who would show them the way. She wanted to be that for all of them.

"This battle is over," she said. She was no longer asking. She was no longer requesting input. She was telling. "I still need you, though. It pains me because while this battle is over, this war continues. Lady Grustmiener has ensured that, but we are done fighting each other. I would like you to join me. To help us fight for all our futures."

"King Theaus," a man said flatly without question.

"He will no longer have an army. And there will be no one left for him to fight," Aura said.

"What if he is unwilling to surrender?"

"He doesn't have the option," Levi chimed in.

"He will be presented with the facts, and if he is still unwilling to see reason, I will have no choice but to capture him. He will be dealt with in our court," Aura continued.

She was glad Levi stood by her side, but she felt strange when he spoke for her kingdom. She knew he'd risked a lot over the years for her home, but she still felt possessive over it. But what if her home became their home? What would happen when the fighting was over once and for all? She pushed such daydreams reluctantly from her mind.

One by one the group in front of them put their weapons away and slowly made their way toward them. Aura held her breath, her skin crawling. She ignored the scream in her head and her racing heart. Could this be a trick? Could they be lulling her and her army into letting their guard down before they attacked and killed them?

Aura felt Levi press into her side. It was clear he had the same apprehensions. Soon both armies were so mingled, it was impossible to draw lines around either one. Aura locked eyes with Milskar. She was relieved to see him there. He nodded at her and began to push the crowd toward the castle. She still felt like she was in a slight daze as they streamed by her. Milskar squeezed her shoulder as he brought up the rear of the procession.

Once the area around them was clear again, Levi took her hand. Aura looked over at the dead bodies lying on the ground. It seemed so pointless, all this death. There was no reason for it. She wondered what their stories were. What made so many people have such intense hatred in them to make them want to go to war?

"You okay?" Levi asked, snapping her back to the present.

"Yes, yes, of course," she said automatically as her hand absentmindedly rubbed her throat.

"Let's go find the others, all right?"

She nodded her agreement.

Word must have spread through the forest because the noises of battle faded away as they picked a path through the trees. Anytime they came to a group of people, none appeared to have weapons as they walked with a purposeful, yet dejected, determination. Few even glanced their way. The fighting had taken its toll, and it seemed like everyone was trying to put as much distance as possible from it.

"How can I ask these people to fight again, to fight for me?" Aura asked, stopping Levi.

"I don't think they will be fighting just for you. They know what will happen if they don't fight. They know what she will do to them. Whatever she's promised, they have to realize she was never planning on keeping her word."

"And why would they trust me? What would make them think that my word is worth anything?" she asked.

"Because," he said, touching her face lightly. "Your heart is easy to see. Anyone can take one look at you and know you will do everything in your power to be truthful. Come on."

He pulled away and followed the thinning crowd toward the castle grounds.

Chapter 14

Disrespect

They'd been sitting in the house for practically an entire day when Lady Grustmiener broke. The adrenaline from the battle had fully worn off, and she was exhausted. She also couldn't quite put her finger on it, but there was something about this place that unnerved her. In the other world, even when she was at her weakest, she still felt like her possibilities were endless. Her future felt wide open. In this world, she felt closed in.

It was as if she didn't belong here, and the environment itself was fighting her presence. Every inch of her felt sluggish, like she was moving through too-thick air. Cecily seemed to pick up on her distress.

"You don't belong here," she said simply.

"I beg your pardon," Lady Grustmiener said. The more time she spent with this woman, the more and more she disliked her.

"Everything works a little different here," Cecily continued. "Time is much slower than in your world. Most can't feel it. In the short term, it actually makes little difference, but those who are so strongly tied to the other world seem to be affected more than others, especially those that are of both worlds."

Lady Grustmiener decided right then and there to not let this woman see how it made her feel weak. She would prove her wrong, prove to her that she was part of any world, every world. That she could rule them all. That she was to be feared, no matter the location.

"I do not know what you speak of," she said. She sat up straighter in her chair and set her jaw. "If anything is wrong with me, it is the fact that we are doing nothing but sitting in an old house while we should be doing a victory tour throughout both our worlds. I did something amazing, I pulled off something no one has been able to pull off for hundreds of years. I defeated the Four Corners."

Cecily laughed lightly and rose from her chair. "Of course, you did, my dear." She walked forward and patted Lady Grustmiener on the shoulder, as if she was an obedient dog, and left the room.

Lady Grustmiener could hear her talking in low voices with Respin as he moved around in the kitchen. Dishes and pans clattered in between her words, making it difficult sometimes to hear them. Only pieces filtered through.

"But…time…here…days."

She was unable to decipher what they meant. She'd been fighting for so long, she foolishly thought that once she broke over into the other side, it would be over. That Doyenne Cecily would be so pleased with her success, she would, what? Give her rule of the Four Corners? Of course, that was what she wanted, deep down, but she thought maybe she would rule under Cecily's direction until she could prove herself. At the very least she thought she'd be welcomed with a warm reception and riches.

There was something off about the reception she was given. Winester—it pained her heart to think of him—had told her late at night, as they lay in her bed, that the new ruler of Lady Amadea's world was searching for a way to break in. Cecily had clearly picked up the hunt as well. She'd inherited the curse from her predecessor's predecessor, forbidding anyone solely from their world coming into Lord Vertrous's world. Her hands were tied. She desperately wanted to but needed some connection to make it happen.

Once Winester told her about the boy named Levi and how, ultimately, he could help them rise to power, she was fully focused on their goal. His ties to both worlds enabled him the luxury of going where he pleased. That power and knowledge could help them. When she lost Winester at the hands of that wretched sorceress Resbuca, it didn't dampen her motivation. If anything, it made her work harder. She lost both her husband and her lover and was left with Abaddon, the brilliant yet crazy man that became her biggest ally. Together they had gotten her here. Together they were able to do what no one before had. They united the Four Corners by destroying it. Now she was left to pick up the pieces and rule the lands however she saw fit.

Cecily seemed to care little about what sacrifices Lady Grustmiener had made or what was owed her.

It was clear what was going to have to happen. In the kitchen, the din reached its crescendo, the occupants having no idea their lives were about to end.

Chapter 15

Forgiveness

Levi sat heavily on an upturned tree. Every inch of him ached with the stress and strain of the last several days. He longed for a soft bed, something warm to eat, and for all of this to be over.

"Have you figured out your game plan yet?"

Levi jumped at the sound of Amaline's voice. He turned to look at her. Her left eye was swollen shut and a small cut ran to the side of it, but she had a smile on her face. She hesitated for a moment, then walked toward him.

He rubbed his tired eyes and felt Amaline sit next to him. The upturned trunk was barely big enough to hold the two of them, and she sat at an awkward angle, almost half on him.

"Have they found King Theaus yet?" he asked her.

"Not yet, but Calanthe sent out a team to look for him. It is only a matter of time."

"I hope he comes without any more fighting."

She had a sad little smile on her face. "Now that may be too much to ask."

"And Omire?"

She shook her head.

"Maybe he went home. Maybe he went to check on Grustmiener and any of the people who are left there." Levi tried to sound reassuring.

"Maybe."

"Now I guess we have one last hurdle to climb," he said after a long pause.

"I wish we could just enjoy this for a while first. It is a shame."

"A shame?"

"That you cannot celebrate what has been done," she said and gestured around them. "What you and Queen Aura have accomplished has not been done for hundreds of years."

"What's that?"

"You unified our world," she said.

He looked at her, a broken, yet jubilant, woman. Someone who helped lead an army. Someone who may not look like they had the kind of abilities they did. In short, someone like him. Levi reached out and grasped her hand.

It was strange and confusing being here with her. Amaline had been the part of the catalyst that put them in this mess. She, along with Omire, had been the ones to kidnap him when he entered this world all those years ago, but her remorse was plastered on her face every time she looked at him.

"Oh, Levi."

"You didn't know," he said.

Tears glazed her good eye, but didn't fall. He forgave her. After everything they'd been through together, it was the only thing to do. She'd saved him a few times, and he could tell she was genuine in her actions. It was clear she regretted what she'd done and carried that burden around with her ever since. She worked harder and longer than any of the other soldiers.

Forgiving her felt like a blanket lifted off both of them.

"I'm afraid what we accomplished won't make a difference if Lady Grustmiener is able to destroy my world," he said and dropped her hand. "I'm happy things here are good, don't get me wrong, but is it going to be at the expense of the people over there?"

"I hope not." Her bad eye was facing him, and it pained him to look at it.

He gestured to his own eye. "How'd you do that?"

She leaned in and whispered. "You know, there is this war going on. Some fighting and such."

He laughed, despite himself. "You should get that checked out."

"There are many more much worse off than I am. It will heal. But more importantly, of course, she will not destroy your world."

"How can you be so sure?"

She sat up straighter and visibly brightened. "You have a whole bunch more people fighting with you. We will find her. We will defeat her once and for all, together."

As if this sparked some deep-rooted idea in her head, Amaline sprang up and, before he could say anything, vanished. His side was still warm from where she pressed against it so reassuringly.

Chapter 16

A Plan

What should our plan of action be?" Aura asked. She looked around the room, but no one would meet her gaze.

It was late at night, and they were in her chambers. It felt like old times, like the battle hadn't even happened yet, like no time had passed. Calanthe was sitting in a chair watching the fire. Amaline was rocking from foot to foot as Milskar and Levi sat in hushed conversation together. For a moment, Aura looked around for Theirra, then her throat caught, and she had to look up at the ceiling to prevent herself from crying.

"We cannot just sit here idly," Aura said after she regained her composure. She slapped her hand on her desk. It was louder than she'd anticipated but produced the desired effect.

Every pair of eyes momentarily turned to her. "Sorry, my queen," the room said in unison.

"We need to go to the other world," Aura said. Only Levi would look her in the eyes.

"How many do you want to bring with you?" he asked.

"It is too soon," Milskar said. "We are in no shape for another battle."

"Which is why we will go together. This needs to be done," Aura said.

"And leave everyone here? It is too fragile," Milskar said. "It is not a good idea to leave these people to fend for themselves. We risk another battle breaking out in our absence."

"No one wants to fight anymore," she said.

"They may not *want* to," he continued. "But with no one left in power and tensions still high, it may naturally progress that way."

The room returned to silence as each member weighed the options.

"I will go," Amaline said. Everyone turned to look at her. She looked silly in her defiance with her black eye and beaten up body. She looked about as ready to fight another battle as to run from one end of the kingdom to the other.

"Amaline." Aura's voice softened.

"It makes sense. Send me and a few more people. Lady Grustmiener is sure to be on the lookout for you, Queen Aura," she said. "But no one will be looking for me. Send me and a few of the strongest fighters left. We will have the element of surprise and can end this once and for all."

"I will go as well," Levi said. Aura immediately bristled.

"Absolutely not," she said.

He raised an eyebrow at her. "I don't think you have many options. Or many people who have the faintest clue how to maneuver around my world. You're a bit stuck."

"It is far too dangerous. You are the one she is after," Aura said, trying to hide the pleading in her voice. "We will send a party there. And if needed once they access the situation and find her, they can send for reinforcements. At that point, we can ask people to join and fight with us again. It will give them a break while Lady Grustmiener is located. Then we can figure out our next step, but you need to stay here where you are safe."

Levi moved and sat on her desk, taking her hands. "I will be fine, but I have to do this. We need to end this, and we both know that I need to be a part of that."

She found it difficult to meet his gaze and turned her attention to the rest of the room. It was true that they looked battered and battle worn, but their eyes were bright, and they were sitting in front of her. They were alive, and she desperately wanted to keep them that way. If she sent them away, if she split them up, there would be no way to keep an eye on them. No way to aide them in their safe return.

"We will all go," she announced. She dropped Levi's hand and stood. "I will place Emily in charge while we are gone." She saw Milskar start to protest. "The people trust her, and Nikolas needs her. She will be fine. Then she can organize the fighters that will meet us— volunteers only—from any of the armies."

"I have someone from home that I can bring here to assist her," Calanthe said. Aura nodded her appreciation.

"And how will we get through the portals? Our scouts have reported back that they are still closed," Milskar said.

"Lady Grustmiener found a way," Aura said. "We must find the same way. We must find who helped her and convince that person it is in their best interest to help us as well."

"I think I have an idea," Amaline said in a hesitant voice. She looked over at Levi. "I got to thinking after our conversation."

She moved to stand closer to Levi. Aura had a strange feeling as she watched them.

"What is your idea?" she asked. She tried to keep the focus on Amaline.

"So, Lady Grustmiener is totally evil." Amaline began to talk and then hesitated a moment.

"I think we can all agree on that one," Calanthe said. The room broke out in relieved chuckles. It felt good to let some of the tension of the past months go.

Amaline continued, gaining vigor with her voice after each word. "So, she spent a lot of time in what we presume was the northern woods of Grustmiener or something like that, hiding out and plotting her revenge. She had no one with her—no support, no followers, no one."

"I don't think I'm following," Levi said.

"Witches!" Amaline said brightly. "She must have come across some in the north or even traveling in Omaner. They must have helped her gain some of her power back. I doubt she could have done that on her own. Even if she just had one witch working with her, that is all it would take. Just one ally. And I am sure she would have made promises or whatever." It seemed like she was on a roll now. "That must be it. And the powers that boy had with the dead, maybe the witches gave it to him."

"Now I think we are getting a little ahead of ourselves," Calanthe said.

"Well, either way. Who is the best person to unlock a portal?" she asked the room.

"A witch," Milskar said.

Amaline beamed. "A witch!"

"So, all we need to do it find a witch and that will solve all our problems?" Calanthe sounded skeptical.

"It is a start at least," Amaline said.

Aura paused and thought this over. It was as good a plan as any, she decided. The occupants looked at one another for several moments.

"So that's it then? We are going and fighting?" Levi broke the silence.

"We are going. We are putting an end to this," Aura said and strode from the room.

Chapter 17

Lost and Found

It caught Julia off-guard when she saw her own face. It wasn't that she had changed, quite the contrary, she was frozen in time. It was just how unexpected it was.

She was on her way to the bathroom in the small diner where Toli and Deserae had taken her to when she saw the bulletin board. It was strewed with pieces of paper in various degrees of fading, and there she was, staring back at herself.

The photograph was a few years old—they really couldn't find a more recent one?—but she was instantly recognizable. The word MISSING topped the paper. She quickly looked around, and, after confirming no one was looking at her, ripped the sheet off the board and crumpled it into the nearby trash. Just as she was about to turn, another face leapt out at her.

Jada didn't smile. He stared straight through at the camera. It made him look about ten years older than he was. His was a more recent picture, and there was a plea for a safe return and a reward for more information.

Julia's chest tightened. There was no reward on her photo.

She took Jada's picture down as well and let it join hers in the trash. She did another quick scan but didn't recognize any of the other faces.

As she passed by the board on her way back from the bathroom, she looked straight ahead, fighting the urge to glance at the bin which held the weak plea for her return.

Toli and Deserae were just as she'd left them, deep in conversation over cups of coffee. Their food was still untouched at the table. Julia had scarfed hers down and wondered as she sat how she could broach the subject of eating Deserae's toast.

"So, I think we need to leave the city," Deserae said when Julia sat.

"Leave?" Panic rose in her. "I can't leave, how will they find me if I leave?"

"What makes you think they are going to come for you?" Toli asked. There wasn't malice in his voice, but it still hurt Julia deeply. Why did she think they would come for her? They didn't owe her anything. Heck, they barely knew her. A small part of her wanted to jump up, grab the paper out of the trash, and call the listed number.

"They will come. They know Lady Grustmiener is here. They will come." This she was sure of. If not for her, they would come to finish the war once and for all. She could figure out where she fit into the mix when the fighting was over.

"Well, if that's true, and they are on their way," Toli said.

"I want to be as far away as possible when that fight breaks out," Deserae finished.

"You won't be here? You don't want to fight? What was all that talk before?" Julia asked.

"If this group is what you say it is," Deserae said.

"They won't need us anyway. I'm not going to risk my neck unless I have to."

Silence fell upon them. Julia could have screamed in frustration. It was mere hours ago that the two sitting in front of her seemed ready to pick up the fight and carry on with just the three of them. Clearly, something had changed.

"What have you heard?" Julia asked. Neither would meet her eyes. "What happened when I went to the bathroom?"

"We came to our senses," Deserae said.

"Bull," Julia replied. "What happened?"

"All right," Toli said. "We got word from someone we know in the Four Corners."

Julia stiffened.

"There is a battle raging there. All the kingdoms are fighting. Julia, I'm sorry, but I don't think anyone is coming here any time soon. And if that's the case, if it is up to just the few of us here to go up against her, I don't think we have the manpower to do it," he continued.

"So that's it? It might be too hard and too dangerous, so you're going to give up? You aren't even going to try?"

"It's not that simple," Deserae said.

"Oh, I think it is."

"It's not," Deserae said firmly. "Yes, we do want to fight, but we also need a world to live in when this is over, and if the Four Corners is burning and this world is burning, there isn't any place left to go."

"I think we are better off lying low for a little bit," Toli said. "See what happens, see where all of this goes. Maybe Lady Grustmiener won't resurface for a while. She is going to need to gather some sort of following. That could take months. In that time, who knows, maybe the fighting will be done over there, and they will be able to come help."

"You are more than welcome to sit here and see if others will do the work for you," Julia said. She got up and moved toward the door. "But I am not one to idle around and let others do what's hard while I sit and wait."

The bell jingled as the door shut behind her. It took every ounce of her strength not to burst into tears.

Chapter 18

The North

Aura's breath cut plumes of smoke through the frozen air. Heza's breath was visible beside her, the dragon's eyes sharp with focus. The world was silent as they moved through the open expanses.

Aura looked to her left and right. Levi and Amaline held the line with her. He smiled weakly, though she could see all over his face he was freezing as well. Amaline had lost some of her pep but looked the most alive of the bunch.

Flanking them were Milskar, Jada, and Calanthe. Aura thought back to the fit Emily had thrown when Milskar informed her that she had to stay behind.

"There's no way I'll allow you to go on your own. If anything, I'm more useful than you are. I actually know how to read a map and drive a car," she said late two nights before when they were in Aura's office.

"Be that as it may," he said flatly.

"Don't patronize me," she shrieked. "You know it's true. You know you need me." She turned to face her cousin, her anguish palpable in her expression. "Levi."

He shook his head. She had hot, fat tears in her eyes. Aura felt torn but tried to keep her face relaxed and expressionless.

"I can't let everyone I love risk their lives while I sit at home and do nothing," she said. She turned to the group around her, but each of them, in turn, lowered their eyes. "Please."

"Emily, listen, I cannot risk losing you again," Milskar said. "I cannot risk something happening to you."

"So, it's okay for me to lose *you*?"

He sighed. "No. None of it is all right, but Nikolas…"

Their son's name hung in the air like a flag. Neither spoke, but, eventually, Emily nodded and promptly left the room.

"I—" Milskar started.

"You did the right thing," Aura said. "I will speak with her tomorrow. I need someone to look after the kingdom while we are gone, and if—" She broke off, unable to finish her thought out loud.

Early the next morning Aura, Milskar, and Jada went to find the portal that Lady Grustmiener and Julia went through. As expected, it was closed, but they were surprised to find a woman lying still on the ground close by. Milskar bent over her, studying her face.

"Witch," he confirmed.

"Amaline was right," Aura said. He nodded.

They gave her what they thought was a just burial and returned to the castle to continue preparing for their departure. Early the next morning, the team of six departed. Emily walked to the edge of the castle grounds with them, having come to terms with staying behind, bolstered by Aura's heartfelt request.

It was painful to watch the good-byes between Emily

and the rest of the group. Nikolas was still sleeping. They thought it best not to make a big show to him and risk upsetting him when he couldn't understand what was happening anyway. When the group turned to leave, Emily ran forward and grabbed Aura's hand, pulling her back.

"Just as I have promised to keep your world safe, you must promise to do the same for me." Her eyes bore into Aura.

"I promise," Aura responded firmly. As she walked away and mounted Heza, she wasn't entirely sure what she'd agreed to. Was it to keep her physical world safe, the home she came from, in which her family still lived? Or was it the world that was mounting an adjacent dragon? Aura vowed to do her best to save both.

The creatures cut their travel time substantially, but it still took the better part of three days to reach the northern rim of the Morski forest in Omaner. Along the way, they flew over the charred remains of countless villages, reminders of the destruction of Lady Grustmiener. Aura closed her eyes and said silent prayers to the heavens for those lost souls.

The air grew thinner and colder, and she wondered if they should have brought only the griffins instead of the dragons. To her right, Levi was riding Gilbert, and behind him Calanthe was astride another griffin, but the others were on various dragons. She knew how upset Heza and the rest would have been at being left behind, and let that cloud her better judgment. When they touched down on the far side of the woods, Aura's fingers and face were frozen. The feathered beasts were the only pair that looked comfortable with the temperature.

They rested in the tree line, huddled around a fire Heza had made from a pile of frost covered fallen trees. Levi pressed himself tightly against Aura, Amaline to the other side of him. The memory of seeing the two of them on the fallen trunk churned in Aura's stomach, but she pushed the thought away. The dream felt like a million lifetimes ago, but just as vivid as if she'd just awoken from it.

"How much farther?" Calanthe asked, her teeth chattering.

She had about seven layers of clothing on but acted as if she had none. The south never saw cold weather, and she evidently wasn't prepared for the shock of it. Aura's heart went out to the woman, normally so strong and formidable, reduced to a shivering mess. She sat so close to the fire, Aura worried about her safety. Milskar and Jada looked miserable, but not too worse for wear.

"We follow the open plains through the mountain passes, and they should be there," Aura said.

Calanthe looked at her with murder in her eyes. "*Should?*" she asked through clenched teeth.

"W—Well," Aura stuttered, not prepared for her tone. "They do travel, but they typically stay in that area. Theirra said—" Her voice broke off.

She hadn't said her friend's name in what seemed like ages. It felt foreign on her tongue. Levi squeezed her knee while she brushed tears from her eye.

How she longed to see her friend again. How she wished Theirra was on this journey with them. Calanthe opened her mouth to say something but shut it again after a sharp look from Milskar.

"I do not think we are far," Amaline said brightly. "I have also spoken to those who have traveled to the witches and wizard territories and what Queen Aura said is correct."

Silence fell over them. Puffs of smoke rose into the air, a mixture from the fire and their own breath. Aura tried not to think about how cold she was. She locked eyes with Jada and wondered if he'd invaded her thoughts and knew what little truth her words held.

It had been years since she'd heard of the location of the witches. If they weren't where she thought they were, she was out of options for their future. She kept this fact to herself. Levi had told her that Jada made your mind feel cold when he looked inside, but with how cold she already was, would she even know? If he did know, or even suspected, he didn't let on about it and went back to rubbing his hands together.

She looked over at Levi and then the huddling mass of creatures in the tree line. The dragons kept opening and closing their wings in a desperate attempt to generate heat. The griffins slept soundly.

"Levi," she whispered, not wanting to disturb the rest, in case they were able to sleep. "Can you do something to heat them?"

Levi looked in the direction of the dragons. "I—I don't think I have those kinds of powers Aura, I'm sorry."

"Please, can you try?"

His face morphed into a pained concentration. His complexion purpled and Aura was worried he was going to pass out. He flinched next to her and then sagged.

"It's so cold. It's hard for me to concentrate. I tried to enclose them with some warmth from the fire, but it isn't working. Aura—" he broke off.

She raised a frozen hand and placed her finger tips against his cold lips. "Shh. It is all right. Try to get some rest. We will stop for about a half hour. I am afraid if we wait any longer than that—" She moved toward him and lowered her voice even more. "—we will not be able to start again."

He nodded and followed her gaze once again to the large masses. "They'll be okay."

Aura tried to sleep, but even with the fire, she was still so cold. Her body was also unable to relax. She wondered if there would ever be a time when she would feel safe again. Even if they were able to defeat Lady Grustmiener, would life ever go back to normal? Had she reached the threshold for loss where she could no longer recover from it?

Levi shifted next to her, and her heart tightened. If she lost him, too, lost anyone else from this group pressing in around her, she feared there'd be nothing left to fight for.

Chapter 19

The Witches

The cold was so all-consuming, it was like a permanent part of him now. Levi felt as if it was an extra appendage. Did frostbite exist here? His magic was sluggish, which made him worry about their vulnerability. If they were attacked now, they'd surely perish.

They were planning on resting for about an hour, but after only twenty minutes, Aura called for them to pack up. None of them were sleeping anyway, the fire was doing a frustratingly poor job of keeping them warm. They lied and told Heza how great it felt and how thankful they were for her help.

She'd lit some fires for the other dragons, but it seemed to have little effect on them as well. It pained Levi that he wasn't able to help them. It made sense once Aura told him, but he never thought about the lizard-like creatures needing the warmth for their cold blood. Could they freeze? They seemed so strong but looked smaller somehow huddled together. Would Heza and the others ultimately fall out of the sky, leaving Levi and Calanthe to scramble and try to save their fallen riders before they plummeted to the earth?

The image was heavy in his thoughts when he approached Aura as she stared at the fire, a pile of snow in her hands over it.

"Should we double up on the griffins and leave the others behind?"

"Leave them?" Her voice was full of confrontation.

"Just the dragons. Aura, they look like they're going to freeze to death. Which, frankly, will kill more than just them."

"We are not leaving them. We are not leaving anyone." She dropped the snow, and it sizzled as it extinguished the flames.

They wordlessly mounted their creatures and took to the sky. Since they didn't have as far to go and needed to be sure of their travels, they flew much lower. The air was warmer than the last time, but just slightly.

Levi buried his hands in Gilbert's feathers. The heat that radiated from the griffin burned as it thawed his digits out. He fought the urge to burrow his entire self in the warmth.

The topography shifted below into spectacular juts of rocks and ice formations. Gilbert's pace quickened, and he took over the lead position. It was clear from his determination that he recognized a familiar place in the distance and wanted to travel there quicker.

He swerved and dove through impossibly small spaces between the huge mountains. The adrenaline coursed through Levi's body and brought with it some warmth. It awakened and strengthened him, allowing his powers to increase it until he was finally, blissfully, no longer freezing.

After a particularly impressive aerial act, Levi let out

a whoop. Gilbert must have appreciated his enthusiasm because the animal sped even faster. Levi now understood the deep affection Kolas had for this magnificent creature. For a moment, he was able to forget that the whole world was in danger and just live completely in the moment.

Levi stole a glance behind him. He wanted to beam at Aura, to share in one bright moment in the darkness that surrounded them. To convey without words that they'd be okay. They were going to get through this, he was sure of it, but she wasn't there. He scanned all around. No one was there.

The warmth evaporated, and the cold wind rushed around him, roaring in his ears. Where was everyone? Where was he? Had they just gotten so far ahead, or were they lost? Or worst, was Gilbert taking him someplace else?

"Where are we going?" he hollered.

He was pretty sure the griffin understood English, but there was no wavering in speed or direction to indicate that he'd heard. Though as Levi looked around, it was clear they were purposefully losing altitude.

The air got about a degree warmer, and it felt heavenly. The shock of not seeing the rest of the group had broken his concentration, made it that he couldn't regenerate the warmth he'd been enjoying. The lower they got, the more noticeable the temperature increase was. By the time they'd touched down, beads of sweat were forming on Levi's forehead and under his arms. He shifted the heavy clothing around to try to get some relief from the building heat.

He dismounted and stood next to Gilbert's head. The griffin pranced in place, his chest puffed out. It was clear he was pleased with himself, but Levi wasn't immediately sure as to why.

He patted him on the shoulder. "Good job, thank you, Gilbert." There was a palpable obligation to praise him, though for what was still left to be seen.

Gilbert strode forward, his paws making no sound as they padded over the snow. He stopped and turned his oily eyes to Levi before walking again. Speech or not, it was clear what he wanted, and Levi obediently moved to follow.

The ground undulated under foot, and several times Levi pitched forward and fell in the deep snow. His feet weren't as adept at moving through this place, and the going was slow. He was about to call out for Gilbert to wait when the griffin halted, eyes fixed and sides heaving gently. Once Levi caught up, he was about to ask where they were going when he saw black specks darting in and out of the formations surrounding them.

He'd been so concerned with where he was placing his feet, he hadn't realized they were walking into a dead end. They stood in a low bowl shape, mounds of earth, snow, and mountain on three sides of them. He turned to go back the way they'd come, but there were five hooded figures blocking their path.

They were surrounded.

Speech boomed around them, bouncing off every available surface. Levi couldn't understand what was being said.

"I'm sorry. I—I don't know what you're saying," he called.

Maybe they spoke a different language here. Was he going to meet his demise because he didn't have a magical world translation book? He stepped closer to Gilbert, embarrassed by the reflex to hide.

A form to the left of him stepped out. The woman's skin was as dark as her cloak, her eyes cutting white ovals in her face. She was stunning. She moved down the slope and stopped a few feet from Levi. He was rooted in place, by fear or magic, he wasn't sure. Gilbert trembled next to him, causing his senses to perk up even more.

She spoke in a low tone, and the griffin bolted forward. He kicked up snow as he flapped his wings around the woman. Her fingers moved over his golden body before giving him one final pat. He moved to stand beside her, their eyes both focused on Levi. His mouth was dry, and he found it difficult to swallow.

"Who are you?" She spoke clearly and without a hint of an accent.

"L—Levi," he stuttered. He could feel countless eyes watching him, but forced himself to stare straight ahead.

"Why have you come here? What are you doing with this precious creature?"

Was it Levi's imagination, or did Gilbert stand even taller at her words? He looked behind himself and momentarily locked eyes with one of the women before turning back. "I came with others. I don't know what happened to them." He felt very alone and begged for Aura and the rest of them to appear.

"Why have you come here?" the woman repeated, her voice even.

"I—we—" He stumbled over his words as he tried to form them. "The kingdoms are in trouble."

"We do not concern ourselves with the other kingdoms. For centuries, we were driven out of our homes, away from our families. We were forced to live in this frozen land. We have been exploited and used. We have received little help and kindness from the kingdoms. Therefore, we feel little obligation to help them."

"I am sorry that happened, I truly am, but you may soon have no home. We all may have nothing." Her silence was encouraging, and he rambled on, hoping to buy himself time until the others could arrive. "The portals, there is something wrong with the portals."

"What do you need with the portals?" Her tone was indignant.

"Lady Grustmiener, she got through. She's gone to the other world." Soft murmurs trickled around him. "We have to go get her. She's killed the king in the south."

She moved closer to him, and he fought the urge to back up. "King Piester is dead?"

"Yes, she killed him. She thought she killed me too and then escaped to the other world. I think she is going to try to take that one over as well."

"Why does thinking she killed you have anything to do with us?"

"Because—" He paused. "—I am the Missing Link."

The air cooled as his words echoed around them.

Chapter 20

Interrogations

Once back at the safe house, Toli and Desi bombarded Julia with hundreds of questions. After about thirty-six hours, they realized they had gotten any truths Julia had out of her. She had told them everything she knew. How she came to the magical world. Queen Aura and the battle she fought against Lady Grustmiener. How Levi was killed. This part still seemed unbelievable to her. The image of him lying on the forest floor unmoving. It didn't seem real.

She told them about the other hybrid kids and their powers. How she was using Jada's to help the others find her.

Deserae and Toli listened intently and were now busy planning their next moves. Julia was hopeful the two would now be willing to join her in finding Lady Grustmiener and fighting. They walked back and forth throughout the room, but never once looked at her.

She tried to keep out of the way, but it she was annoyed that they continued ignoring her. She'd picked through what little food they had, her patience reaching its end.

"All right, enough," she said, her voice echoing around the large space. Toli and Deserae stopped mid-conversation and looked at her for a second before resuming what they were talking about. "Enough!" she said louder. It had the desired effect.

Deserae strode purposefully toward her, making Julia shrink back. "Let the grown-ups handle this situation." Her voice was laced with sarcasm.

"I don't see you doing much of anything," Julia squeaked.

Deserae pressed her nose to Julia's. "What did you say?"

"Desi," Toli warned.

She wheeled on him. "No, you keep out of this. You've tried to run this show, but where are you running it to? We've been talking for two days. She's given us next to nothing. We've gotten nowhere, no closer to a decision on what to do."

"Deserae, we are figuring out our next move *together*. We will go *together*. Julia's included in that. She's given us quite a bit of information. Just..." He paused, carefully choosing his words. "...just calm down, please."

She took a step back, but her chest still rose and fell in short, quick successions. Julia felt a reprieve and released her own held breath. The three stood in a triangle, equal distances from one another. Each seemed on the verge of speech, but silence persisted. Toli sneezed, breaking a sort of spell that had befallen them.

"Bless you," Julia said. "So, what is the plan?"

"We need to get out of town, head to the country, and try to form a game plan with other hybrids in our area and figure out what our next move should be," Toli said.

"Leave?" Panic bubbled hot in her chest. She shook her head vigorously. "No, no way. I can't leave. I told you, I can't leave here."

"Oh, your 'friends'?" Deserae asked, putting the last word in air quotes. Toli gave her a pleading look.

"They know I am here. I can't leave. I know they're on their way, and I have to be here when they arrive." She hoped the doubt wasn't apparent in her voice. She'd felt the cold arrival of Jada on several occasions, so she knew he was at least keeping tabs on her. She just hoped that this information was being relayed to the rest of those in Esotera.

"Oh, right, your mind-reading friend. And how long are we supposed to wait for them to arrive? Until the war is totally over there? When they finally decide to come over here and take care of the problem they created, the evil they let go and stumble into our world to destroy it? At what point can we, say, cut our losses and take matters into our own hands?" Deserae asked.

"We can't stay here forever. We need to move," Toli said, his tone regretful.

Julia's vision swam with tears. "I can't leave."

"We can't leave you here," Toli said.

"Why? Why not? I thought you trusted me? Just pretend you never saw me then. I'll go my separate way. It will be like we never met."

"You know we can't do that. We want to trust you, Julia, we really do, but I think it's in everyone's best interest that we stay together right now. We can leave a message. That way when they get here, they'll know where to find us. Or you can just get them a message, read a piece of paper that lets them know we left."

"If they're even coming," Deserae repeated.

"Cut it out," Toli snapped. "Just cut it out, Desi. She's obviously lost and upset. She's trying to help us, so let's help her, too. We will figure this out together, but I don't think it's safe for us to stay here right now. We have a safe house about sixty miles north east of here in the country. We sent word for others to meet us there. It will be too noticeable for everyone to come here."

"And having people come to the middle of nowhere will go unnoticed? Don't you think lots of people in a city can blend in easier than in the boonies?" Julia's mind was whirling, trying to figure out any way to make them stay.

"Please, trust us. We'll meet out there and then travel back here once we have a plan, once we figure out what to do. This will work. This will be the best way. We'll get you reconnected with your people." Toli stared at her without blinking. She wanted so badly to believe him.

"And think," Deserae said. "By the time they get here, all the fun may already be over, and you'll be the hero." She cackled as she walked away.

Chapter 21

Esotera

It was strange how the kingdom could feel empty and yet be filled with so many people. Emily tried to bring everyone back to the castle grounds, but while Queen Aura had called off the fighting, there were still eastern and northern sympathizers who would not give up the battle willingly. Just when it seemed like things were beginning to settle down, she would hear word of combat and would rush with several guards to that area, trying to disarm the participants before others needlessly died.

Most of her days were spent running from place to place, putting out literal and figurative fires. Even the disappearance of their ruler did little to quell the Omaner people. King Theaus, after sending word that he wouldn't stop fighting, had melted into the darkness and hadn't been seen in days. His people, currently ruler-less, didn't want to return to their inhospitable homelands, preferring to stay in the more idyllic Esotera, but they didn't want to be under the rule of the woman they considered a murderer. They also wanted nothing to do with Grustmiener, associating that with the rule of the terrible woman who dragged them into this war. They were backed into a corner with no way out but through.

Most of the time, Emily could relocate the combatants farther north. The air was colder there, so most Esoterans avoided it, but it proved to be a reasonable compromise for most of the Omaner's. Some wished to go farther south, closer to Vertronum, but for the time being, she was trying to keep them all in about the same location. Quan, who had been placed in charge of the southern kingdom in Calanthe's absence, agreed. Really though, she wondered if he just didn't want fighters that close to his people's lands. She sympathized.

Emily wondered if a sovereign state could be set up, a sort of safe-zone, where people would be granted lands the kingdom didn't really want anyway in exchange for promised peace. She made a note to talk about it with Aura upon their return.

The referring was exhausting work, though, if there was one silver lining to the activity, she had little time to worry or miss those that left. If her mind wandered, she felt herself spin into a black hole, but was quickly pulled out by someone needing her help somewhere. She made a point to try to come home each night and kiss Nikolas and read to him. She wondered what his memories of this time would be. Would they be filled with resentment, his parents never around for him? Or would he be proud of what they accomplished, how their sacrifices helped secure his future?

She hoped both she and Milskar would be around to explain it to him. To make him understand why they had to spend so much time away from him. He was too little now. He lashed out in anger at her and pleaded for his father. It broke her heart, but she knew that this was the right thing to do. One day, one day, he would understand and hopefully forgive them for their absence.

Emily hadn't received any word from the group since they'd left and she wasn't sure if she should take that as a positive or a negative sign. Communication wouldn't be at the forefront of their thoughts, but she still expected Milskar to send a message, at least, that they arrived at their destination. She sent a jadwiga the day before, but it returned with her letter still clenched in its beak, body hunched in shame.

"That's all right," she said, stroking the white feathers. "I'm not sure where they are exactly. I should have given you better information."

"He got lost," Kiya informed her.

"Lost?" Emily had never heard of a creature in these parts not knowing exactly where to go. She assumed it was part of the magic of this place, that all the beasts knew right where everything was.

"Yes, he is really upset about it," she continued. "Something about the pull he normally feels not being there. I think the burned land also has something to do with it. He seemed disoriented."

"Have any of the other animals complained about this?" If so, she wondered how the dragons and griffins were fairing on their journey.

"Not that I can tell, though I haven't seen too many creatures around lately."

Emily had noticed that. It was as if, now that the battle was over, they melted into their surroundings. Maybe they were mourning their own losses? Or worried that they would be tasked with some other mission? On her travels, she noticed that the woods seemed quieter than before. She hoped they were just laying low and it wasn't that so many had been lost, their recovery was impossible.

She tried to keep who remained of The Kids engaged, but there was little for them to do with the main fighting over and the gathering of the dead being handled by the healers and townspeople. With the portals still closed, the group was stuck in Esotera. Emily was traveling so much, they were left for long stretches unsupervised. Tab had been absorbed by the search party guards tasked with traveling to as many villages to see if any inhabitants were left and if any of them needed help.

It was sad, slow work and she was grateful he agreed to partake. Maybe it was easier for him since he had no real ties to this land, but she couldn't imagine walking from outcrop to outcrop, picking over charred remains to see if anyone was still alive. Those that were injured were transported back to Esotera, and the healers did their best, but they weren't always successful.

The remaining of the children spent most of their days helping with the cleaning efforts, though it was clear they were just trying to keep busy until they could return. Jada was a last-minute addition to the group that left with Queen Aura. Aura had thrown a fit at the suggestion when Emily made it, but Levi agreed that it was the best thing to do.

"He is our only link to Julia, and possibly our only link to Lady Grustmiener," he said reasonably.

"Absolutely not. I am not putting a child at risk, in danger," she stated.

"No more danger than he has been in since he arrived," Calanthe said.

Aura stared daggers at the woman, her opinion not asked for.

Jada must have seen them meeting for he appeared in the doorway of Aura's office. "I want to go," he said. "I need to do something. You may not find her without me."

"You are fifteen," Aura said, as if this was argument enough.

"Yes, I am."

"You were—" Milskar began.

"Yes," Aura cut him off. "No one needs to remind me. I know exactly how old I was."

She looked at the faces surrounding her and realized that while she was technically their ruler, she was out-numbered. She somberly nodded. The group loaded up supplies and left the next morning, leaving Emily in charge. The notion both thrilled her and turned her stomach.

Each morning Emily noted that the children who were left behind gathered in the castle grounds and paired off with different teams, not returning until well in the evening. Galina always stayed behind.

Emily had tried to make friends with each of them, especially now that she was the only one left in power, but Galina proved impossible to crack. She walked the castle grounds in some sort of pattern known only to her. She'd walk several steps, get to a predetermined place, turn around, and do another lap. Never the same path each day. Never a clear rhyme or reason to her pacing. The only indication that she was even present was the ever-changing weather.

She'd heard about the girl's abilities to control the elements, but seeing it front and center was, at times, alarming. Emily could return from a shorter mission, arrive back before dark, and what was blue skies and cool weather would be transformed when she arrived home. Dark clouds would sometimes greet her. Once, much to Nikolas's delight, piles of snow littered the ground. Everyone talked about it, wondered what to do, though no one dared approach the girl for fear of what repercussion may happen.

Emily was deep in thought as she rushed into the castle that night, fighting her way through the cold rain that pelted her surroundings, when she heard a shriek behind her. The hair stood on the back of her neck as she turned around. A flash of white cut through the storm as the bird dropped a rain logged letter. It fell heavy at her feet. Emily fought the urge to tear it open, afraid that she might damage the soaking-wet paper. Instead, she calmly walked into her office and lit a candle. She held the envelope out and let the flame dry it as best she could.

After five minutes, her patience could take it no longer, and she gingerly peeled the flap back, exposing the contents. Most of the ink had bled and smeared. It was difficult to make out any of the letters, but the print was unmistakably Milskar's. Her heart leapt as her eyes strained to read it.

Through the blotches, three words jumped out at her: *We lost Levi.* Her heart dripped to the floor along with the water.

Chapter 22

Doyenne Cecily was deep in conversation with Respin when Lady Grustmiener entered the room. The two didn't stop talking or even look up at her appearance. Lady Grustmiener took long, even breaths, trying to calm her boiling blood and shaking hands.

She'd had a dream the night before about her late husband again. It was the same dream she'd had each night since arriving in this place. No matter how she tried to change the events, it went the same way each time.

She was walking in the woods but was disoriented and didn't know if she was back home or in this horrible place. The noises of the woods sounded all wrong, the animals large and strange and like nothing she'd heard before, but there was a familiarity about it that she couldn't quite place. She was chasing a small white creature as it darted from tree to tree until it disappeared under a series of thorny bushes. Something deep within her told her she had to talk to the animal. She needed to know what it knew. It was the key to everything. It was the only way she could find a way out.

Pulling back branches, she cut her fingers, but while blood oozed from the tips, there was never any pain associated with the marks. At last, when she was sure she could reach through and pull the creature out, a hand would touch her shoulder. She was expecting it, especially after the fourth or fifth time she'd had the dream, but it still made her jump every time. Turning around, she'd come face to face with her husband.

"I need you to help me," she told him. "I cannot do this by myself. I need someone to help hold the branches so I can get to him."

"There is no hope for you," he said in his cold, dead voice.

"Yes, there is, I just need to get the creature. He will help me get out."

"There is no getting out. There is no hope."

She'd reach for him, but as soon as her fingers made contact, he would vanish, as if made of smoke. In his place, faceless figures stood. One she thought was Winester while another was King Piester. The others she could not name, though they also seemed familiar. Were they people she'd killed? Was one of them Levi?

She'd wake in a start, angry that no one would help her, angry that she was never able to find out what the creature knew. And she was never able to alter the events. No matter how long she held off, she always had to touch him. No matter how fast she ran, the creature always made it to the bushes before she could catch him.

The dream put her in a perpetually foul mood, though little notice was taken by her companions. She wanted to wring their necks. Wanted to make them acknowledge her. To make her face the last they would see. To have them die in regret of underestimating her.

Time, she told herself. Just give it time.

"All right," Cecily said. Lady Grustmiener startled at being addressed. They'd spoken to her little, typically Respin only addressed her when the sporadic meals he prepared were ready. Today when she arrived at the table, there was only an apple and a knife. She picked it up and began slicing off chunks of the sweet, green fruit and dropping it into her mouth.

"What?" she kept her voice cool and smooth.

"We will travel soon. You may accompany us if you wish." This last piece was said as an after-thought. Lady Grustmiener clenched and unclenched her fists.

"Are we moving to a new cabin? Would you prefer one on a lake this time? Or perhaps at the top of a mountain?" Her voice shook from anger, and she took a deep breath to steady herself.

Cecily ignored her tone and said brightly, "Oh, heavens no. We are moving on."

"On? I do not understand."

"No? We are crossing over, moving to the other world. Heading to the Four Corners. Do you understand, or do you need me to speak more clearly?"

The image in front of Lady Grustmiener's eyes burned red with her hatred. Who was this woman to speak to her this way? After what she had done, after the work she'd done to secure the mission, she dared talk to her in this condescending manner? She looked forward to killing her more than she had to ending Levi's life.

"I did what you needed," she replied curtly. "What you asked Winester to do that he was unable to. Why do you need to travel back there, especially now? Let the other kingdoms take one another out. Fighting is still happening there. Let them burn it to the ground and walk through the ashes."

"I can't rule a land if I can't be there," Cecily said.

"Rule?" Lady Grustmiener's blood turned cold and sluggish in her veins.

"Are you hard of hearing today? Yes, rule. I need to see what is left and what to make of it before I can determine how to move forward."

"I did not..." Lady Grustmiener hesitated over her words, trying to pick them carefully. "...I did not know that you planned on traveling there. I assumed—"

Cecily laughed, and Respin joined in. The sound was infuriating. "Did you think—did you think that I was going to hand over the entire other world to you? Oh, heavens. Oh, heavens, you silly girl."

The laugh was still caught on Cecily's face when Lady Grustmiener deftly moved forward, slicing Doyenne Cecily's throat in one movement with the knife, the handle still sticky from the apple she'd been cutting.

Chapter 23

The Dead

Luther felt the dead all around him as he moved through the charred forests. They whispered to him, asking if he needed their services. He tried to quiet them, to make them shut up, but they wouldn't.

"Luther," they breathed in the wind.

"Luther," the leaves whistled as they flew by his ears.

He wasn't sure where he was headed, but he felt a deep urge to keep moving. As if the ghosts would catch up with him if he stopped for even a second. He was sure he'd seen Unna about a dozen times. She would flash at the edges of his vision, but when he turned to look, she was already gone. The anger that pumped through him waned as he put more distance between the battle and himself.

Tiredness and doubt replaced the adrenaline, causing his thoughts to wander. He longed for home, longed to be anywhere but here, to pretend that none of this had ever happened.

Why had he ever left his home? Ever thought that there may be bigger and better things out there in the world for him. He saw what he needed to see. The power he held frightened him. It was exhilarating when Unna was beside him. Part of him knew it was wrong, knew he shouldn't do what the crazy woman bid him to do, but he was scared of her. Scared of what she could do to him, and desperate at the same time for how she could help him. She promised him love. It clouded any better judgment he may have had.

But now with Unna gone, with that horrible woman having killed her, there was only one thing left on his mind. Revenge.

He'd seen her, was certain he was going to kill her, but was thwarted. He ran. He was embarrassed that he was unable to stay and fight and be brave, but he ran. Now he would give anything to be back in those woods face to face with the red-headed woman. He swore he could still see Unna's blood on her hands.

Instead, he was lost in this strange land. He'd gotten himself turned around and now hoped he could retrace his steps back to some place familiar. A branch snapped behind him, and he froze.

"What have we here?" a familiar voice said. Luther wracked his brain but was unable to place it. He whirled around, but no one was there. Was he losing his mind again?

"Show yourself," he called.

The voice laughed. "Ah, now you are giving orders. You ran away, a scared boy, yet you are suddenly a man? Suddenly able to tell another man what to do?" The voice laughed again. The woods were still. Luther's ears strained to place where the noise was coming from.

A man stepped out from behind a tree and Luther searched his memory for the man's name. He knew he'd seen the stocky person before, but had he ever known what the guy was called?

Luther knew he was aligned with Lady Grustmiener, but wasn't sure where his loyalties were now that she had vanished. He hoped they were still on the same "team."

"Where are you running away to?" the man asked.

"Not running away," Luther said. "I'm trying to find someone."

"Your little girlfriend?"

Luther's hands were around the man's throat before he knew what he was doing. The man's eyes bulged with shock as he fought for oxygen. His lack of struggle is what brought Luther back to reality, and he loosened his grip.

The man broke away, coughing and panting. Luther took a step forward, and the man put his hand up to stop him. "You made your point. You are a big tough guy, I get it," the man choked out.

"Who are you? Why are you following me?"

"Achan. And I am not following you, not really. The battle disintegrated, but I was not done fighting. I barely got to do any of it. I saw you, you looked like you were on a mission, I decided to see what it was."

Another snap was heard nearby, and Luther whirled in its direction.

"Oh, now you come out," Achan called. "I almost got killed, and you kept hiding."

"Maybe I was hoping the boy would be successful." Lieal stepped out into the light. He had blood caked over one side of his head and had a slight limp, but spoke in a clear, unwavering voice.

It was silly, Luther knew, but seeing a familiar face made relief wash over him. If he didn't think it would get him killed, he could have hugged the man.

"So," Lieal continued. "What is this little party about. Are we on an adventure?"

Achan gestured toward Luther. "You will have to ask the boy-genius."

"I need to find the red-headed queen."

Lieal's eyebrows raised. "Interesting. Why?"

"I need to kill her."

"That, my boy—" Lieal stepped forward and put an arm around Luther. "—is the first intelligent thing I have heard you say."

Chapter 24

The Abyss

It was difficult for Levi's eyes to adjust to his surroundings. The white of the snow coupled with the blankness of the sky made everything blend into itself. It was disorienting, and he struggled to get his bearings. He tried to place his feet in the prints already made in front of him and kept his eyes on the ground. It seemed like he was the only one making any noise, the rest somehow moved silently. Gilbert's feathers ruffled from time to time, the only indication that he wasn't alone on this journey.

After the murmurs died down after his announcement, the hooded figures appeared from all over the clearing and stood behind the woman in front of him. No words were exchanged, but they moved in a single file line through a break in the side of the mountain Levi hadn't seen before.

The woman who first approached him turned around and curled a finger at him. Gilbert trotted behind her as she turned to leave. Levi shut his eyes, hoping for a sign, hoping for some indication of what he could do. He was so far from home. So far away from everyone and everything he knew. He'd followed countless people into the unknown in the last several years with various, and often times disastrous, consequences.

Levi took a deep breath and stepped forward. What was one more bad decision?

They'd been traveling for days. Or was it hours? Minutes? The cold had made his mind sluggish, and he wasn't able to get his bearings on time. His feet ached, the ice had long frozen through his boots. He tripped several times and once thought about not getting back up. His thoughts drifted as he lay on the freezing ground. How easy it would be to simply close his eyes. To allow the cold to permeate through him until it pulled him out of the world. How selfish. How terribly ungrateful these feelings were. They burned his insides. Adam gave up his life for him, and here he was, lying on the ground acting as if it meant nothing. As if his sacrifice was meaningless. Levi rolled and stood, following the line of black specs contrasting against the horizon.

He asked, on several occasions, where they were headed but received no answer. Once he raised his voice, worried that maybe they hadn't heard. Gilbert turned around and made a terrible, guttural squawking sound. He heard laughter up ahead, but still, no response.

Was it his imagination, or did the sun not set here? He wondered where they were in relation to his world. The north pole? Did this world work the same geographically as his? He knew that if he walked through a portal it brought him to a specific location, or at least it was supposed to. It unnerved him that Julia came out in a different place than where they started. Would they go through a portal and plummet off the edge of a cliff? Or be hanging in space, the world dissolved around him? He wished Jada was with him so he could ask what the progress was in the other world. And Aura.

His heart ached to see her. To run his hands through her fire-colored hair. To kiss her pink lips and hear her whisper his name. He had to see her again. The universe couldn't be so cruel to take her away from him again. They'd found each other after so many years apart, that couldn't be for nothing. That couldn't be a meaningless exercise. No, he would see her again. He just had to keep walking.

Levi looked up, but he no longer saw the black specs. Gilbert, too, had vanished. He looked around, thinking that maybe he moved off the path, but he'd been stepping in the fresh snow marks all along. He was sure he'd been going the right way. He felt like a blind man, walking through a world of white instead of darkness.

He placed one more foot in front of him in the perfectly made impression of a paw. The print was twice as large as his foot, yet it appeared so delicate, six small circles atop a larger one. Six? Gilbert had six toes?

The thought was skimming over his mind when his foot touched the ground and went straight through it. He fell through the earth, the ground opened like a chasm beneath him. He was sure he screamed, positive of it, but the sound was swallowed up by the darkness that devoured him whole.

Chapter 25

Searching

Aura tried to hold her breath to better hear any noise from her surroundings. Heza puffed gently next to her, and it took incredible effort not to admonish the dragon into silence. The others seemed to sense her alarm because they didn't utter a word. She heard their clothing rustle in the wind, but otherwise, no noise came from their direction.

Where was Levi? How did they get separated so quickly? She knew they were heading in the direction that Gilbert flew, but they lost him so fast doubt nagged at her. She turned to the other griffin, begging her to indicate where they may have gone, but her deep amber eyes stared blankly at Aura as if she didn't understand the language she was speaking. What Aura wouldn't give for Kaya's powers right now.

They'd touched down in a small clearing at the edge of a mountain ridge. Formations rose up around them, and the snow was powder soft and untouched. She swore this was the direction he'd traveled. It was where she was told the witches would be. She was warned that they would come to this place, and they would be greeted and moved to whatever location the rest of the clan was residing. Blankness surrounded them, blending in on itself.

Tears sprang to her eyes. Could they have missed him? Could he have fallen, Gilbert traveling too fast for his frozen hands to hold on to, and plummeted to his death somewhere between when she saw him last and here? Should she go back and search for him?

With the countless miles they'd traveled, all the adventure and danger they'd encountered in these last months, this couldn't be how she lost him. She wouldn't have it. They needed to find him.

"Maybe he fell?" she questioned the group. They didn't look at her. She knew what they were thinking. What fool's errand had she taken them on? Why did she insist on them all coming? Couldn't she have found the witches by herself and brought them back to Esotera? Open up the portals by them and travel together to the other world? But she felt like they needed to do this, needed to be in once place so when the portals were open, they could get a move on right away. There was no time for hesitation. Lady Grustmiener could have been anywhere in the other world, and they needed to find her.

Jada informed them that Julia had been stuck in the same room for several days now. She was there with two people, but he wasn't able to get a good look at their faces. He could feel her frustration though, and fear. He tried to stay as long as he could, to reassure her that they were concerned about her, but he was never able to for more than a few minutes. They had to keep moving. Stopping was a luxury they couldn't afford.

Aura knew this. They needed to keep moving on, but she couldn't do it. Levi's loss had her rooted in place and confused as what to do next. She'd been so confident when they left. Sure that this would be, maybe not an easy journey, but a safe and straightforward one. She never once thought they may lose someone, not now. Not here.

"Can you see Levi?" Milskar's rough voice cut through her thoughts as he called to Jada and brought her back to the present.

"No, I don't feel anything," Jada said with an apologetic look in his eyes.

"What does that mean?" Aura asked. She tried to keep the panic from her voice but wasn't sure how successful she'd been.

"Might not mean anything. Might mean he is too far away or in a place where my powers don't work."

"Too far away?" Amaline asked skeptically. "But you can see Julia." Milskar gave her a stern look that Aura was pretty sure she wasn't supposed to see. "I mean…" Amaline tried to recover but didn't know what else to say, her unfinished sentence hanging in the frozen air.

"Or someplace I can't see," Jada repeated.

"Or he could be dead." Aura hadn't realized she was the one who said the words until everyone looked at her. "We need to keep moving. We are on a mission, and we need to complete that. Calanthe, would you please do a small circle back and see if you see anything? "

"Of course," the woman said and mounted the griffin. In two huge flaps, the dark brown beast took to the skies, flying low over the horizon.

"We will keep moving forward. She will catch up with us." Even as Aura said the words, part of her knew she would never be able to walk a step forward. The others filtered by her, but she stayed, rooted in place.

"My queen." Milskar's voice and touch were soft as he passed her. "He will be fine. He is probably up ahead.

We need to go meet him. He will be wondering where we are.”

She wiped tears from her eyes but did not move.

“Calanthe will find us,” he said, as if that was the reason she didn't want to leave. His hand tightened on her forearm, and he pulled her slightly forward. She stumbled after him, tears unapologetically running down her face.

Chapter 26

Carrying On

When Emily and Nikolas exited the castle early the next morning, she saw Galina walking the perimeter grounds. Emily and her son were planning on going for a stroll and to visit the horses in the stables. Several of the old king's horses had stuck around after the battle, and the barn was full with the sounds of their munching hay and the warm, musty smell of their bodies pressed two to a stall.

Emily had grown to love the horses and enjoyed visiting them. It was a much-needed break after a sleepless night. She couldn't get the words Milskar had written her out of her head. How could they have lost Levi? Did something happen to the group? She'd scribbled a letter back and asked the tired bird to please fly it back. Kiya disapproved of her asking so much of the weary creature, but Emily needed to get in touch with the group.

She tried to push these thoughts from her mind and focus on the present, but there was a sadness about the barn that pulled her in even another direction. Gustado had been the head groomer since Theirra's rise to Aura's confidant, but the place still reminded Emily of the woman. Theirra's death was like a black cloth pulled tight over the building. It felt like something was missing, no matter how full the structure was.

Nikolas enjoyed feeding the horses carrots and apples he snuck from the kitchen. It had become their morning ritual on days when Emily was home. She knew she needed to release them back into the wild. They had been set free after the death of their previous owners, and she didn't want to break that thread by keeping them locked up, but it seemed so final. She wasn't ready yet to let them go. She told herself it was because she was waiting for the others to get back, that they would probably want to be witnesses to the event, but she wondered if there wasn't some deeper, unspoken reason she was afraid to address. As if releasing them would erase her last remaining ties to Aura and Milskar. If letting them go would seal the fate of those she loved. She knew it was completely ridiculous, but in the stable, they still resided.

Nikolas broke away from her and ran ahead to Galina. Emily caught up when they were already mid-conversation.

"I don't feel like it," Galina huffed.

"Oh, please. Please. Pretty pleeeeaase," Nikolas whined.

"Nik," Emily warned. "Leave Galina alone."

"Wanna come feed the horses with us?" he asked.

"No."

Nikolas's wide eyes looked her up and down. "Why are you such a sour puss all the time?"

Galina sighed. "Okay, fine. Whatever."

He jumped up, clapped his hands together, and sprinted ahead. Emily didn't know where he got his nerve sometimes. She and Milskar were usually so reserved, trying to always say and do the right thing, to be the kind of examples that people in the kingdom looked up to. Nikolas, on the other hand, had a wild streak in him that made Emily think of Levi.

It had been so nice to have her cousin back in the kingdom. Even through her fog of madness when she was first released from Lady Grustmiener's grasp, she'd realized how much she'd missed seeing his face. They'd spent their entire childhood together, and while she had ultimately decided to stay behind when he returned home all those years ago, it still pained her.

A small part of her thought maybe he'd stay behind, too. That he'd wait and see what this place may hold for him. If he could etch out a future that wouldn't be possible for him back home. Instead, he left.

She was pleased that he'd made something of himself while he was gone. She'd received occasional updates from her parents that he'd finally found a direction in life and success, but part of her ached for him like he was a missing limb. Selfishly, and at the horror of her own thoughts, she wanted something to happen to pull him back to her. To make him return here. She got more than she could have ever asked for.

Being imprisoned by Lady Grustmiener was the darkest period of her life. She still woke in cold sweats from time to time, picturing the faces of the people that were killed right in front of her. The screams of that little boy before he was mutilated. She saw Nikolas and thought of the children ripped from their parents and murdered, and for what end? So, Lady Grustmiener could spill blood here and leave? Leave this place to recover without her?

She wished Milskar was here and could wrap his arms around her. Whisper in her hair that everything would be okay and he would protect her. Though he failed. He wasn't able to keep her safe. Emily would never, never, say that to him, but she saw it every time he looked at her. The knowledge passed between them like a bird, and all they could do was stare at it, neither one wanting to give it a name.

Galina walked a few paces in front of her, eyes on the ground. Emily had tried to engage her in conversation before, but the response was never favorable. Her heart went out to the girl. She'd obviously had deep feelings for Adam. It might seem silly to some, but Emily knew more than most how quickly a person could change your life. Could make you look at the world in a whole new way, and you wanted to always look at the world that way. Always have them there to remind you of a particular time or moment. *If I lost Milskar...*

No. She couldn't entertain the thought. The knowledge of his existence in the world was the only thing that kept her going some days. Admitting that he could not be there was not an option. Him leaving her, really leaving her, couldn't happen.

Emily walked quickly to match strides with the girl. "Galina."

"Don't," she said.

"Galina, please."

The girl whirled around and faced her. It took Emily by such surprise, she about crashed right into her.

"Whatever you are going to say, save it. It can't help. It won't make the pain better. You got what you wanted, and I didn't. That's what happened, and nothing you can say will make it not have happened. You don't understand." As she talked her eyes reflected forming tears, but they didn't fall.

"I understand a little."

"Humph." Galina turned and began walking toward the barn again.

"That's why I'm even here," Emily said, matching pace with her. Whether she wanted to hear it or not, Emily needed to say it. It needed to be said. Galina needed to know, no matter how much she might feel it, she was not alone in this place. "I met Milskar here, and I couldn't leave. I didn't even know him for very long, but that didn't make my feelings not real. Didn't make what we had not true."

"Yeah, and you got your happy ending. Congrats." Galina raised her hand swiftly to her face several times.

"I'm just saying…" She paused, trying to piece together the correct words, as if there was such a thing. "I know what it's like to meet someone and know that you will do anything for them. That they mean something to you that you aren't sure anyone else can mean to you in that same way. And I'm here. I'm here just like you, and he isn't—"

"Yeah, but he's coming back," Galina retorted.

"I hope he is," Emily whispered.

Chapter 27

Foe

"What's our game plan?" Luther asked.

"Oh, so now you need a plan?" Lieal said lazily.

Luther's skin crawled being around these two. He knew they were his connection to finding Unna's killer and Lady Grustmiener. It just would have been great if someone else had found him. Even the creepy old guy probably would have been better than these two.

They bickered constantly. Lieal was much younger but was in a higher position of power than Achan. Each time one spoke, the other rolled their eyes or gave dirty looks. It was like two siblings vying for the attention of their parents. Luther was sick of it, but he didn't have a lot of options.

He felt his anger building into a force. He worked on bottling it, pushing it deep within him as if there was a cavernous reserve that he could fill until the moment when he unleashed it. Luther could picture the woman—Lieal called her Queen Aura—and his anger would crescendo. After much concentration, he was able to take a deep breath and put the pressure down into the deep abyss inside himself.

She'd better watch out. He was preparing. When he met her, he was going to kill her. He was going to raise each dead person around him until they crushed her under their weight. His revenge would be complete, and then he would meet whatever fate resulted.

"I say we go back to base." The other two looked at Lieal as the man spoke. Achan was about to say something when Lieal raised his hand. "Let me finish. The other side, they don't know that's where we were. That's where Lady Grustmiener hid."

"Do you think she may be back there?" Luther asked. Why hadn't he thought to go there?

"Oh, no. No, she is long gone. That is a dragon that has flown long ago, and we were not on it. But others may have gone there. Anyone who's left, that is where I would think they would meet up. I think that is our best bet for regrouping and deciding what to do from there."

It seemed logical to Luther, but he could tell Achan wasn't pleased with the idea.

"How far do you think that is? Did we leave any supplies back there?" Achan absently rubbed his belly when he addressed Lieal.

"How have you made it this far in life being as lazy as you are?" Lieal asked.

It was clear there was some history between the two by how they looked at one another, but Luther wasn't interested in settling scores or working out differences. He had one focus, and either these two could help him on that mission, or they couldn't. In which case, he'd have no use for them.

"Lead the way," Luther said.

The others looked at him and hesitated for a moment, not sure if complying would mean they were following orders. And if they were, if they did, did that put Luther in a position of power over them? He was the one with the plan. He was the one with a mission.

Lieal chewed on his lip for a minute before nodding. "All right, foreign boy."

He turned and walked the opposite direction Luther expected him to go. Achan followed directly behind.

The buzz that had been coursing through him was momentarily tampered down by having a plan. Luther felt like he could think for the first time in days. They needed supplies—and not the normal kind. Sure, they needed food and water, that kind of stuff, but he needed to be thinking about what *he* needed. What he was going to do to gather his own army. Luther hoped that some animals had either been left behind at the old base or fled back to it once the fighting had commenced. He would need a cart and something strong to pull it. Then they would have to travel over the lands between here and Esotera, gathering any dead bodies that were left behind. He would build his army one by one. Pluck each member out of the woods and pile them up. He wasn't sure how long it would take. How many would be left behind in the woods, but he knew at this moment that finding them was the next step.

If he had any hope of defeating Queen Aura, he needed something to control. An image flashed across his mind, and it was so sharp, so realistic looking, he didn't immediately recognize it as a day dream.

He pictured himself walking through an open field much like the one he found Unna in. Cowering around him were men and woman, each of them looking at the ground. Any that he passed that had perished, he collected, bid them to join him. They rose obediently.

Luther marched on toward a single glowing image. Standing at the edge of the clearing, red-flame curls covering her head, stood his nemesis—the woman he hated so much he was able to have every dead person in the kingdom behind him. They marched slowly forward, and while she should have been too far away for him to tell, he could see the fear in her eyes.

"Pretty boy," Lieal's voice cut straight through the image. "Get a move on."

Luther jogged forward to fall in line behind the other two, the vision still buzzing in his head as a wicked smile tugged at his lips.

Chapter 28

Demise

Respin didn't go down as easily as his beloved Doyenne Cecily. Lady Grustmiener had taken the latter by surprise, but Respin had a moment to prepare, to anticipate her attack on him. She probably should have killed the bodyguard first, but the opportunity to fell Cecily happened so quickly, it was as if another person had completed the task entirely.

Lady Grustmiener slashed at him, but he pushed back from the table, causing Cecily's lifeless figure to crash to the floor. He didn't have a weapon on him—how foolish!—and moved to the fireplace to grab one of the metal instruments propped against it. Lady Grustmiener reached it first. The poker slid easily between two of his ribs. Staggering back, he collapsed against the table as she moved forward, pushing the rod deeper into him. He reached out and put his hand around her neck, but his grip felt like a whisper. His eyes went wide then slacked along with his fingers. She stepped back, and he clattered onto the floor, resting near his charge.

There was a primal instinct within her that told her to run, but she fought against it. They were alone in the woods. No one was coming. No one could hear them. That was actually the point of coming here. She laughed out loud to no one at the pair's stupidity. They'd underestimated her, and as often happened when people did that, they paid for the mistake with their lives.

It didn't have to be this way. She hadn't planned on killing the woman when she first traveled here. She'd planned on coming to her, telling what she'd done, and receiving her blessing to rule over what she'd won. Not that she needed permission. Not that she needed the woman, but she considered it a professional courtesy. How she was treated was completely unacceptable. Like she was some kind of hired hand, the help. Like what she did meant nothing and that woman could just swoop in and take all the spoils for herself.

Lady Grustmiener bent down to examine the bodies. Respin's eyes stared unfocused and unblinking at the ceiling. There was no way she was going to be able to move the body on her own. He was a huge man. A huge, stupid man. His counterpart was a different story. It was as if she were made out of bird bones for how light she was.

Lady Grustmiener started to drag her when a noise emitted from under her arms. She recoiled, dropping the woman back down. Blood soaked the front of her shirt, but the woman's eyes followed her own. A gurgling sound came out of her throat as her mouth moved silently.

"You are going to die," Lady Grustmiener said. "There is no use."

The woman mouthed more words, and Lady Grustmiener lowered her ear to the moving lips. "You. Will. Not. Win," Cecily gasped.

Each word was spoken with a halting wetness. Some blood sprayed on Lady Grustmiener's face, and she moved her hand up quickly to wipe it away.

She stood and laughed. "Oh, but I have won. Can you not see? Has death brought blindness to you?"

She bent over with laughter. This foolish woman! This old hag. The gurgling stopped, and she looked over. The woman was dead, her mouth still open in speech.

Lady Grustmiener left the two there, deciding against moving the woman again. She went to the sink and turned on the faucet, her hand smearing blood on the shiny chrome handles. She was covered in it, a mixture from both victims she was sure. It was dark and cracked at the edges where the air had already started to dry it. It washed away so quickly. She marveled at how fleeting life could be. *Others lives*. Not hers. Her demise had been thwarted so many times, she was convinced of her immortality. How else could someone live through what she lived through? Survive what she'd survived?

With the blood rinsed off, she splashed her face one last time with water and took off her stained clothes. She walked up to her room and stood in front of a full-length mirror naked. It had been years since she'd seen her whole form like this. My how her body had changed. Her breasts, never having been suckled by a babe, stood high and firm. Her stomach, while flat, had a softness to it that hadn't been there the last time she'd checked. Though while age may have given her more lines, it couldn't take away from her clear strength. Her muscles were visible under her skin, lean and strong. She was invincible.

She turned, put a dress over her head, and fixed her hair into a bun when a knock came to the door.

Her whole body froze. They were in the middle of the woods. She'd scoped out the surroundings the last few days since she had little else to do. They were at the end of a long, dirt road, no other buildings for a mile in either direction. That was why they'd picked this place, she was sure of it. There wasn't supposed to be anyone around, thus no risk of being accidentally found.

The knock came again and sounded like it belonged to a large, heavy fist. She turned and grabbed a sword from next to her bed and a small dagger which she tucked into the belt at her waist.

She tried to move quietly down the stairs, but the wood squeaked under her weight. The outline of a figure was visible through the frosted glass at the front door. It shifted and moved in such a way, she wondered if there were two people behind standing on the other side. The grip on her sword tightened.

"Oh, come off it," the voice, male and with an accent, said through the closed door. "Let me in. I came as soon as you asked. It is hell to get up here."

So, they had called for help. She knew Cecily and Respin had lied. They weren't going to be alone. She wondered how many more there would be and where their loyalties were. Did they care about the dead woman lying bleeding on the other side of the door? Would they avenge her death, or would Lady Grustmiener be able to convince them of her cause? Promises could go a long way, she knew. There was little she could say that wouldn't convince at least one person to pick up a sword and join her. She'd done it hundreds of times. Thousands probably.

What was one more?

Chapter 29

Levi's head throbbed, yet he still couldn't keep himself from rubbing the bump forming on it. The fall had taken his breath away, and he'd lost his orientation. He landed with a painful thump, worried for a few moments that he'd broken a leg or something equally bad, but he just had the wind knocked out of him and an egg forming on the side of his head from the impact.

The witches covered their hands to hide their laughter. Gilbert floated down behind him, his wings catching the air as they plummeted.

"Thanks for the help," Levi said through clenched teeth. The griffin looked smug and stood by the women as Levi gathered his legs beneath him.

"What is this place?" Levi's voice sounded hollow. No echo bounced around the open expanse they were in. He looked up and could see a hole of sunlight pouring through from above.

They'd fallen, that much was clear, but where they

were now wasn't. The place looked strikingly familiar to where they'd just come from. White surrounded them on all sides. More white against white. The sun hit them the same as well. Where was it coming from? How could they have fallen through something and come out the other side just the same?

"Is that the question you want to ask us?" the woman asked. She stepped forward.

"Where are my friends?"

"Ah," she breathed, white puffs disappearing into the color-less background.

Noises infiltrated his ears. A soft shuffle at first, but the din grew louder and louder. Over the horizon, figures appeared. They approached at a crawl, indicating whatever was coming toward them was doing it on the ground. They varied in sizes, and Levi hoped, hoped so hard it made his entire body clench, that it was his friends.

The sun hit a glint of red, and he broke into a run. His limbs and head screamed in protest, but nothing was going to make him slow down. He saw her mouth moving, but couldn't hear what she was saying until he was upon her.

"Oh, Levi, oh my. Oh, thank the heavens," Aura sobbed into his neck as he lifted her up into an embrace.

He heard Amaline laughing behind her. "Told ya he would be all right. No one ever believes me." The group ignored her but moved forward to slap him on the back as they filtered pass. Even the creatures looked happy to see him.

Gilbert made a loud noise, and the other griffin trotted forward to greet him. Levi tried to pull back, but Aura clung to him. He felt her shudder in his arms.

"Shh," he whispered in her hair. "Aura, it's okay. I'm okay. Shh."

He combed his fingers through her hair. It had fallen out of her braid and spilled down her back. Her grip loosened and he took a step back, putting a small space between them. Her eyes were red-rimmed and her face lined with worry. His heart broke and swelled at the same time.

She moved her head in a measured nod. "I know, I just, I just thought—"

"I know. I thought so too, but it was fine. We're both here." She nodded again and held his hand as they walked to where the others were standing.

A conversation had already started between the witches and Amaline and Calanthe. Amaline was animated as she talked, in stark contrast to the calm demeanor of the hooded figures. It wasn't until they were upon them that Levi could hear the conversation.

"You do not seem too interested in helping us," Amaline said.

"That is not it. It just does not appear to benefit us," the woman said. Levi thought it was strange that she was the only one who'd spoken this whole time. He wondered if she was their leader or maybe the only one who spoke English.

"You," Aura said. She stiffened and halted without warning, pulling Levi back and making his ribs ache with the quick movement.

The woman bowed. "Queen Aura."

"You know each other?" Levi asked, having recovered enough to talk.

"She was present the night my father died. I am sorry to say that I did not get your name and have been unable to properly thank you for what you have done."

Recognition lit Milskar's eyes as he looked from one woman to the other. "Yes," he said. "I remember seeing you in the castle. I did not know…" He trailed off.

"Of my abilities?" the woman finished his thought.

"The king was desperate. He knew his final sleep was imminent, and he had some affairs he had to put in order." She looked over at Aura. "My name is Filia."

"You helped keep him alive so he could speak with me." Her tone was a statement, not a question.

"I did not know that was what he needed, but yes, I helped him hold on for longer than his body wished."

Aura nodded, tears reddening her eyes once again. Levi squeezed her hand, and she returned the pressure without looking at him.

She sniffled and wiped her nose before addressing the witches. "There has been a great evil threatening our homes and our future."

"Our homes have been threatened for hundreds of years."

"We had no part of that," Amaline said defensively.

Calanthe put a hand on her.

"Be that as it may," Aura said to Amaline before turning back, "sometimes children must pay for the sins of their fathers. This does not erase the pain they caused, far from it, but may it be a start to healing. To bridge the gap. You helped my father. I do not know what your reason for doing that was, but I ask you to consider doing the same for me."

The woman was silent, but she also didn't disagree.

"Please," Levi asked. "The whole world is in danger."

"You will be welcomed back to whatever home you wish. There will be no restrictions on your travel or your residence." Murmurs rippled with Aura's words.

"You do not have the power—" the woman started.

"I do. The rulers of the Four Corners have fallen. Those who opposed you no longer have control." She dropped Levi's hand as she spoke, and he couldn't keep his eyes off her.

She stood tall and confident. Her words were firm, and whether they were true or not, Levi believed her. As far as he knew, they hadn't received word yet about the fate of the king of the north, but it didn't matter. Levi knew they'd defeat him. Defeat all of them. Standing there, shoulders back and eyes straight ahead, he saw their future laid out in front of them. Aura would rule with her kind hand. The world would flourish. She would make sure of it. He was so proud of her, proud of the woman she'd become since he first met her those many years ago. No longer was she a scared girl. This strong woman replaced her, and he loved every part of her.

"Anywhere?"

"There will be no restrictions," Aura repeated. "In this world or any other."

A smile broke out on the woman's face. It was clear this last part pleased her. Did Aura mean what he thought she did? Had she just promised to open travel up between the worlds? This wasn't the time to question her, to ask her what she was thinking. They needed these witches to help them. Needed their powers to aid them. They could figure out the logistics later.

"Yes," the woman said.

"Oh, thank goodness," Amaline said. Calanthe shushed her loudly.

"I also have some unfortunate news I must share with you," Aura added. "It seems that one of your own, I do not know her name, was helping Lady Grustmiener with the portals. It appears that she was killed for her troubles. I am so sorry."

Filia's composure waned for half a heart-beat before she regained it.

"Yes, we were worried that might have happened. Neski sought power. She did not like her rankings in our midst, and I am sure promises were made to her that tempted her desire too much for her to refuse. She will be mourned." Filia paused. "I appreciate you not using this information to coerce us into assisting you."

Aura nodded as the witch fell silent.

"When do we leave?" Calanthe unceremoniously broke the somber moment, her lips trembling in the cold.

A smile broke out on the woman's face. "Oh, we are already here."

"What?" Levi asked.

"You have been here for some time. We had decided to help you the moment you walked into our midst. We passed through to the other world a few yards ago." The woman took a step back. Levi looked around and noticed the other figures were gone. She began to fade into the whiteness of the surroundings as well, only her voice remained. "Good luck, Queen Aura of Esotera, Queen of the Four Corners. Good luck."

The voice rose and faded, leaving the small group to look dumbfounded at one another.

Chapter 30

New Information

Deserae came into the room in a flurry. Her arms were filled with papers that jutted out in every direction. She dropped them on the table with a thump as she spoke without taking a breath. She was pulling her gloves off—she'd complained all morning about how the temperature was dropping too early—as she continued with her rapid rant.

"I can't understand you," Toli said in a bored voice. He didn't even look over his newspaper when he spoke to her.

Julia sat up straighter, it was clear something had happened. "What is it?" she asked.

"I received word that she was on the move," Deserae said. Her hair had partially fallen out of her pony tail, and she was struggling to push the fat curls behind her ears.

Toli lowered the newspaper. "Who's on the move?"

"Seriously?" Her voice sounded exacerbated. "Umm, the person we've been searching for days for. Lady Grustmiener."

"One the move where?"

"Northeast, though not as far as New York. Country, I think."

Toli stood at full attention now. "You think?"

Julia wondered if she should leave the two alone to talk about the matter but decided she was as much a part of this as anyone.

Deserae sighed. "Look, there isn't a lot of information out there. And it's even harder to gather when I can't be straight about it. 'I'm looking for a woman, but I can only give you a vague description of her. She may be with a man or another woman as well. Nope, can't describe them either. So, have you seen them?' We don't want to tip someone off and have word get out to Lady Grustmiener or Doyenne Cecily. From what Julia said, neither knows that Lady Grustmiener was followed here, and I'd like to keep it that way." She paced the room and rolled her eyes as she talked.

"Desi, this is serious. Where did you get this information? Can it be trusted?"

"Yes." Her voice was firm.

"Where did you get the information?"

She grabbed a browning banana from under the stack of papers and began to peel it, refusing to look at Toli.

"Where?" he repeated.

"Oh, fine. But you're not going to like it." Toli raised his eyes brows. She took a large bite of banana before speaking. "Heffi," she mumbled.

"Who?"

She made a show of swallowing. "Jeffrey. Okay? Jeffrey."

"Why in holy—" he started.

"Who's Jeffrey?" Julia interrupted. The two looked at her as if she'd just crashed some party they were hosting. "Who's Jeffrey?"

"He's a friend," Deserae said to which Toli huffed. "Well, he *was* a friend. Toli and him had a bit of a—" She paused, looking at him, but he gave no indication he was going to offer anything to the conversation. "—falling out, if you will."

"And what does this Jeffrey do?"

"Well, it's sorta complicated." Deserae looked at Toli again.

"He is one of the gate keepers," Toli finally said.

"Gate keepers?" Julia hadn't heard the term before.

"For the portals. They keep track of the time tables and do routine checks on them. Not all of them, there are too many for one person to keep on top of every single one, but in some of the busier cities or the busier ports, they have a person who keeps an eye out," he said.

"And this Jeffery person, he does that here?"

"Sorta," Deserae said. "He was stationed farther south in Maryland, but he noticed the portals were real quiet for a few days in a row, which wasn't normal for that particular one. When he investigated, he found it was closed."

"Yeah," Julia said. "The one I went through in Dallas closed as well. We weren't able to go home."

"Right, so he did some investigating, called up a few people he knew, and confirmed that as far as the US was concerned, all the portals here weren't open."

"There are portals in other countries?" This was the first she'd heard of it, or thought to ask.

"Oh, sure," Toli said. "The other world is large, just like ours. Parts saddle up against each other all over. I heard there is even one place that is part of the oceans, water everywhere."

"The south," Julia said. "That's where King Piester lived."

"Yeah, I guess he does," Deserae said.

"No, I mean *lived*. He was killed during the battle."

The two were silent for a long time.

"It was bad, wasn't it?" Deserae asked. Julia nodded. "Do you know what's left there?"

"The battle was still going on when I followed Lady Grustmiener. For all I know—" She paused. "I don't know what's left."

"So, what did *Jeffery*—" Toli said the man's name as if it was a sarcastic jab at Deserae, "—say happened."

"He didn't know. He started moving up the coast, wondering if maybe a forgotten portal was still open. He made it all the way up here."

"Convenient," Toli said.

Deserae ignored him. "He saw a woman go through who looked suspicious. He followed her for a bit but didn't think a whole lot of it. Jeff—"

"Jeff?" Toli interrupted.

"*Jeff*—" she said again. "—said he saw her go into a house. He kept tabs on it here and there. Luckily, he didn't catch Julia's escapades, but he did see the woman leave with an older woman and a man earlier yesterday."

"And he didn't know who any of the people were?" Julia asked.

"It's not like their pictures are distributed throughout our world. Doyenne Cecily tries to fly under the radar. I didn't even know she was in Philadelphia until you and Lady Grustmiener got here."

"So, did he see where they went?" Toli asked.

"He followed them up the highway for a bit but gave up once they headed into horse country. Said there aren't any portals for miles, so he wasn't too worried that they'd be crossing back over. He wanted to get back to see if anyone else was going to come through in Philly."

They sat quietly for a while. Julia wanted to ask a hundred questions, but she didn't want to interrupt whatever thought process the other two were working through. Finally, Toli spoke.

"So, it's settled then."

"I think so."

"What's settled?" Julia asked. They rose at the same time as if choreographed.

"We're going to have to go after her," Deserae said. "If she's here doing what you say she's doing, we need to make sure we follow her every move until the right moment presents itself where we can stop her." Julia took a step forward. Deserae put a hand on her chest and laughed. "Oh, no, not you, little lady. You stay here and wait for your friends."

"But I thought you said I had to stay with you, that I wasn't allowed to split up from you two."

"That was before, when we were going to go into hiding and figure all of this out, but now, now we need to act. We got the information we needed from you. I think we can trust you aren't really a spy for the other side and will tell them our plan." Deserae shrugged. "I guess I trust you enough now to leave you."

"No. No, I have to go," Julia said. Her insides squirmed. There was no way she could stay behind. She needed to do this.

"Oh, yeah, and play the hero, how exactly?"

The table lifted high in the air and slammed back into the ground. It smashed and sent its contents scuttling across the room. Deserae laughed.

"Well, you better hope wherever we're going has lots of dining sets. Look, you were the one concerned with your friends not being able to find you. But if you want to ditch them, I don't care. The more, the merrier."

Julia felt a coolness enter her mind. "They'll find me," she said confidently. "They'll come, and we'll lead them right where they need to be. They'll come, and we'll defeat her together."

"I like your hope, little lady," Deserae said, and it was hard for Julia to figure out if she was being sarcastic or not.

It didn't matter. She was going either way.

Chapter 31

Assistance

It seems that people are filtering out of the castle grounds," a man said to Emily late one night. She couldn't remember his name and felt embarrassed.

Her mind was still scattered from time to time, and it was difficult for her to concentrate. She'd made remarkable progress since returning back to the relative safety of Esotera, but she still had her struggles. It was difficult with Milskar gone. Emily would wake in the night covered in cold sweat, convinced she was still in the underground bunker. Without him there to assure her, it took several minutes for her to get her bearings and remind herself that she was safe.

She'd had too many conversations with the man standing in front of her for her to be able to ask his name now. They were past the point of no return. She'd have to find some way to get the information and then hope she would retain it.

Emily was part of the very small counsel Aura kept along with Milskar, Omire, and Amaline, so Emily had to scramble to assemble those who could help her with the day-to-day running of the kingdoms. Right before the others had left, they'd received word that Omire had returned to Grustmiener. She thought it strange that he left so soon and without informing them of his decision, but he claimed that he was needed back there to help inventory what was left. She missed seeing a familiar face she could trust and made a note to send him word to return to Esotera as soon as he could manage.

For now, the south was a no-man's land. With Calanthe traveling, their affairs fell to Emily as well. Luckily one of Calanthe's aids, Quan, was willing to help out until his new ruler returned. Emily liked Quan. He was quiet, but strong, and the other inhabitants appeared to respect him, despite him not being quite middle aged.

They communicated daily through letters the jadwiga brought, though for one of the first times since arriving in the Four Corners, Emily longed for some of the modern convinces of home.

The birds were quick and incredibly capable of finding their intended recipient, but what she wouldn't give to pick up an ordinary phone, press a few buttons, and be connected instantly. There were some arcane communication devices that worked with the other world, similar to telephones, but for some reason, they never got adapted here. She made a mental note to push the issue with Aura when they returned.

"Emily?" the man asked, jolting her back to the present.

"What? Oh yes, I'm sorry." She hesitated. If only she could remember the man's name. "That is good, right? They are feeling safe enough to return home."

"Possibly…" The man's voice dropped off.

"What are you thinking?"

"King Omire and Quan have not reported an influx

of numbers. And as far as we can tell they are not appearing in the north either."

Emily felt her eyebrows pinch together. "Then where could they be going?"

He shook his head. "Your guess is as good as mine. Should I put some people on any who leave to follow them?"

"No, not yet. Let us wait and see. We are already stretched thin in the search for King Theaus. I would hate to pull scouts off of that mission and task them with following various townspeople. They may be traveling slowly or checking on lost homes or friends before returning to where they came from. If we are still seeing the same drop in unexplained numbers tomorrow, I will send a few parties out to investigate. Please keep me informed."

The man bowed and exited the room.

Two women entered behind him, one from the south named Hai and one from the east named Edda. They'd stuck around after the battle, and Emily found them in her office with more and more frequency. They were smart and strong and had become confidants of hers. She greeted them warmly.

An idea popped into her head. "Do either of you know the name of that man?" she asked hopefully. They shook their heads. "Rats."

"Where?" they asked in unison, eyes darting around the room in alarm.

Emily suppressed a chuckle. "A figure of speech. Never mind. What can I help you two with?"

They looked at one another quickly, then down at the floor. Edda spoke up. "The animals?" Her tone was questioning.

"What about them? Are they all right?" Alarm prickled at Emily's skin.

"Oh, yes, yes," Hai said. "But they are restless. If there is nothing left for them to do here, can they start going back to their homes? We believe the bodies have been gathered and large graves have been dug. Trees and brush have been cleared and toppled houses cleaned up. I do not think there is much need for them anymore. We are afraid they are going to get bored and look for other…" She paused. "…outlets."

"They are quite large, some of them," Edda added.

"I will address them this afternoon, inform them they can leave tonight or travel in the morning, whichever they are most comfortable with." Both women looked relieved. "Are there any that we should ask to stay? Any need you can see of them?"

"The griffins have been useful," Edda said. "We only have four, but with a few of the dragons gone, it may be nice to keep them in case travel is needed."

"Good thinking," Emily said. They hadn't lost many beasts in the battle, but when it came to the larger ones, even a single one's passing was felt. The dragons and horses were relied on so heavily for travel, the half dozen that never made it home again were a serious blow to Esotera. Emily had sent one of each with Omaner when he returned to Grustmiener and Aura and her crew took a mix with them, making the addition of the griffins a welcome relief in logistics for travel.

"I will ask them if they are willing to stay," Emily added. "Thank you again very much."

The women nodded and turned to leave. Hai turned back before walking out the door. "I will try to find out the man's name," she said.

"I will be forever grateful." Emily felt a rush of affection and relief. Official or not, she was developing a pretty good group of aides all on her own.

Chapter 32

Hidden

Should we bring them with us?" Amaline asked, concern etching her face. "I think there is still time to send them back."

Aura looked over at the dragons and griffins huddled together a few feet away and hopefully out of ear shot. When the witches left them, the group had stood frozen for what felt like hours before Levi turned and started to walk. To what, they didn't know. None of them had any idea as to where they were, which made Aura feel incredibly vulnerable.

"I don't see how we can take them," Levi said. "But I also don't know how we are going to move without them."

Jada stood just outside of their little circle, a vacant expression on his face. Aura wasn't sure if he was trying to see Julia or anyone who may give them a clue as to their location. She still didn't know exactly how the boy's powers worked but hoped he would be able to bring some clarity to their situation.

"Will it matter? If someone sees us?" Milskar asked as he blew into his hands. It was warmer here, but still not close to the warm temperatures they were used to in Esotera.

"Oh, if we just walk into a city with a bunch of magical creatures?" Levi asked sarcastically. "Yeah, I think it will matter."

"Hear me out." His voice was even, not rising to Levi's bait. "If Lady Grustmiener is planning on staging a battle here, if she is planning on fighting for these lands as well, is it not inevitable for people to figure that out? Will a few 'magical creatures—'" He used air quotes and looked directly at Levi. "—really matter? I think we may have bigger problems to deal with than the general public getting their first look at a dragon."

"You've never been to Philadelphia," Levi muttered.

"Milskar may be on to something," Calanthe said.

"I am not endangering these animals," Aura cut in. "I will not put them at risk."

"Oh, because they have been so safe up until now?" Amaline said. They wheeled to look at her. "What? Seriously, we have all been risking our lives this whole time. They are intelligent creatures. They know what they signed up for and what they are getting themselves into. Do you really think they will just, what, walk home now? If that is what you want, I nominate you to tell them, because I am not going to be the one to say that we no longer need their services." She was speaking directly to Aura now.

"But—" Aura started.

"I know," Amaline interrupted her. "I know you want to keep them safe. You want to keep us safe. Of course, you do, and we are thankful for it, but it is also not going to happen. Not everyone is going to get out of this alive."

"I know that." Aura felt the losses press against her bones, crushing her. But she wanted those deaths to be the end of it. Childish, she knew, but she still wanted to be able to save everyone else, to not lose a single thing from here on.

"Sacrifices are going to have to be made, and all who are standing here are aware of that. You all know what may happen, am I correct?" Amaline looked around and was met with nodding heads.

She was right. Aura couldn't protect them. She probably never could. But that wasn't an argument for being reckless. With her own life, maybe, but not with the lives of others. Not with the lives of those she cared about. She looked back at Heza, Gilbert, and the other massive beasts, their eyes on hers. They didn't look scared. They didn't look defeated. They looked defiant. There was no way she could ask them to go home.

"They will stay with us." The creatures must have been able to hear the whole conversation, because with her declaration, a chatter began between them. Whether they could understand each other wasn't clear, but they made noise that each species comprehended.

"Well, if we are going to storm the city with them, might as well let them give us a ride," Levi said. Aura locked eyes with him, and he nodded. For the hundredth time, she felt secure in his presence. Felt like he was a sounding board for her fears and frustrations and allowed her to see them with clarity and overcome them. She never thought she'd find someone like that in her life. It wasn't that he completed her. No, it was that she was able to be a whole person, and he met her with his whole self, too.

"They're leaving," Jada said.

"What?" Levi stepped forward. "Leaving, where?"

Fear was in Jada's eyes. "I don't know. She looked at a map, but I couldn't read it. I saw a highway and bags. They are packing bags."

"The people she is with are going too?" Aura asked, alarm rising in her. "Are they forcing her to go?"

"No, she wants to go. They don't want her to, not really, but she insisted."

"Where could they be going? How will we find them?" The panic bubbled in Aura, but she refused to give in to it. She felt a hand on her shoulder.

"It will be fine. If they are traveling by car, there is only so far they can get in a few hours. We can move quickly once we are in the air. We are going to have to be high, so we aren't spotted, but we need to watch out for planes," Levi said.

"Planes?" Amaline asked.

"Flying objects," he explained.

"Like birds?"

"Sort of, but they are mechanical, like machines."

"How do they fly?" She was enthralled.

"I'll explain it to you later. All you have to know is they are dangerous, we have to avoid them, or we could get seriously hurt." Levi looked at each of them and waited for them to nod before he dropped eye contact.

"Keep checking in with her," Amaline told Jada. "If you get a new location, tell us immediately if we need to change course." They'd reached the dragons and griffins, and now she addressed them specifically. "We need to stay together. It is very important that we are not separated. We will fly east, but we do not know where or how far yet. We are trusting you."

They mounted and took to the air, fast becoming black specs against the bright sky.

Chapter 33

Visitors

The man was startled when Lady Grustmiener opened the door. He looked her up and down, and stared hard at the side of her face before he reached for his sword. She lifted her hand and wiped away a drop of blood she'd missed before. She made a tisk, tisk noise, freezing him in place.

"I would advise against that. Please, come in." Lady Grustmiener stepped aside and motioned for the man to follow her. She quickly looked around but saw no one else with him.

"Who are you? Where's—" His husky voice broke off as he entered the dining area.

She followed close behind him, her hand firmly gripping the hilt of her sword. "They are dead."

"I can see that. Who the hell are you?" His voice rose, a mixture of anger and fear.

"Lady Grustmiener. Ruler of the Four Corners and now—" She looked down at the slumped bodies. "—this world as well, I presume."

The man's brows knitted together. "But—but I thought you were killed?"

She laughed and smiled at him. "Oh, no. That rumor has persisted, but it is false, as…well, as you can see."

She pulled out a chair and sat, motioning for him to do the same.

He did so, but cautiously, throwing glances at the floor every few seconds.

"In a moment, I will ask you to help me with moving them, but for now, I need you to answer some questions of mine. And please, hands on the table," she warned when she saw his right arm shift infinitesimally. He chewed on his inner cheek but complied.

"Okay, what is this? Did you kill them?"

"Obviously." She laughed again brightly. "Who else would have? Who else would have had the power to do so?"

"And now?"

She leaned in conspiratorially. "And now, I rule everything."

He nodded slowly and glanced at the floor again. "Okay."

"Now." She slapped a hand on the table, and he jumped. This pleased her. This whole exchange was pleasing. Here was a man, strong, willing to take up arms, yet he was reduced to someone who could be directed with mere words. The thought of his endless uses tugged one corner of her mouth up.

"What?" he asked.

"Who are you? You know who I am, but I know nothing about you. What brought you to this place? How did you even know about this place? Enlighten me. What is your name?"

"Xavier." He spoke slowly as if he was unsure of the answer himself.

"Xavier. Wonderful. And what has brought you here?"

He looked at the floor. "I was summoned by Respin. I was informed the operation was moving to this location and that I should come right away."

Lady Grustmiener clapped her hands together, causing Xavier to jump again. "Operation? Oh, how wonderful, and what was this *operation*?"

"I don't know, not really."

"You came without knowing what you were being called for?"

"I did work for Doyenne Cecily from time to time," he said. "I figured there was some trouble and she needed some help."

She laughed. "If only you had arrived an hour ago."

Silence hung between them. He looked at the bodies again.

"Remove them, then we will continue talking," she said.

"What?"

"Remove the bodies." She spoke in halted words, enunciating each one. "It is clear they are a distraction to you. Remove them, and we will continue." She did not want to have to ask him again.

"And if I don't want to? If I just want to get up and leave?" He pushed his chair back but made no attempt to get out of it.

"It is too late for that. You served one master, that master is dead. You serve me now."

His motion was fluid. He rose and deftly drew a knife out of the sheath around his waist. Xavier brought it crashing down in the place where Lady Grustmiener had been. Had.

He cried out in pain as her blow hit the back of his head. His knife crashed and skidded across the floor, coming to rest in a dark corner on the other side of the room.

"There is only one way you will get out of helping me." As she spoke, she lifted his head by his hair and placed her own blade to his neck. He made a short movement in agreement. "Fine. Move these bodies."

He scrambled to his feet and rubbed his neck.

"How many more are coming?" she asked as he hoisted under Doyenne Cecily's arms and pulled her toward the back door.

"None," he huffed.

A knock came at the door.

She held up her pointer finger. "That is one. If you lie to me again, it will be the last thing you do." She turned to greet their next visitor.

Chapter 34

Spies

It feels like we've been driving forever." Julia tried to keep the whine from her voice but was having little success.

"Seriously?" Deserae asked without taking her eyes off the road. Toli held a map fully extended.

"Do you not have GPS?"

"Doesn't work well," Toli said.

"They have basically every road in the world," Julia said. And, she thought, it would give an estimate for when they may arrive.

"No, doesn't work well with us. Technology like that, our powers seem to disrupt the wavelengths. Didn't you ever notice that? Signals dropping, calls getting lost?" Toli asked.

Julia could feel her cheeks heating up. "I've never had a phone."

"Are you reading that thing right? I'm going to pull over and ask," Deserae chimed in.

"No, I can read it just fine. Keep driving. About a

mile up there will be a dirt road, turn on it."

"Wait." Julia sat up straighter. "We are going straight there? Right now?"

"Element of surprise," Deserae said as she slowed the car. "Plus, don't worry. It's not like we're going to march up to the door."

"We could," Toli said.

Deserae laughed. "And say what? 'Oh, hey, we're here to kill you. Please don't put up a fight.' You think that's going to go over well?"

"I just meant we could have the upper hand," Toli said.

She shook her head. "No way. We do it just like we planned. Scope out the situation, get a feel, and wait for back up. We have contacts, but we've got some time. I've already requested a few people to meet us which may take a day or two anyway."

"Including?" Toli paused.

"Oh, cut it out," she growled.

"How long are we going to watch?" Julia asked. "And from where? Don't you think there will be look-outs?"

"Honestly," she said, "no. I think they tried to come in quietly. Too much movement would cause suspicion. This isn't a heavily populated area. Too many people would get noticed."

"And how are we not going to get noticed?" Julia asked skeptically.

"Ah," Toli said. "That's where I come in. I have some talents with memory and blocking charms."

"What are those?"

"I can either make someone not see what's right in front of them or I can talk to someone and convince them of something else. Plant an idea and make them think it was theirs. While you two check out the house, I am going to go to the town and turn a couple blind eyes if you will."

"It's what we were going to do to you," Deserae said over her shoulder back to Julia.

"Desi," Toli warned.

"What?" she asked. "It's true."

"Excuse me?" Julia asked.

"We didn't think you were going to come with us," Deserae said. "We couldn't have you wandering around the city. What if you fell into the wrong hands?"

"Wrong hands?" Julia's voice was rising.

"I don't see what the big deal is," Deserae said. "I mean, we brought you with us."

When they turned on the road, Deserae pulled the car into a small clearing. She opened the driver's door and got out while Toli slid over. He adjusted the seat and mirrors and looked back at Julia, eyebrows raised.

"Right," Julia said and scrambled out of the car. He put it in reverse and backed out the way they came. Silence hung in the air. Not even the birds were signing. It made Julia's skin crawl but made her think they were in the right place.

She looked up and saw that Deserae was already walking into the woods, paralleling the road. Julia jogged to catch up as she felt a coolness wash over her mind.

Chapter 35

Travel

Levi's heart raced, and his palms were slick with nervous sweat as he clung to Gilbert's feathers. He had no idea where they were going or even where they started from. It was cold, so obviously somewhere north, but where in the north? Alaska? The North Pole? Canada? Buffalo? He hoped it was at least in the western hemisphere, but there were no land markers that he recognized.

"Jada," he called. "Can you see anything?"

"They are in the woods. She showed me the name of a town. If we were there, I could find her, but I didn't recognize it."

"What was it?"

"Bridge Township?" he said it like a question. Levi shrugged. "No, wait, Bridgeton Township. Bridgeton."

"Never heard of it."

"They have a map, but it's hard for me to read it. Though I'm pretty sure they're still in Pennsylvania. I'll keep checking in with her. Hopefully, she'll get the hint that I need more of a clue than what she gave me. Maybe she doesn't know we are traveling to her."

"Thanks, Jada, for everything," Levi said. The boy nodded, and they flew on in silence.

Okay, so they had a connection to Julia, however limited. They would find her. Doubt ate away at him, but he pressed it down. They could not give up. He didn't know what it was, what Julia symbolized to him, but he needed her to be okay. He needed her to be safe, for them to find her, and to whisk her away from danger. It was childish, he knew, silly even, but she'd infiltrated him. Crept into him somehow and he couldn't just leave her to be alone or die, or worse be captured by Lady Grustmiener. He hoped she knew they were coming for her. That they would defeat Lady Grustmiener once and for all and go home.

And where would home be? Surely the cover of the magical world would be broken. Dragons and griffins aside, there was no way a large-scale battle could break out unnoticed. Levi assumed that all of the portals were re-opened now. Hopefully, inhabitants of the Four Corners were flooding into his world and heading toward, what? To hopefully find them when they themselves didn't even know where they were headed? To assist in a battle that he himself didn't know how it would pan out?

He couldn't concern himself with that now. Little things. *Concentrate on what you can control*, he told himself. *There is only so much you can influence, the rest is up to everyone else.* He needed to find Julia, then they could re-group. He needed to keep Aura safe. There would be no world without her.

The thought crossed his mind before he even registered the words. No world? No world because Esotera needed a ruler, or no world because he didn't know what life would be like without her? It was as if his body had a beacon that was tuned into her. He felt her presence at all times whether she was right by him or not. It was like a comfortable pressure, and he didn't want it to leave him. He cared for her more deeply than anyone he had in his life before. Sure, he loved his parents and Emily, but this was different. They were his family, blood or not, caring for one another went along with the territory, but Aura was different. She didn't owe him anything, not really. She was there because she wanted to be. She kissed him back because she wanted to.

He didn't know how his life would be without that, and he didn't want to find out.

Aura made a movement in front of him, and they began descending. The air was increasingly warmer, and he looked forward to taking off a layer or two of clothes. He was too unsure of his balance to do it in the air. The others appeared to have the same idea because as soon as they touched down, they began ripping off sweaters and hats, leaving them in a wooly pile on the ground.

"Do we need to keep these with us?" Amaline asked, eyeing the articles as if they were covered in slime.

"I do not think so," Aura said. "Hopefully, the portals are open, and we will not have to travel back the way we came."

Amaline laughed. "If we could even find the way."

Nothing seemed to faze her, Levi marveled. They'd traveled through horrible conditions. Went through a bloody war that was probably still being waged. They were marching toward, what, none of them knew. And there she was, cracking jokes as if nothing had happened.

They'd stopped by a gigantic lake, and the animals drank in deep, loud gulps. Levi also dipped his hands in the cool water. The relief radiated throughout himself as the liquid brought much needed moisture to his insides.

Amaline sidled up next to him, a groan emanating from the back of her throat as she drank.

His belly full to the point of sloshing, Levi sat back on his heels and closed his eyes. Maybe he could convince Aura to let them sleep here for a while. There were woods nearby that could give coverage, and he didn't recall passing any homes on their way here. He was desperate for sleep.

"I think that is the best water I have ever had in my life," Amaline said. She sat on the ground in a huff next to him, her legs stretched out in the last bits of dying afternoon sun.

"How do you do it?" Levi asked her. He opened his eyes and faced her puzzled expression. "It's as if the last few months, or year, or whatever, never happened. I can't see any of it on you."

The corners of her mouth tugged. "What choice do I have?"

"Plenty."

She shook her head. "No. I cannot atone for my sins and then be ungrateful for the chance at redemption."

"That's what this is? You're here because you think you owe something?"

"Of course I *owe* something, Levi, but maybe not the something you think. I came from a land where I was nothing. Omire took me under his wing and together we discovered dark things about our home. Dark things that we were a part of—"

"But," he interrupted.

"We were a part of them," she insisted. "Willingly or not. But Aura gave me a chance to put it right. I never would have had that back home. And so, I took it, and I vowed to never let her regret it."

"I think she knows."

"She does, but not everyone else does. The people from my old kingdom, some from Esotera, they see me, and they see someone who does not belong. Who has no real home. So, I try to make everywhere home. I try to make myself the home. Then no one will feel the pressure of having to provide for me. They can simply listen, and if they like what they hear, follow. It is what makes me good for training the new recruits. They are just as lost. I let them know that lost is all right."

A feeling of warmth and affection filled him, and he reached over and took her hand. A throat cleared behind them. Levi turned as saw Aura's ashen face staring, not at him, but at his and Amaline's entwined fingers. He dropped them immediately and got up. Tears rimmed Aura's eyes, and it made Levi's heart ache with pain.

"Aura."

She shook her head. He repeated her name again and tried to take her hand, but she snatched it away.

"We will rest here for the evening. Sleep wherever you want." She gave a pointed glance at a confused Amaline and walked away.

"Did I..." Amaline's voice trailed off.

"No, it's okay, I'll go and talk with her. You rest here and watch the sunset."

He caught up with Aura as she was relaying the message to Milskar and Calanthe. He reached for her and again she pulled away from him. She marched into the woods, and he followed in silence. She stopped, and it was hard for him to see her. The thick trees blocked out what was left of the light of the day. The moon hadn't gotten high enough to assist, but he could see her shoulders rising and falling.

Levi came behind her and encircled her with his arms. She did not pull away this time but melted into his hold. Her knees bent, and in one swift movement, he was carrying all of her weight. He lowered them both slowly to the ground, his arms still around her.

"Shh," he cooed into her hair. "Aura, please. Aura."

She sniffled and turned to face him. "Do you—do you?" She could not form the question, but he knew what she wanted to ask.

"Do you think Milskar loves Calanthe?" He was unable to see her reaction, but her silence indicated that she was caught off-guard by his question.

"No, no, of course not," she said.

"And why is that?"

"Because he loves Emily. Loves her truly."

"But he spends a lot of time with Calanthe."

She was silent.

"Aura, I love you." He picked up her hand and kissed each finger. "Amaline is trying to make amends for what she did, and I am trying to let her. But she doesn't hold my heart."

Aura's body shook again as tears took over. "I do not know why I am being so silly. I just—I had this dream…"

It gushed out of her, and she told him everything. Her insecurities, her fear for the future, of losing him. It was difficult to understand each word as the sobs muffled some of them, but he understood.

"Aura. I am here. I am here, and I'm not planning on going anywhere. I'm not planning on leaving you again, ever again." His eyes had adjusted, and he could see her outline, made blue and silver by the full moon placed firmly in the dark sky. He leaned forward and kissed her.

She tasted salty from the tears and kissed him back, her hands moving through his hair. They broke away and clung to one another.

"Do you promise?" she whispered over his shoulder.

"Yes," he said into her neck as he kissed her once again.

Chapter 36

Decisions

Julia and Deserae crept along the tree-lined road. They would walk a few paces before pausing to listen intently to their surroundings. Each time a vehicle crunched down the road, kicking rocks and dust in its path, they froze. Julia felt like a hunted animal. Hunted by what, she didn't know.

Deserae motioned to the other side of the road and darted across before Julia was able to say anything. She disappeared behind a tree, leaving Julia feeling very alone and vulnerable. Julia wondered if she should she stay where she was or continue to travel the way they'd been going?

She was just about to take a step when a branch snapped behind her. She whirled and came face to face with Deserae, only her features were strangely upside down. Her whole body was actually upside down, and she was hissing and spitting like a cat. It took Julia a moment to realize what had happened. She hesitated before letting Deserae down, unsure of the reaction she'd get.

"What in the holy hell was that?" Deserae seethed in a quiet, yet harsh, tone.

"Sorry, it sorta just happens sometimes," Julia said. She could feel her cheeks burning. "You scared me."

"You do that again." She moved forward and spoke with her nose literally touching Julia's. "And I'll show you my talent."

"What are you planning to set on fire?" Toli's cool voice cut in from behind them.

"This little show-off twerp," Deserae said under her breath. She was still angry but backed away. "What did you find?"

"No much," Toli said. "Literally. This is a pretty small town. Which is good. Containment will be easier."

Another car rumbled down the road, causing them to duck where they stood. Julia peaked over a short hedge and noted three passengers in the vehicle. That brought the total to fifteen since they'd arrived. Not a huge amount so far, but still troubling.

"A fair number of cars for such a sleepy place," Deserae said, as if she could read Julia's thoughts.

Had Lady Grustmiener called these in? Or maybe Doyenne Cecily? Julia yearned to be a fly on the wall in whatever building resided at the end of the lane. Maybe she could run ahead, climb a tree, and stay hidden as she spied. She felt a tap on her shoulder and turned to see Toli and Deserae slip deeper into the woods. Julia was torn. She wanted to stay and watch. To keep counting cars, but she turned and dutifully followed.

"What do you think?" Deserae asked.

"Well, we definitely need more people. The element of surprise is one thing, but there must be a dozen people in there."

"Fifteen."

They turned to look at Julia.

"Fifteen people have arrived."

"Right," Toli continued. "Fifteen."

"We need more people," Deserae echoed his previous words.

Ice washed over her thoughts. It had been happening with increased frequency. They must be getting closer. Julia made up her mind.

"I'll go," she said.

Toli looked at her. "What?"

"My friends are close. You should wait here for them and the others you call in. I'll go with Lady Grustmiener, then you'll know for sure where she is."

"What makes you so sure they're close? Or that we'll find you?" Deserae asked.

Was it possible that her feelings toward Julia had thawed?

"They have a boy named Jada with them," Julia said. "I can make sure he sees what I see. I can make sure you'd be able to find me, find us."

"And you are sure this boy is with them?" Toli asked.

"Yes." She spoke the words firmly, but was she sure? She assumed Jada was with them, why else would he be invading her mind? She'd have to hope that he was and proceed as such. The time for doubt and second guessing was slipping away. Lady Grustmiener wasn't going to stay in one place for long, that much she was sure of.

Toli and Deserae looked pointedly at one another. Whether or not they thought it was a good idea, or even the only valuable idea, they appeared visibly torn. Deserae chewed on her thumbnail, neither of them speaking.

"I will be fine," Julia said.

"How will you contact us if you get in trouble? Can you communicate with this Jada person as well?" Toli asked.

"Are you serious?" Deserae's voice was exacerbated. Toli looked at her and raised an eyebrow. "She is a child. There is no way we are letting her in there by herself to be swept up by that monster."

"Desi," he began, but she promptly talked over him.

"No, this is ridiculous. There is no way she can waltz in there unnoticed and just be along for the ride."

"I'll say that I heard about it. That my family didn't want me to go because of my young age, but I slipped away anyway. I will sound like a desperate run-away. There's no way she won't accept me."

"She'll probably accept you with open arms, that's not the problem."

"Desi, she will be okay. She's a tough girl. You forget, she's the one who came here, who followed Lady Grustmiener in the first place. Without Julia, we wouldn't even know there was anything to worry about."

Julia stood up straighter as Toli talked and tried to keep the pride off her face.

"She's right, we need someone in there. They aren't going to stay here forever, and when they move, we can't be right on their tail without them noticing us. She's young, yes, but she knows what she's doing."

Julia beamed at him. She reached out and touched Deserae's arm, but the woman shook her off. "I'll be okay," Julia said. The chill came over her again. "They will be here soon, I know. Contact anyone you know, gather as many as you can. In the meantime, I'll be watching her and reporting back. Then you'll meet up with me, and we'll take her down once and for all."

Deserae turned on her heels and marched back toward the road. Julia looked hopelessly at Toli.

He shrugged. "She acts like she's all tough," he said. "But she's scared. She doesn't much like fighting."

"Does anyone?"

"I know one person who does." They stared in the same direction where the cars were traveling. "She has the power to make fire."

"Lady Grustmiener?" That didn't make sense, she'd never used that during the battle, and it seemed to be a deadly power.

"Deserae. When she was young, she burned her house down, killing her parents and little sister."

Julia's heart fell into the pit of her stomach and turned into churning acid. She didn't want to ask the question but had to. "How old was her sister?"

"A few years younger than Desi. Maybe eleven or twelve."

The pit grew to a cavern. No wonder she had such mixed feelings about Julia. She was the same age Deserae's sister was when she died. This must explain the sudden turn of emotion when Julia announced her plans. Her *dangerous* plans.

"What happened?

"She ran away. Police looked for her for a while. She was a suspect for a little bit, but when the fire marshal completed the investigation, they couldn't find a source of the fire. No accelerants, no red herrings, so they said it was an accident, and they stopped searching. She was eighteen, so there wasn't anything they could do. We lived in the same hometown, but she was two grades below me in school, so I knew of her, but I didn't really know her. But for some reason, she sought me out a few months after it happened. I don't know what she did during that time. She's never talked about it, but we left our home and moved to Philadelphia. We've been there for the last ten or so years. Until you found us."

Julia had no words. She sympathized more than most could. She knew what it was like to lose one's parents at a young age, but she had no idea what it felt like to be the one responsible. Julia had merely stumbled upon her parent's death where Deserae was the catalyst. If sympathies taught her anything, it was that saying that you knew what the person was going through was the last thing they wanted to hear. No one knew your own pain better than you, and she didn't want to act like she did.

Without words, she left Toli and walked back to the road. Deserae was sitting down, her back leaning against a large pine tree. The branches were heavy and partially obscured her. It was a good hiding place.

"Hey," Julia said. She sat down with her knee inches from Deserae's. There was no response to her words or her presence. "I am going to be careful. Everything will be fine."

Deserae stared straight ahead. "You can't promise that."

"None of this is going to be safe, none of it is going to happen without some risk."

"You don't think I know that?" Deserae still wouldn't look at Julia.

"I know you know that. But that doesn't change that this is the best thing to do. I want to be a part of this, I want to help. I want to have a chance to make a difference for once in my life."

Deserae turned and looked right at her. "Then you better get going."

The words stung, no matter how much she wanted to act like they didn't. Julia told herself it was just a defense mechanism, a way that Deserae was able to distance herself in case something happened, but Julia was still hoping that there would be a more formal goodbye. A good luck, be careful…something.

She rose and marched down the road, refusing to look back, no matter how much she wanted to.

Chapter 37

Rain

A drumming sound woke Luther with a start. He listened intently, trying to decipher where the beat was coming from. Rat, tap, tap. Harder and faster until he realized it was rain pelting on the roof above him. The air felt damp and heavy around him as he dressed.

The barracks somehow felt small this time around even though there were less people than before. Maybe it was that the emptiness filled each corner the way no bodies could. He heard a new sound now, muffled, but clearly voices. He opened the door and noticed several people standing at the end of the long, dark hallway.

"What's going on?" Luther called.

"The rains have started," Achan answered. As Luther approached he saw the men were wet, their bodies hunched at the shoulders, resigned expressions on their faces.

"So?" Luther asked when he reached them.

"So, so we have to hunker down," Achan said in a

way that implied the response should have been obvious.

"I don't understand the problem. We'll wait until it lets up and then get on with our day." The group laughed. Luther clenched his hands into fists. He was about to say something, to yell something, when Lieal spoke up.

"They are not going to stop. Not for a while at least. It is the rainy season. It turns on like a faucet and off again about six months later, more if we are unlucky."

"And if we're lucky?" Luther asked.

"We are never lucky," one of the other men said.

Here, standing before him, were a group of large capable men. Each of them looked like strong soldiers. Each found their way back here from the battle despite any injuries they may have endured, and yet. And yet they were afraid of a little rain?

It was ridiculous.

"It's raining in the whole kingdom?"

They nodded in the affirmative.

"Good. We'll gather more as we go. We need to gather as many carts as we can and as many creatures as we can muster to pull them." Luther's mind was planning three steps ahead.

"As we go?" Achan asked, though the expression on his face showed that he was pretty sure he understood.

"Do people typically travel during this time of the year?" Luther asked.

"No, never," Lieal said. "We usually stay underground, hence all the low-lying buildings."

"Then they won't be expecting us," Luther said. "The rain will cover us and clear our tracks behind us. We will be a complete surprise."

A smile broke out on Lieal's face.

Chapter 38

Arrivals

The men and women who stood before Lady Grustmiener didn't appear very assuming, but she hoped that would work in her favor. Once she had tried to win a war with the strongest-looking army she could gather, and it had ended in near disaster. Then she stole an army. Kidnapped it from their homes and forced the people together, and she'd still almost lost it all. Maybe it was time to change tactics. Plus, these were people who literally showed up on her doorstep.

None were particularly impressive, none stood out as a leader, but she didn't need leaders. She needed people who would follow orders, and if the scared glances they threw to one another were any indication, she would have no trouble with this bunch.

"We need to travel," she said.

"Travel, where?" one of the women squeaked.

"What is the most populous city in your world?" she asked.

"New York," the woman answered.

"Then we shall go to New York." The name sounded good in her mouth, strong, important. New York.

"Just like that? We pack up and waltz in?" a man asked.

"And what do we do when we're there?" another piped up.

"We will destroy it, of course," Lady Grustmiener said.

Had these people no vision? No plan for the future? Sure, she was technically ruler of this world, but of what? No one knew she was ruler. There would need to be a message, strong, clear, and loud. What better place than this New York to announce her claim?

"How will we go?"

"We will take your horseless contraptions." Her voice was even, but she was frustrated. They did not seem eager for her mission. They stood around like they were debating if they were going to go, as if they had a choice in the matter.

"And when will we leave?"

"I believe we should wait a day or two. I want to make sure everyone who was going to arrive here has. That will also allow you to tell me everything you know about this place. How it is fortified. What weapons they have. I do not want there to be any surprises."

Again, they looked at one another before the first man who arrived, Xavier, stepped forward. "New York is a huge city with millions of people."

"Wonderful."

"It is not fortified," he continued.

"Then it will be that much easier to take."

"I don't think you understand."

"No, *you* are the one who does not understand." Lady Grustmiener rose as she spoke. "The previous ruler of your world is dead." She pointed to the corner as if they needed a reminder. "I am now in charge here. You obeyed her, and now you obey me. I do not know what kind of army Doyenne Cecily maintained, but I rule one that follows orders." They shrank back as her voice rose.

"There—" The woman paused. "—there just aren't enough of us. There's no way we can march into the middle of Times Square and declare war."

Lady Grustmiener leaned forward and put her pointer finger in the middle of the woman's chest with a firm pressure. "Then you must figure out a way. Each of you must have powers. Otherwise, Doyenne Cecily would not have called you here. You must have known that she wanted you for some type of battle."

"Powers?" a woman asked.

Lady Grustmiener did not hide the frustration from her voice. "Yes, powers. Abilities. Whatever you want to call it. A reason why she told you to come here."

"We thought we were crossing over," one of the men said.

"And you will." Lady Grustmiener made her voice low and sweet. "When we are done here, you will have your choice of land. There is an entire world, and I rule it. Helping me will help you in the end."

"Whatever land we want?" he asked.

"I will even take the land out from under your enemy and slaughter anyone who tries to stand in your way. Follow me, fight for me, and you will have riches beyond anything you could have ever imagined."

They talked in excited whispers now. It was so easy, manipulating people. People always wanted the same thing. Power. And those not strong enough to take it for themselves were happy getting a small scrap of it thrown their way. They would fight for her, and whether they knew it or not, they would die for her. For she knew the lust for power better than anyone in any world, and she'd be damned if she was going to share it with anyone.

A knock came to the door, and each person in the room froze. They hadn't been expecting anyone else, even if Lady Grustmiener was holding out for hope that more would arrive.

She moved to open the door, as it was clear no one else was going to. Pulling back the heavy wood, she saw a small girl. She had medium brown skin and dark, practically black, hair which matched her eyes. The girl stood as tall as her small frame would allow and stared straight ahead.

"What have we here, child?" Lady Grustmiener asked.

"My name," the girl said, her eyes still focused on a point just over Lady Grustmiener's shoulder, "is Julia. Julia Jones."

Chapter 39

Broken

They had been riding for the better part of a day when it happened. It had taken years, but Emily finally got used to being on a horse. She'd even begun to enjoy the rhythmic rocking motion. Serenity's muscles tensed and rippled under her as she felt the mare stiffen.

The day before, with Kiya's help, Emily addressed the creatures that had resided in Esotera for the last few months.

"You have done such wonderful and brave things," Emily said. She felt a bit silly talking to the animals, but Kiya was encouraging. Frankly, she felt awkward anytime she addressed a large group. This wasn't her role. This wasn't her place. Sure, she was a fixture in Aura's group of aides and helpers, but she never considered herself high up. Now she was basically running the kingdom.

"I thank each and every one of you for your service," she continued. "Esotera and the rest of the Four Corners owe you a debt of gratitude. You may stay here as long as you like, but you are also free to go to your homes." The animals shifted, changing the mood around her. She turned to Kiya with a quizzical look.

"They think you are making it sound like they weren't free to leave before. Like their help wasn't given on their own accord," Kiya whispered.

Emily roller her shoulders back in an attempt to remove some of the tension. "What I mean is—" She paused. "—your service is no longer needed." As soon as the words were out of her mouth, she knew they were wrong. She turned to Kiya, desperate for help.

"What Emily means on behalf of Queen Aura—" Kiya spoke up loudly over the thrums of disapproval. "—is that she understands the deep sacrifices that you made in coming here. You left your homes, you left your families. You lost friends. We mourn with you. They will never be forgotten. The battle is now over, though. As a token of our appreciation, you may stay here as long as you wish."

This appeared to appease the creatures, but Emily wasn't sure why. Wasn't it the same thing she'd said?

"Telling them they can stay," Kiya said in Emily's ear, "is a roundabout way to let them know they can go, but it makes it their idea."

"Whatever," Emily said, then remembering her manners, added, "thanks."

As they stood, a small creature moved toward them. It hopped hesitantly on its back legs like a kangaroo, but it had thick plates covering its body.

"It's a pangolin," Kiya said.

"A what?" Emily whispered.

"Pangolin. We have them in our world, or, my world. But they are hunted so most escaped here for safety. He said they hide in the woods of Grustmiener."

It sat back on its long tail when it reached them, front legs tucked up under its long, slender chin.

"Can we help you?" Emily asked. She knew Kiya would answer, but out of respect, she stared at the animal directly.

"He says the war is not over."

"Not over?"

"He said with the rain will bring more fighting. The rain will wash an army here. It is a little difficult to understand him." Kiya knelt down, and the animal positioned itself to be face to face with Kiya.

They stared at each other for some time before it moved back into the woods.

"They can see the future." Awe laced Kiya's words.

"*That* can see the future?" Emily asked incredulously. Then she chided herself, remembered where she was. "Sorry."

Kiya waved her off. "He said a great army will march to here, *through* here."

"Through here to where?" Her heart quickened. Powers or not, she was pretty sure what Kiya was going to say.

"The other world. We have to warn them. The pangolin said he saw a great battle, a large city burning, and a statue with a woman holding a golden flame falling into the sea."

"You mean—" Emily couldn't finish her question.

"Wherever the rest of them are, the battle is moving there, and from how he described it, I think they're heading to New York."

The conversation whirled around Emily's head as they went out on a scouting mission the next day. If there was an army moving, there would be a trace of it. Thankfully, word had gotten around that the war may not be over after all, and most of the animals stayed behind.

Emily wasn't sure what to do with them, should she march them into New York and hope that a battle was actually happening? She could risk endangering their entire world in an effort to save hers. Or what used to be hers.

She was torn. Where did she belong? She felt connections to both places, but Esotera was her home now. The Four Corners was where she resided. Part of her family was here, and part of her family was there. Would crossing over risk losing them both?

"I need to speak with King Omire," Emily said. They were close to the buried castle anyway, and she wanted his opinion on the matter.

As they got closer, a level of anger began to build in her. Where had Omire been this entire time? How could he have left them? Left her, without any word, and hid underground. She needed him. Here she was, running a kingdom all by herself, trying to make decisions that affected literally every person she ever cared about, and he wasn't there to help her.

The castle grounds were silent. Thinking back, she realized the roads going into Grustmiener were also empty. A feeling of foreboding entered her. Could something have happened Omire? Did she just speak ill about someone who may be—

The thought broke off. She was unable to complete it even in the safety of her own head.

She had the others stay outside while she entered the half-buried castle. The guards protested, but Emily said that she needed them to keep an eye out. Truthfully, she didn't want any witnesses to what she was planning on saying if she found Omire. She didn't need it getting out that the temporary ruler of Esotera yelled at the King of Grustmiener.

The same quiet from the road filled the halls. Had

she made a mistake? Would she be ambushed at any moment?

It took her ten minutes to find her way to the Omire's office. She'd only been here once or twice before and got lost easily in the dim light. The door was ajar, letting a sliver of light through into the hall. She knocked lightly before pushing it forward. Omire looked up at her without expression. His left arm had a bandage wrapped around it, yellowing and dirty. It made Emily's own arm itch.

"Have you come to bring me back?" he asked in a measured tone.

"Bring you back?" Emily was so taken aback by his strange demeanor, she forgot to launch right into her speech lambasting him for deserting her.

"I know the fighting is still going on. I know I am still needed."

"We are well beyond fighting. What have you been doing here? Have you cut yourself off from the outside world?"

"There is no one left here. I came home to an empty kingdom. Please send my apologies to Queen Aura."

"If I ever see her again, I will." Emily let her words hang.

A glimmer of interest sparked in Omire's eyes. "What do you mean?"

"Did you not get any of my letters?" He gestured to a pile of sealed envelopes at the corner of his desk. "So, you ignored me, too. Well, at least I feel better that you didn't even open them. Here I was thinking you'd read them and still decided not to help."

"Where is the queen?" He stood, came to the other side of his desk, and leaned back. The wood creaked under his weight.

"The other world, *my* world. She crossed over."

"Crossed over? Why?"

"To follow Lady Grustmiener. She's brought the war to my home. She'd taken the next step just like Levi thought she would."

"Lady Grustmiener? But the portals? With who?" He spoke in fragmented questions.

"Levi, Jada, Calanthe, Amaline." Shock registered on his face as she forced the last name out. "And Milskar."

"Emily," he breathed.

"I needed you." The anger toward him melted away. Or was it never there in the first place? She didn't want to yell at him, she wanted him to help her. To make sense of what was happening and what to do about it.

"I am preparing to follow them to my old world," Emily continued. "But I need your help. There are loose ends here. King Theaus, for one, but I don't have time to find him, I need to go and help the others. I received a letter that Levi is missing. I need to help. I need you to help me so I can help them."

"I cannot help you," he said. He rose and moved back behind his desk.

Frustration bubbled in her. "What do you mean you *can't*. More like won't. Why are you hiding here? What are you doing buried in this tomb? You aren't dead, but those you love may die. You can help stop that. Help me." Her voice had lowered to a desperate whisper.

"Listen," he said, annunciating each letter and refusing to meet her eyes. "Just because someone is older doesn't mean they are better equipped to handle something. That is the thing no one tells you." He looked up at her. "Fear doesn't disappear just because you are no longer young."

"So, that's it? You've lost your nerve? There isn't time to lose your nerve. Don't you think I'm scared?

Don't you think I walk around with a ball of fire in the pit of my stomach all the time that threatens to consume me?"

"I cannot help you," he repeated. "Not anymore." He sat back in his chair.

She wanted to cry and scream and throw something at him, but the way he sat hunched over, she couldn't bring herself to do any of those things.

"I am going. I have to go. Can I leave you with one task?" She hoped he could do one last thing for her.

"Emily…" He trailed off.

"I need you to keep an eye out for King Theaus. He doesn't have to be killed, just captured. Just held until we can get back and Aura can deal with him. That's it. You don't have to fight him."

"And you think it will be that easy?" he asked, looking up at her with pain in his eyes.

"I do," she lied. Of course, it wouldn't be easy, but she needed him to do this. And more importantly, she needed him to think he could. "And if there is anyone who can do it—"

He cut her off. "I am a different man. A different man than I thought I was. I was brave. I remember being brave once, but now…"

"You are still the man I know," she said with firmness and finality in her voice.

"I will do what I can." He nodded to himself and began to busy his hands with some papers on his desk. She left without another word and wove back through the darkened tunnel.

"Let's go," Emily said when she excited the castle in the late afternoon sun.

"King Omire?" one of the guards asked.

"We are on our own," she said without emotion. They didn't question her further.

It was now up to her and the small group that was left. She had to figure out what they were going to do. They walked for miles, checking the various portal markers. While she'd anticipated what they were going to find, she had to confirm it for herself.

The portals were open. That meant that Aura and Levi had been successful. The witches had agreed to help them. It also meant that anyone else could get through now, too.

The woods were eerily quiet. No people marched. They stopped by several villages that had been burned in the attack, and they were empty as well. Not even the dead remained.

What is going on? she asked herself.

Just then a rumbling sound started in the distance. Serenity continued to shift from foot to foot, nerves making it difficult for her to stay in place. The other horses pranced as well.

"I think it is time to go back," Emily called to the five other riders with her. They nodded and wheeled their horses back the direction they came. They were about to cross the border from Grustmiener and Esotera when the skies opened up, and the rain poured down upon them.

The image of the pangolin flashed in her mind along with his premonition. Dread filled every crevice of Emily as the liquid seeped in.

Chapter 40

News

Aura tapped her foot while she chewed on her inner lip. She looked up at the sky and tried to determine how much time had passed with the movement of the sun, but it moved too quickly here and disoriented her. It was her first time crossing over, and it felt strange, like gravity was a degree stronger here than she was used to. Maybe it was.

The areas they flew over became more populated and then thinned out in an indeterminate pattern. They had to stay up high so they wouldn't be spotted, but she could still see areas below them where hundreds of houses and buildings dotted the terrain and barely any trees were visible.

"Was there a plague here?" Aura called to Levi.

"A plague?" He looked down, but shook his head when he looked back over at her.

"The trees, there are no trees."

He smiled sadly. "Yeah, I guess you notice it more from up here. No, they cut them down to build the houses. There are some wooded areas though, it's not all buildings."

But she noticed them like wounds through the landscape. Trees and vegetation dotted here and there, but everything else looked so similar she wondered if they were flying in circles instead of a direct line.

Aura, Amaline, Milskar, and Calanthe found a rare open field and decided to land. Levi and Jada left to walk to something they called a hass station. Or was it gas? She didn't know what it meant, but Levi said they would have documents that could help them determine where they needed to go.

They tucked the dragons and griffins in between the trees as best they could and sat out on the edge of the open land. The sun was setting, and it painted the most brilliant colors she'd ever seen in the sky. This place couldn't be that bad if it was able to create something so beautiful. The four foreigners sat together and stared upward, speechless.

A noise tugged through her and it took her a while to register what it was. She stood and looked around, but couldn't see anything. Was her mind playing tricks? How could it even be possible?

Milskar got up quickly with alarm and unsheathed his sword. "What is it?"

"I thought I heard something," Aura trailed off. Amaline and Calanthe stood as well. The noise got louder, and the creature became visible just above the tree line.

Thankfully it was white. Otherwise, she may not have seen it in the dimming light. "How did you get here?" she asked the jadwiga as it sloped down and landed heavily on her out-stretched arm.

Milskar stepped forward and took the note from the bird. It hopped off Aura and landed on the ground. Heza, happy to see a creature she recognized, made a noise deep in her throat which caused the bird to click back to her.

"What does it say?" Aura asked. Milskar was alarmingly silent, and she turned to see what was stopping him from speaking. His face was ashen.

"The war is not over," he said in a mechanical voice.

"Well, yeah," Amaline said. "That is why we are here."

"The war is not over *there*."

Aura's blood turned to slush in her veins. "What?" Her voice sounded so small and far away.

"They are coming," he trailed off. "They are coming here."

"Who? Who is coming?" Calanthe took a giant step and stood in front of him. Milskar's eyes were unfocused. She repeated her question, but he didn't answer her, his expression still far away. Before Aura could stop her, Calanthe raised a hand and slapped Milskar across the face. She raised her hand again, but he grabbed her wrist before she could make contact. He snapped out of his stupor and let go.

"There are still fighters in our world. They are crossing over to come here," he said.

"And our people?" Aura asked even though she wasn't sure if she wanted to know the answer.

"They are coming too." He lowered his face into his hands and dropped the letter. It fluttered to the ground.

Aura moved to pick up the paper and grabbed a writing piece from her bag. Emily's distinct, sloping handwriting took up one entire side. She flipped the page over and scribbled a message before she handed it back to the jadwiga.

"I know you are tired, and I have no idea how far you have traveled, but I need you to go back there right away. I need you to give this message to Emily, quickly please. Thank you so very much."

The bird took off and was immediately swallowed by the night, all the beauty in the sky having been erased.

Chapter 41

Escape

It was strange being back in a city, no matter how small the one they'd stumbled upon was. As they were flying, Levi spotted the gas station sign and signaled they should land in a nearby clearing. He took Jada with him so they could first off find their way back and second, he was the only one who wouldn't stick out like a sore thumb.

They'd left the dragons and griffins, obviously, and set off on foot toward the direction he saw the building. Levi's legs felt sluggish as they moved along a paved road. The firmness of the ground was jarring in a way he hadn't remembered before. Did it feel this strange when he came back the first time, all those years ago? Jada must have been feeling similarly for he moved with short, dragging steps.

Levi moved his head from side to side, cracking the joints in his neck in a satisfying pop. A rumble sounded behind them, and he froze before he realized what it was. He turned and put an arm out to pull Jada from the road.

His eyes were glazed over before focusing at Levi's touch. Levi was about to ask what was going on with Julia when the truck came around the bed.

It was the color of rust, or may have been made of rust, and rattled as it moved forward. Levi nodded at the driver and hoped it would pass them by, but he heard the brakes squeak as it approached. The man leaned over and cranked the passenger side window down.

"I didn't see a car back there," the man said. "You boys lost? Or run out of gas?"

"No, sir, but thank you," Levi said in a casual tone.

"Where you headed, you don't look familiar, and I know pretty much everyone around here."

"Out of town. We're heading to the gas station for a map."

"Map?" Skepticism laced the edges of the man's question.

Levi shrugged. "Phone died."

"You kids rely on those things too much. Once you find yourself without them, you're hopeless." Levi shrugged again. The man looked from Levi to Jada and shook his head. "All right, here, take mine. I've got more back at the house."

He opened his glove compartment and handed him a worn Pennsylvania map.

"Any general direction I can point you in?" he asked.

"No, thank you. And thank you for this, you're saving us a lot of trouble."

"Sure I can't give you a ride?"

"No, sir. But thank you again." Levi took a step back and hoped that would end the conversation, and the man would keep driving.

The man looked directly at Jada. "How about you?" Jada looked up at being addressed as if he just realized he was in the middle of a road conversing with a stranger in a truck.

"Me?" Jada stuttered.

"You all right? You not in any kind of trouble, are you?" The man looked pointedly at Levi.

"Huh? No," Jada said.

"All right, let's go. Thanks again, sir." Levi folded the map and tucked it into his pocket. He gently took Jada's arm and tugged him back the way they came.

Levi could feel the man's eyes watching them as they moved away. *Please don't call the cops,* he repeated in his head. The last thing they needed was some law enforcement looking in to see if Jada was some kidnapped kid.

And it hit Levi. Jada *was* a kidnapped kid. Just being here with him could put them in danger if he was spotted and recognized. Looking back and forth over the road, the truck still idling in the same place, Levi pulled them into the woods. They'd have to leave here, and quickly. They got what they'd come for, and now it was time to move on. They couldn't afford losing any time, good intentions or not from the local law enforcement.

"Jada, we have to move quickly. I'm pretty sure that guy thinks something's up."

"Something is up," Jada pointed out.

"Well, yeah, but we don't need them to know that. Come on."

They half walked, half jogged through the woods. The going was slower than the direct path of the road, but it felt more normal to be dodging trees then pounding the pavement. It took them nearly twice as long to return as it did to leave. Levi was just about to turn to Jada, to confirm they were going the right way, when he saw movement out of the corner of his eye. The animals had blended in reasonably well, but once Gilbert heard his voice, he popped his head out from around a tree, causing his amber eyes to glow even in the fading light.

In what felt like a blink the sun set, and Jada bumped into him as they picked their way through the trees. The moon gave off such little light it was hard for his eyes to adjust. After the third tree he crashed in to, he felt a large presence in front of him. Reaching out his hand, he was met with soft feathers and fur and breathed a sigh of relief.

Levi grabbed Jada's hand and let Gilbert lead them to the others. They were a little easier to make out since they were standing in a field softly illuminated, but they still needed the griffin's guidance to reach them.

Aura wrapped her arms around him and breathed into his neck, "Oh, I am so glad you are back."

He pulled away and looked at her, trying to read her face, but her features blended together. "Why, what happened?"

Milskar's voice came out of the darkness. "We received a letter from Emily."

"Did she say all the portals are open?" Levi asked.

"It appears that way," he answered.

"Why does it seem like you aren't telling me everything?"

"The war is not over," Milskar said in a calm voice.

"I don't understand," Levi said slowly.

"We do not fully understand either, but Emily said that the fighting is moving here. We do not know who is still leading an army there, but they are heading our way. I can only assume they are going to rendezvous with Lady Grustmiener. We need to find Julia. We have to get there first." Milskar moved so close to him he could see the white reflected in his eyes.

"I found a map," Levi said, holding up the piece of paper. "But it is too dark, I can't see."

"Heza," Aura called into the darkness. "Can you please light some embers for us? We do not need a whole fire, just some light, so we know where to go."

A rumbling could be heard in the distance, and Levi wondered if the truck driver had followed them by some path in the trees. He looked around but didn't see any headlights. Plus, the sound was very far away, but clearly getting closer. It was rhythmic, like a…like a—

"We need to get out of here," Levi called, stuffing the map in his pocket.

"What?" Aura was startled at his abruptness.

"The driver of the truck," he called to Jada. "Can you see him? Did he call the police?"

The woods were silent except for the stead thrum of the approaching helicopter.

"Yes," Jada called out. "They're on their way."

"We need to get out of here right now." Levi didn't try to hide the panic from his voice. They weren't moving with enough urgency. He wanted to shake Aura, to throw Milskar on a dragon, to drag Amaline and Calanthe toward the griffins.

"Levi," Aura said.

"There's no time, now. Move. Now!"

They scrambled up, and the animals took to the skies. Levi hoped the creatures were able to see in the dark. Hoped they could sense the approaching danger and realize they just needed to fly as quickly as possible. Just needed to put some distance between themselves and whatever was coming for them. They would figure out direction later. He'd spread out the map, they'd figure out where they were and where they needed to be, but for now, they needed to escape.

Lights flashed and scanned before them. They'd left with seconds to spare.

"We need to get a bit higher," Levi called. He wanted to be safe. Wanted them to be cautious.

Up and out the creatures flew until the only light was the moon and stars, the ground below them a dark abyss.

Chapter 42

Lady Grustmiener

The mood in the room shifted when the small girl entered.

Lady Grustmiener eyed her, but the girl moved through confidently as if she'd belonged there the entire time. None of the other inhabitants seemed to recognize her, or move forward to acknowledge her, but she didn't seem to mind. She gave a fleeting glance at the blood stain on the floor and took a chair at the empty table.

"How did you find us?" Lady Grustmiener asked.

"I felt a large concentration," the girl named Julia said. "There aren't many people that live in this town, so I knew something was going on, and I wanted to be a part of it."

"And your parents?"

"They won't even notice I'm gone. And if they do," Julia said, "they won't care." She let her eyes drop to her hands on the table.

Was the girl crying? Lady Grustmiener hoped she wasn't going to be a problem. Wasn't going to get too emotional to be of use. But she was intriguing. She looked unassuming and small, like she could easily blend into a crowd. Out of the various people standing in the room, this Julia may end up being the most beneficial to her.

"I am so sorry to hear that," she said softly.

The others in the room shifted and looked at one another, confused by the change in tone. Lady Grustmiener ignored them and sat next to Julia at the table and took the girls hands in her own. They were cold and clammy, and it took a lot of inner strength to not drop them in disgust.

Julia sniffled. "That's okay."

"It is not," she said. "But it will be. You are welcome here. We are going to do great things, and you are going to be able to be a part of that. How exciting will that be?" She gave false excitement to her voice.

"I want to be a part of anything. Anything that will get me away from here. That will let me make something of myself," Julia said.

Lady Grustmiener was pleased. This was exactly what she wanted. This is what she wished the others would have said to her. Instead, they were groveling and mourning the death of the pile of flesh and useless bones lying on the floor. That woman was nothing to them anymore. She was nothing to them before. Someone so strong should not have fallen so easily. Lady Grustmiener was the superior one, they had to see that. They had to recognize and want to be a part of it, but she still sensed their hesitation. This girl was different.

"We must leave right away," Lady Grustmiener called to the room.

"Leave? Now?" one of the women repeated.

"Yes." She was unable to hide the annoyance in her voice. Maybe they would see her treating the girl well and realize that a little humility would help them go far. Would put them in her good graces. Questioning her would certainly not.

"And we are off to New York?" the man asked.

"Yes."

The girl shifted uncomfortably next to her and took back her hands. It was a momentary break in her façade, but it was there. Was there doubt in this person? Lady Grustmiener would have no room for doubters, useful or not.

"Is there a problem with New York?"

"N—No," Julia stuttered. "No, ma'am. I have never been to New York before, that's all. I've always wanted to go, but my parents called it a sinful place. That it's no place for a young lady."

"Well, it sounds like it is good you were able to leave those close-minded parents of yours then." She smiled at the girl who returned it with a crooked one of her own.

"Yes, yes, I think it is."

Lady Grustmiener looked up, and the room exploded into movement. The men and woman rushed around, picking up objects and placing them back down. And always, always turning to look at the dead bodies on the floor.

"We will leave them," she said. "We will leave them with a message for anyone who finds them and wants to join the right army, the one they should have sided with from the beginning, they can travel to New York."

"Where exactly?" Julia asked.

"Excuse me?" Lady Grustmiener didn't attempt to hide the annoyance from her voice.

"I am not trying to be rude." Julia lowered her eyes as she spoke. "But New York is a very large city. How will they know where to find you? Do you have a land-mark location or something?"

A man stepped forward. "The girl is right, there are millions of people there, millions of places. Where do we begin?"

"In the heart of the kingdom, of course."

They looked at one another, confused expressions wrinkling their faces.

"Times Square," Julia said. "The heart of every-thing."

"Times Square," Lady Grustmiener repeated. "That seems as perfecta place as any to take over the world."

Chapter 43

Luther

The rain was coming down in great sheets, turning parts of the ground into rivers beneath their feet. Luther was wet in places he hadn't even known existed. He was tired and miserable, but in the middle of himself burned a candle, albeit faint, that fueled him.

He knew others may think of him as ridiculous for this crusade. Heck, he even questioned his own sanity, but Unna had changed something within him. Made him feel something that no one else had made him feel, and he owed it to her to avenge her death. He hoped she would have done the same for him. No one had looked at him the way she had. He was terrified no one ever would again.

Achan and Lieal flanked him, followed by several hundred marchers. They'd been collected from all over the region. Most of those who'd joined did so because they weren't ready for the fighting to be done. Some were left without a kingdom or were hoping to get theirs back. Each was searching for something. They were hungry for whatever personal reason drove them. Luther didn't care why. It didn't matter to him what brought these people to follow him, just that they did.

They could be fighting a hundred separate battles, but they equaled part of the same war, and that was what he needed. He was going to kill Queen Aura and destroy everything and everyone she loved.

As they marched, his hatred toward Lady Grustmiener built as well. She had filled his head with dreams that vanished along with her. He'd make her pay for what she'd done to him. For what this war did to Unna.

He sent one of the members of their growing militia to Esotera to act as a spy. Her job was to pretend to have spotted their clan and rush to tell whoever was in charge of the terrible thing they were about to do. He wanted to draw as many of them out as he could. He wanted them to cross over into his world. Luther knew Lady Grust-miener was there, knew that anyone he couldn't finish off she would. Then the Four Corners would be, for all practical purposes, empty. Then he could do whatever he wanted, choose to live in whichever world he wished, and no one would be able to stop him.

For he planned to kill Lady Grustmiener as well.

She was the one who brought him to this wretched place. Made him fall in love with Unna and then was the catalyst for her death as well. For every ounce of hatred he had for Queen Aura, he held a pound for that other terrible woman. If he was the last man on Earth, that would be okay with him. If both worlds turned red with the blood of those slaughtered, he would pay that price. The revenge he sought was important to him above any-thing else.

As they walked, they collected the dead they found as well. He expected dark and worried looks when he pointed out another one and ordered one or two people to place it on the heavy carts, but they gave it no mind. They knew what the bodies were for. They'd either seen it with their own eyes or heard about it. If they were still willing to fight and follow him, it was clear they were willing to do whatever it took. He liked that about them. It made him feel strong and unashamed of his powers for the first time in his life.

Achan touched his arm, stopping him and his thoughts in place. The man's lips moved, but the rain was so loud and unrelenting, Luther couldn't hear what he was saying. Luther pointed to his ear and leaned forward.

"A few hundred yards up we take a right and follow the edge of the clearing. The portal will be straight ahead there," Achan hollered.

"And where will it dump us out?"

"No idea."

A pit formed in Luther's stomach. He could not, would not, be thwarted. "What do you mean you have no idea?"

"I have not been through this portal before."

"Best guess?"

"I heard it leads to a large city, but I do not know which one," Achan yelled over the din.

"Hopefully it's the right one."

"Luther," a voice cut through the noise. He saw the woman he'd sent as a spy running toward him.

"What have you found out? Did you infiltrate?"

She leaned over and placed her hands on her knees, huffing with each breath. "No need," she said in halting words. "I made it to the perimeter of the castle. They are already preparing. I over-heard someone talking. They are coming."

He straightened and looked around, the others had paused, hands above their eyes forming a brim in which to see through.

"We're nearly there," Luther boomed to them over the rain.

They looked equal parts nervous and afraid, but when he turned, they followed him.

He walked slightly off the path. The ground had been worn in such a way puddles of rain formed great expanses. Luther turned back to make sure the beasts were able to move the cart through with no problem. What was he going to do with them? Surely, he couldn't bring these creatures, whatever they were, through to the other world. They had scales where a horse's mane typically was and talons on the back of each of their six legs. Luther was frightened of them, but he needed them to carry the bodies. It took too much energy to summon the dead for long periods of time, and he needed to conserve his energy for the right moment. Until then, the bodies would need to be carried somehow when they crossed over and left the cart-pulling creatures behind. He'd just have to hope something would present itself as a solution.

"We cannot bring these creatures through," Luther said to the two men. They looked quizzically at him. "There aren't animals like this in my land. They can't come."

"And the bodies?" Lieal asked.

"That is why I am bringing it up." The frustration was palpable in Luther's voice. He was going to be glad to be rid of these two.

"We will be unable to carry them all," Achan said.

Luther sighed. "Yes, I know. Again, why I am addressing this now."

"Osey and Palastrar," Lieal said.

Achan nodded his head. "Of course."

"What is an Osey and Palastrar?" Luther asked.

"They can levitate objects. I think they can help," Achan said.

Why was this information just getting to him now? Luther decided to let that go. He also refrained from asking what other magical powers accompanied them on their journey. In the end, it wouldn't really matter. His was all that was needed.

They marched on and took the right Achan indicated. There was nothing special about the portal, no real indication that it was even there, but one step he was in total wetness and the next, the air was dry and warm. It felt like sweet relief to not have the skies bombarding him with rain.

He moved aside to allow the others to filter through pulling Achan and Lieal over to stand with him. They watched as a large man and woman, presumably Osey and Palastrar, gathered the bodies from the carts and floated them to the other side. *At least that is taken care of*, Luther thought.

"When does this portal close?" he asked.

"I am not sure that it does," Achan said. "I heard a rumor the witches in the north had done something. I was waiting until we arrived to see for myself."

"To see what?" Lieal asked. This was the first time he had heard this too, Luther thought.

"This portal is not supposed to be open now, not for another three hours, but here it is. They must have left them open on purpose."

Lieal looked alarmed. "Then there is free travel?"

Achan shrugged. "Appears so."

"Good," Luther said.

It was good. He could do what needed to be done and return without any trouble. Without any time-table to have to worry about. This would work.

When the last of their group filtered through, Luther took a look around. He hadn't paid attention to where they were, he was so busy talking and making sure everyone crossed over okay, but now he was able to. While he'd never been here himself, the view was unmistakable. He'd seen it in pictures in his text books and dreamed of visiting here.

They were in a large park, a paved path cutting through swaths of green grass and tall, full trees. Wherever they were, it was a less frequented portion, for there were no people around other that the ones he brought. This would be the perfect place to hide everyone until the moment was right. Until he could figure out where to go.

It was even more beautiful than in the pictures, and he took a moment to shut his eyes and listen to the birds calling around them.

"Where are we?" He heard Achan ask.

"A park?" Lieal said questioningly.

"Like no park I have ever seen."

"Not just a park," Luther said and opened his eyes to look at them. "Central Park."

Chapter 44

Daybreak

Aura and Heza followed closely behind Levi and Gilbert, at least Aura hoped they followed close behind. It was difficult to make out the dark shapes against the dark sky, but she knew Heza could see. Knew her vision was just as good in the night as it was during the day. For the millionth time in her life, she was thankful that her father had finally agreed to get her the magnificent dragon.

"Thank you so much for taking care of me all these years," Aura whispered over the purple scaled neck. "I love you so much." A soft, guttural rumble told her Heza had heard and understood her. Of course, she did.

They'd taken to the skies in such a rush, Aura was worried they may have left someone behind in the flurry of activity. Her heart caught in her throat when she only counted the beating of four other sets of wings before she realized the fifth was a little way behind her, the sound of the thumping in her chest fighting to drown out any other noise. She didn't know what Levi had seen and why it was so terrifying. She heard it, sure, but it sounded like some large animal, a hippogriff maybe, but it was strange that a light seemed to emanate from it. She assumed that it was some strange creature that lived here, but it was clear in Levi's panicked voice that whatever it was, it meant them trouble.

Now they followed him. The moon was strange here, not as large and bright as her moon. Were they the same moon? she wondered. Or did each of their worlds have their own celestial bodies orbiting around them? It gave off the faintest light and made Aura long for hers back home.

Home. Would she ever see her kingdom again? The lands of her father and father's father? Would she lay eyes again upon the great waterfalls and creatures that roamed the beautiful lands she was proud to call hers, or see her beloved Serenity one more time? A tightening pull in her chest made her press her hand to it. Her wonderful, brave mare. Her first love. If she never got to see her again, never got to run her fingers through her thick mane, it would be a terrible shame.

She'd lost so much in her life, it seemed silly to be saddened over a horse, but Serenity was so much more than that. She was her friend. Like her other friend who she lost. Who she lost and could never get back and tried not to think about because the pain just may eat her alive.

Aura's tilted back slightly, and she realized they were going to land again. *Good*, she thought. She wanted to talk to Levi and find out what had happened. To know if they needed to worry about something in this word endangering them as well.

The ground came up quicker than she anticipated and she was thrown up on Heza's neck. The dragon faltered and buckled into the ground, vaulting Aura through the air. She landed in a painful crash.

"Aura." She heard Levi's voice call over to her, but she was unable to yell back. Her eyes teared and the air in her lungs, trapped, burned painfully. Just when she thought she'd never take another breath again and pass out from lack of oxygen, it came in great, gasping sprits.

"Shh." She felt soft hands accompany the soft words as he helped her sit up. "You're okay, you just got the wind knocked out of you. Slow, steady breaths. You're okay," he repeated.

She tried to focus on his words as her breathing became easier and less painful. He stood and helped her up, picking a twig from her hair.

"Thanks," she said in a shaky breath.

"You gave us quite a scare," Amaline said.

"Heza?"

"She's right over there," Amaline pointed.

It wasn't until that moment that Aura realized she could see. The sun was beginning to rise, deep orange hues over the horizon. Heza was shaking herself off and looking wildly around.

"I am over here," Aura called, and the dragon bounded forward nearly knocking Amaline down as she pushed past her. "Oh, my love, it's all right. I am perfectly all right."

She patted and cooed until the dragon calmed down, but the beast would not leave her side as they walked toward the others.

"Graceful," Calanthe said. It took a moment for Aura to realize she was joking and give her a weak smile.

"Where are we?" Milskar asked. He was holding a large piece of paper with lines covering it. It must have been the map that Levi searched for, but it didn't look like one Aura had ever seen before.

"We are close to the place Julia said she was. I thought we should land and figure out our strategy before we find ourselves in the middle of something bad. Jada, have you been checking in with her?"

Jada's skin shone the orange of the sun as it colored the side of his face. It gave him a haunting look. "They left," he said.

"Left?" Aura was confused.

"Umm, Julia and a woman." Jada hesitated, not wanting to give them the information. Aura implored him with her eyes. "Lady Grustmiener," he admitted.

"Wait, she is with Lady Grustmiener now?" Amaline asked.

Levi rushed forward and knelt in front of Jada, placing his hands on either side of Jada's arms. The boy nodded.

"What do you mean they left?" Levi asked.

"Julia's with them."

Aura's hand flew to her mouth, covering a soft moan that escaped without her permission. "They kidnapped her?" She spoke through her fingers.

Jada shook his head. "No, she chose to go with her. She wants us to find her friends, the people she was with. I think they will know what to do."

"I do not understand," Amaline said looking around the group. "Why would she go with them? Does she not know how dangerous that woman is? Does she not know…" Her voice trailed off.

"She did a very brave thing," Aura said, putting the pieces together in her head. "She knew they were going to leave and that she was the only one who could go with them safely. She knew Jada could see her and would lead us to her. We need to find that man and woman she was with and hope that they have others meeting them as well."

Calanthe stood and walked a short way off.

Aura considered calling her back, but the woman

looked lost in thought, so Aura decided to leave her alone.

"They're with a lot of people, Julia and Lady Grust-miener," Jada said.

"Then we will need to bring as many people as we can. We will need these people to help us. And, hopefully, they will know some they can ask to join us as well." Aura paused, the task feeling even more daunting than before. "We will gather whomever we can, and while we figure out what we are doing, Julia will be waiting for us. Waiting to show us the way."

"Then we better go," Levi said. He stood and took the map from Milskar who was rooted in place.

"She is just a child," Milskar said. His voice was so quiet Aura didn't hear him at first, but he repeated himself, louder now. "She is just a child."

The group froze in place. A bird called loudly as it climbed in the sky.

Aura turned to face him. "She is."

"She is a lamb in the den with the lion."

"She is in the den with the lion." Aura paused. "But she is no lamb."

Chapter 45

Road Trip

The car rumbled and jolted Julia from side to side as it crossed the bridge. She couldn't get traction on the leather seats and held on to the door to keep from slipping into Lady Grustmiener. The woman sat next to her looking equally uncomfortable. The driver had tried to make her put a seat belt on, but Lady Grustmiener snatched his wrist when the man tried to reach over and buckle her in.

"If you handle this contraption so poorly that I need to be strapped in," she said while the man squirmed and tried to take his hand back, "then I would like another driver."

The man apologized and said she could travel however she wanted, he would just be more careful. They had a convoy of about a dozen cars as they left the small town. Julia looked out the window, hoping vainly that she would catch a glimpse of Toli or Deserae or, maybe, Levi and Aura. There was nothing outside the window but buildings and trees, and soon the latter gave way to concrete walls protecting the residents from the highway.

She tried to focus on each sign they passed as she felt Jada's presence in her head. He was with her pretty much all the time now. She wondered what the others thought, if they noticed his focus leaving them or if they had him in a safe place where he could watch and report and they could take care of everything else.

It was silly, but she so longed to see them again. The lies she had to tell about her parents not caring about her, about them even being alive, pained her more than she thought it would. The lie came out easy, but burned like acid in her mouth and left a terrible aftertaste. Those people from that strange land were the closest thing she'd had to family in as long as she could remember.

As each day passed even the memories of her parents faded away. She tried to focus on them, hold on to how her mother smelled, how her father's beard felt on her cheek, but there were times when she wasn't sure if what she remembered was real, or just a wishful memory of an event that never was.

"Ugh," the driver said and slapped the wheel. "I think we may be lost. Stupid GPS isn't working."

Lady Grustmiener loudly ground her teeth. "I thought you people knew where you were going."

"Well, there is some construction on the Six-Fourteen, so I need to re-route to I-Seventy-Eight, but I don't know how to do that."

Julia didn't know what the guy was talking about, but it was clear that it wasn't the answer the current ruler of her world wanted to hear. How wonderful would it be that a simple act of getting lost could thwart world-wide domination plans? Julia knew it would be too laughable, too easy, yet she hoped for it all the same.

"Let's stop and get a map," the woman in the passenger seat suggested. She'd been silent the whole trip, making Julia wonder if she was mute. Julia wished the woman had stayed that way.

"All right, I'll signal the other cars." He beeped the horn twice and put on his turn signal at the exit before the road was marked closed. They appeared to be in the middle of nowhere, trees and cows dotting the landscape, yet they came upon a rusted sign that read *Mobil* with two ancient looking pumps.

The woman got out of the car when an attendant rushed toward them, waving his hands frantically.

"No ma'am," the attendant said.

"Get rid of him," Lady Grustmiener seethed. Julia's breathing quickened. Would the fighting start already? She wasn't prepared for this. It shouldn't just be them against this poor old man.

"Can't pump your own gas here, you've crossed into New Jersey, didn't you know?" he asked.

"Forgot," the passenger said and got back into the car.

"Get rid of him," Lady Grustmiener repeated.

"Can't," the driver said. He reached next to his seat and popped the gas cover and the attendant set to filling up the tank. He rolled down the window to talk to the man as he worked. "Hey, we got re-routed by the detour."

"Oh, yes. We've seen an influx of cars through these parts lately," he said while looking at the number turning on the pump.

"How do we get back to I-Seventy-Eight?"

"Ah, heading to the city?" he asked. The leather arm rest creaked as Lady Grustmiener gripped it tightly.

"He's going to tell us where we need to go," Julia whispered. "Then we will be on our way." She was shot a scathing look, but no more words were spoken. It wasn't that Julia *wanted* to get to New York, far from it, but she didn't want this innocent man to die either.

"Well, it's easy," the man said. He tightened the screw cap and pushed the gas cover back over, clicking it loudly in place. The driver started the engine. Julia closed her eyes and prayed. "You follow this road a few miles down, then you'll get to where the Old Warwick Farm was, hang a left on Mechlin Corner Road and follow that til you get to the highway. Can't miss it. That'll be twenty-four dollars and fifty cents."

Movement and sound surrounded Julia. She felt herself thrown against the seat as the man's yells reverberated from outside. Julia whirled around in time to see the man chasing them down, but he was no match for the speeding car. She thought about throwing a couple gold coins out the window, but there was no good opportunity to do so. The other vehicles followed closely behind and soon they were speeding down a long country road.

It wasn't the most innocuous pit-stop, but Julia was glad no one got hurt other than the poor man's bottom line. He wouldn't know it, but he got off easy.

Several minutes later they made the left-hand turn. Julia kept waiting for police sirens to find them, but the surrounding area was quiet. They passed houses, but it seemed like no one lived in this town. They didn't see a single person or another car. Maybe her prayers had been answered.

Chapter 46

Saviors

The portals are open," Emily said, addressing the remaining kids. Galina, Kiya, Tab, and Raigan were seated around Aura's office. It felt strange holding a meeting in here without the usual suspects present, but this space was bigger than Emily's office, and she also wanted it to convey the gravity of their situation.

"Thank God," Galina said. "I want to be on the first train, or whatever, out of here."

"It's not that simple," Emily said slowly. She'd gathered them together but didn't have a plan on how to tell them the news.

"Why?" Tab said. "I thought the portals being closed was the only thing keeping us here. Didn't Aura and Levi and the others head to get Julia back? We're not needed for that."

"It's not as simple as getting Julia back."

"Right, you gotta kill that Lady Grustmiener lady," he said.

"It's not that simple anymore, either." Emily let her words hang in the air while she decided on the next ones to choose.

Galina rose. "Why isn't it that simple anymore?"

The image of the jadwiga flying through Emily's window that morning popped into her head. She took the letter from its trembling beak, recognizing her own handwriting. She was about to ask the bird if yet another letter went without finding its intended recipient when she noticed three sentences scrawled on the back in Aura's pen.

The war is advancing to us. Come right away. Bring all that will follow.

The bird was perched comfortably on her vacated pillow, deep in sleep as Emily ran out of her room to make preparations.

Remembering that her office was still filled, she addressed those in front of her. "There is another battle forming. More fighters are going to join her cause." The room turned and watched as Quan, the man Calanthe left in charge of Vertronum, entered. Emily blinked hard, unable to fully comprehend what she was seeing.

"Quan?"

"I received a message from Calanthe. It appears that more help is needed. I came to offer my services."

"Thank you." Emily was overwhelmed. Close behind him followed Hai and Edda.

"Seriously," Galina said. "What in the hell is going on?"

"There is an army being led into your world as we speak. Frankly, they may already be there," Hai said.

"Another army? Where do these people keep coming from?" Tab didn't hide the exasperation from his voice.

Emily laughed softly and rubbed her eyes. "I wish I knew. But they have assembled fighters that were apparently not done defending their homeland or their former queen. They are meeting up with her in the other world. I can only assume they are going to try to take as many with them as they can. I imagine that's why our numbers have been thinning out. Levi was right, domination of the other world was on Lady Grustmiener's mind from the beginning."

"So." Galina paused and narrowed her eyes. "What you're saying, is that we *can* go home, but there may be no home to go to. Or we may be captured. Or killed."

The room was silent.

"What if we want to fight?" Emily was expecting the words from Tab's mouth, but they were much too soft. She turned and saw Kiya standing, staring at her without blinking.

"Fight?" Emily asked.

"I agreed to help in this. The battle clearly isn't over. So, I'm coming with." She stood up taller. Emily could have scooped her up and kissed her.

"I'm in," Tab said.

"Me too," Galina said. "But let me make this very clear." She turned and looked pointedly at each member in the room. "This is just for Adam. For what they did to Adam. I am going to kill as many of them as I can get my hands on, and then I'm going home. I never want to see this place again."

Emily nodded. "Okay. Kiya, will you please help me address the animals again. Edda, any luck contacting the great witches?"

Edda beamed. "Better," she said. "They are here."

"Here?"

"Oh, yes, they arrived before I was even able to send out a jadwiga to look for them. I can only assume they knew you were going to look for them. Would you like me to bring them into the castle?"

"Yes, please, of course." How had Edda kept this from her? She should have burst into the room and announced their arrival. Emily hoped the witches wouldn't feel put out by—well, being put out. "Oh, and Edda, please ask for rooms to be made up for them. The best rooms we have." Emily turned back to speak to the others. "I am going to ask you to leave now. Quan, you may stay. Kiya, can you speak to the animals by yourself?"

"Of course. All of them?" she asked.

"Yes."

"Even the dragons?"

"Especially the dragons. The Four Corners days of being hidden are numbered. We might as well show all our cards in the hope of saving it. We leave at daybreak."

"To where exactly?" Raigan asked. She'd been quiet this whole time. Emily had forgotten she was still there.

"Wherever the witches tell us to go."

They turned to leave.

"Will it be that easy?" Quan asked. "Will they tell us where to go?"

"We can only hope. The fate of the world may depend on it."

Moments later the room filled with hooded figures. One stood forward and spoke, freezing every inch of Emily with her speech.

"We thought you might need assistance," the woman said. Her voice was as cool and perfect as it was the last time Emily had heard it.

She had been locked in a room, convinced she was going to die of thirst, and this woman, this saint of a woman, offered her water. Emily never heard or saw her again and assumed that she'd been killed for her generosity.

Emily stepped forward and embraced her. She felt the woman stiffen under her touch, but she didn't care.

Tears sprang to Emily's eyes. "You," she whispered into the black fabric.

"You remember me," the woman said when Emily released her.

Quan looked confused as did the other witches in the room.

"Of course, I remember you. You saved my life."

"No," the woman said. "You would have been fine."

"Without your kindness, I don't know. Who are you?"

The woman lowered her hood, revealing perfect black skin and a bald head. She was stunning. "Filia."

"Filia, I need your help once again. There was a group of fighters in Grustmiener that might have already entered my former world."

"They have."

Emily tried to keep her face devoid of emotion and her speech even. For some reason, she thought another emotional outburst would only harm their chances of receiving help. "We need to follow them, preferably using the same portal so we can find them more quickly."

"That can be arranged." Murmurs started behind her at her declaration. She turned and faced the other witches, but if words were spoken, Emily could not hear them. The room went silent again.

"We would like to leave in the morning. Until then, I have had our best rooms made up. You will be very comfortable to rest here. I will have a meal made that can either be brought up to you, or you may eat in our dining hall, whichever you prefer."

A smile tugged at the right side of Filia's face. "You are inviting us to stay?"

"Of course," Emily said. "There is nothing too good for friends of ours."

"Friends." The woman rolled the worlds over as she spoke them. "I think I am glad that I saved you."

"I thought she did not need saving," Quan said.

Emily could have slapped him. If he wrecked their chances, she'd have to drown him in his home waters, but the witches just laughed.

Chapter 47

Magic in New York

The contraption she was in sped so fast, Lady Grustmiener wondered if they were actually flying. They must have been in some hybrid version of the one she'd traveled in with Cecily and Respin before. The trees on either side of her zoomed by at such speeds, she found she had to stare straight ahead to keep from getting sick.

The scenery gave way to tall buildings, and she couldn't help but press her nose against the cool glass. She heard the girl shift next to her and turned to see she, too, was taking in the view.

They slowed as they neared a giant hole in the ground. It was swallowing up those in front of them. She was about to call out and voice her concern over the danger when they entered. It wasn't a hole she realized, but a giant tube. They crawled along in the dim lighting. She was about to ask if this city was underground when they came out of the other side.

It was like nothing she'd ever seen. People. Buildings. Horse-less carriages. And the colors! They flashed and moved, bombarding her senses. This would be hers, every inch of it.

"Where should we park?" the female in front of her asked the male.

"There's a garage close. We may have to walk a block or two, but I don't think there'll be another place where we'll all fit."

"What the…" Julia trailed off. They followed her finger. *Maybe this place wasn't so foreign, after all,* Lady Grustmiener thought.

"What day is it?" the woman asked.

"The twenty-fourth, why?" he answered.

"Oh, my, it's *MagiCon.*"

"Oh, God." His voice came out in a gush of air.

Lady Grustmiener had no idea what they were talking about, but if it meant a meet-up of magical or half magical people, she was even more glad they'd suggested coming here.

She saw a man leading a pink colored half-woman, half-large cat creature. She'd never seen something that looked like that before. She was alarmed at first, but the way it obediently followed, it appeared to be tame.

There were witches and wizards too. She would have sworn the only ones left were in the northern region of Omaner. They displayed their wands, and some appeared to be engaged in some sort of faux battle, those around them appearing unconcerned. If only Winester could see this.

Winester. She involuntarily brought her hand up to her chest. She tried not to think about it. His loss was a weakness to her, and she didn't like to feel anything but strong. Late at night, when she was close to sleep, and her mind wandered, she thought of him, but never during the day. Never while it could distract her. She felt an urge to talk to these wizards though. To see if she could recruit and use them.

She opened the door, causing the carriage's movement to cease at one. The two up front yelled and voiced their opposition, but she didn't care. She needed to speak with these fighters.

Lady Grustmiener strode directly into the crowd. Loud noises emanated from the brightly colored carriages as she walked, but she ignored them. She heard another door shut, and Julia appeared breathlessly next to her. Then so did the man and woman followed by the others from the house.

They spoke in excited chatter, their carriages left behind as well. The people and creatures paused to see what the commotion was about. One of the beasts ran up to her and grabbed her arm. It had blue and yellow skin and claws protruding from its knuckles, but it didn't hurt when he touched her.

"Your costume is great," the thing said. She easily broke its grasp and pushed it to the ground. It protested then scampered away, other creatures stepping forward to help it up.

The group she arrived with moved closer to her, forming a circle of protection. She was glad that their immediate response was to guard her. Magical or not, she didn't want any more of those things touching her.

She withdrew her sword, just in case, but held it calmly at her side.

Chapter 48

Calls and Answers

"They are heading to New York," Jada said. "I'm sure of it."

Dread flowed through Levi. The news kept getting worse. He needed to find a phone. Needed to call his agent, Kailly. She could alert the proper authorities. She'd know what to do.

The ground below them was lush and filled with trees. He knew there had to be a landing space, but the foliage was so densely packed, he wasn't sure how long it would be before it presented itself.

Gilbert must have sensed a change in the topography because the trees were getting closer. A break appeared, and the six creatures circled to land. Down below in the middle of the empty space, a man and a woman raised their arms.

When they landed, Milskar, Calanthe, Amaline, and Aura jumped straight down and drew their weapons. Levi was a full second behind their thought process, fumbling with his sword as he dismounted. Jada touched down moments after him. The man and woman looked at them wide-eyed. The combination of dragons, griffins, and armed riders was probably more than they were expecting.

Jada pushed passed and stood between the two groups. "It's okay," he said. "It's them."

"Are you sure?" Calanthe asked.

"Yes. I've seen their faces many times."

Levi relaxed and re-sheathed his sword. The other four did the same. The woman took a tentative step forward then moved back again to stand next to the man.

"I'm Deserae. This is Toli," she called to them.

"I am Aura, Queen of Esotera." She motioned to the rest of their group. "This is Milskar, Calanthe, Amaline, Levi, and Jada."

"We've heard quite a bit about you," Toli said. "It's an honor, Queen Aura." He bowed, and Deserae followed suit after a pointed look from her counterpart.

"Are there others with you?" Aura asked.

"Yes, a few. More are ready to meet us. We assume Lady Grustmiener's group is traveling north." He turned to look at Jada.

"New York. New York City," Jada confirmed.

"I was afraid they may go there. They have a head start, and it will take us an hour and a half to get there, so we should leave right away."

"How many of you are there?" Milskar asked, making no movement to leave at Toli's orders.

Toli hesitated before speaking. "Six. Six total. But more will come. More will meet us there."

"Six is good, we can double up," Milskar said. Toli's shoulders dropped in relief.

Aura nodded. "Please, ask them to show themselves."

Deserae moved, but hesitated, unsure of what was happening. "Double up, where?" she asked. "We only need three cars to drive there."

"Oh," Aura smiled. Levi could see she was getting some much-needed enjoyment out of this exchange. "Flying will be much faster, do you not think so?" She patted Heza absentmindedly on the shoulder. The dragon stood tall and stared straight at Deserae.

The woman swallowed hard and nodded then turned to gather the others.

Levi moved closer to Aura and leaned over her, his eyes still on Toli. "We are going to take them with us?"

"We need all the help we can get. Plus, Julia was with them. Do you trust her judgment?"

He paused, thinking the question over. "I do, actually."

"Good."

He turned to address the man who looked awkwardly between the group and the place where Deserae vanished.

"Do you have a phone?"

"No," he said, startled at being asked such a normal question. "But there is a pay phone in town. I've always had trouble with cell phones working, so I don't even bother anymore. Must be something to do with our powers or something."

Levi nodded. He wondered what kind of power these two had, but decided it might be considered rude to ask.

"I'll be right back," Levi said to the group. Aura and Amaline stepped forward at once to protest. "It'll just take a second, I need to call someone, to warn them. We'll be right back." He stepped forward and lightly touched Aura's hands before kissing her. "I'll be right back, I promise." She nodded.

"Follow me," Toli said.

They walked to a beat-up looking car parked on a

dirt road that split the forest. Levi spotted several figures moving toward them from the north, and he paused before getting in.

"That's the others," Toli said. "We better hurry so we can make it back and leave right away."

The car rumbled and kicked up a swirl of dust when they backed out of the one-lane road. Levi wondered how this, of all places, was picked at the rendezvous point. Sure, it was remote, but it appeared so remote he didn't know how anyone who didn't live here even knew about it.

About a quarter mile down the road a payphone stood outside of small convenience store. The sign proclaimed it as opening soon, but the dust on the windows looked about an inch thick. Levi wondered if the phone even worked. Toli rooted around for some lose change and handed it over as he put the vehicle in park.

"You know the number?" he asked.

"Yeah, yeah I do." Cell phones worked sporadically for him as well. He'd never really thought about it before, but it made sense what Toli said about the magic effecting the signal. As a backup, he tried to memorize any important phone numbers he may need. He knew Kailly's by heart and a handful of other people, including his parents.

His parents. His chest tightened at the thought of them. Should he call them too, warn them that something may be happening? He knew they were far away from the danger, but what if they decided on a whim to travel? See a Broadway show? It wasn't like them, but should he make sure?

He decided to call Kailly first and then go from there. He dropped the quarters into the phone and pressed her number in, his hand trembling.

"Hello?" a questioning voice answered.

"Kailly?"

"Levi? Oh my God! What the hell, where have you been? I've called your phone about a million times."

"I know, I mean, I figured, I didn't get any of your calls."

"What is going on, Levi? I was worried about you. You meet this strange woman and fall off the face of the Earth? I was about one day away from calling your parents to see if they heard from you."

"Did you call them?" Panic rose. They would worry like crazy if they received a panicked call from his agent being unable to find him.

"No, no, but I was really worried. So, where are you? You have an event tomorrow night."

"Kailly, I need you to listen to me."

"If you cancel another signing, I don't know what to do. I don't think the publisher is going to put up with much more of this."

"Kailly." Levi's voice was sharp, and the other end went silent. "Something happened, and I need you to get in touch with the right authorities. I don't know who that may be, but I think nine-one-one may not cut it."

"Cut it? What are you talking about?" Kailly's voice sounded concerned.

"I'm not sure how to say this—" He took a deep breath, gathering his words. "My book isn't a fantasy."

"Are you kidding me right now? Are you seriously asking me to move where you are shelved at the store? Have you lost your mind?"

"I mean, it's not fiction." Silence on the other end. "Kailly, I know this sounds crazy, but I'm serious. It wasn't a made-up story. Esotera is real, the Four Corners is real, and worse, Lady Grustmiener is real. Only she isn't dead. She's here. She's in New York. I need you to help me. I need you to contact someone and tell them."

"Levi." She spoke his name slowly as if each letter was its own syllable. He shut his eyes, knowing what was coming. "I know you have been under a great amount of stress and part of that is my fault. I set you up with a grueling tour, and I know it's been hard, but I need you to keep it together for just a little while longer. A few more weeks and you can go rest on an island somewhere. I promise I won't call you or anything."

"I'm telling the truth. I went there. I'm the Missing Link. It's a real thing, and I'm him. Lady Grustmiener thinks she killed me, but she didn't, obviously. And she moved to our world, thinking she can take over. I think a lot of people are going to die."

A sigh met him on the other end.

"I know you don't believe me, I know it seems crazy, but something bad is going to happen. Please. Please just call someone and let them know. I need to go."

"Wait, Levi, wait. We will figure this out together. Please don't go."

"Aura is waiting. We need to get to New York. We need to stop her." He gently placed the phone in the receiver, ignoring the loud yells emanating as he set it down.

"How did it go?" Toli asked when he got back into the car.

"Not well, I don't think, but nothing more I can do. Hopefully, she believes me and calls someone who can help, even if it's just to have me committed. Maybe they will listen. At least I can say I tried." Levi shrugged, knowing the hope was useless, but wishing all the same.

"You need to call anyone else?"

Levi looked over at the phone, two quarters burning a hole in his hand. "No," he said and hoped he wouldn't regret the decision.

Chapter 49

The City

Jada had become a permanent fixture in her mind now. She barely noticed the coldness in her head. Whether they were close or he simply couldn't look away from what was happening, Julia didn't know. She wondered if he could feel the terror she felt.

When the car slowed as they neared Times Square and she saw all those people in costume, for a moment she thought Aura and her team, or Toli and Desi had successfully gathered a mass of people to fight. When the woman said they were just regular people dressed up, her heart sank. She found it difficult to take in a full breath of air, the pit in her stomach so large it took up half her body cavity, leaving little room for oxygen.

She wanted to scream at the top of her lung for these people to run. To flee the terror that would surely befall them, but where would they go? And she didn't want to risk outing herself as something other than what she was pretending to be. Aura and Levi and the others were counting on her. She didn't know how she knew this, but she did. She would be strong for them. The vision of them in her mind was the only thing that made her put one foot in front of the other.

When Lady Grustmiener pushed down the boy in the Wolverine costume, the group formed a circle of protection. Julia wasn't sure if they were protecting Lady Grustmiener from the people, or vice versa. Either way, she stood with her face to the crowd. People moved to help the boy up, and several yelled jeers at them.

"What are you doing, psycho lady?"

"Hey, he's just a kid."

A man in a Chewbacca costume moved threateningly at them. "What's your problem?" he yelled in a muffled voice through his mask.

Julia looked around. Where *were* the others? She pleaded with the heavens that they'd found a way through the portal and would be spilling into the streets any second now. She tried to calm herself. Of course, they would come. Of course, they would not leave her alone in this situation. She scanned the horizon for police officers as well. Maybe they would come running, arrest, them, arrest them all if that's what it took to neutralize Lady Grustmiener. Anything. Anything to prevent what Julia was certain was going to happen next.

Maybe it was the way they were standing that drew more attention to them. Or simply the way Lady Grustmiener looked, but the crowd started to press in on them. Julia tried to hold her ground, but she was little, and she knew it wouldn't be long before she was knocked over. They must have been creating quite a sight, this group of masked people poised for a fight, but no one seemed to be paying attention to them.

It was strange how it happened, how the fates could make a move that you might never have seen coming. Just as people were pushing in toward her, one stepped aside to engage the man on Julia's left. It happened in an instant, but at that moment, she spotted a man standing down the street. Not just a man. A group of men. A group of men she recognized and not because she'd seen them before, but *where* she'd seen them. On the battle fields of Esotera.

ⲉⲟⲉⲟ

Luther took five of the men with him, including Lieal, to check out the city. Achan was spitting mad at being excluded, but Luther needed him to stay behind.

"No one is going to mess with you," Luther had told him. "I need someone people will leave alone. It will look strange with all of you here in this park with these horses and especially the dead bodies. I need someone who looks menacing enough, that no one will even want to come into this part of the park. You must hide the others before my return and ensure their safety." Luther moved forward and lowered his voice, pretending that he didn't want Lieal to hear. "You are the only one I can trust with this. I am counting on you."

Achan grudgingly agreed.

They walked up Seventh Avenue. It was strange being back in a city again, much less one of the busiest cities in the world. The other men with him stayed close, but Luther doubted it was because they were trying to protect him.

Luther had to throw out a hand to block Lieal from walking straight into a yellow taxi cab. The cabbie blew his horn and yelled some choice words.

"Let me go first," Luther said. He could tell the men were jumpy, hands touching their sword handles. The weapons were hidden under their clothing but could be easily reached. The last thing Luther needed was them showing themselves as armed. They would be stopped by the police before they would be able to do anything.

Down the street, he heard a commotion. He did a double take, not able to quickly process what he was seeing.

"What kind of creature is that?" one of the men asked. A person dressed as, of all things, Big Bird, moved down the street.

"And you were worried that the people here would be concerned about the horses?" Lieal asked.

Luther noted a flashing billboard over his left shoulder. *Welcome MagiCon, Attendees!* The lights proclaimed. It was the best kind of luck he could have wished for.

"Go back and tell the others to join us," Luther said to one of the men, who took off in a run.

The rest of them were waiting at a light to cross back when Luther saw a small mob forming two blocks away. There was a group of people standing in a misshapen circle with a crowd forming around them. He wondered what kind of play fighting these people were doing, when he noticed a single figure stood at the center of it all.

The crowd shifted, revealing a small South American girl who stood directly in front of Lady Grustmiener.

Chapter 50

Happy

Pale light filtered in through the rain-stained windows and threw shadows across Omire's desk. He sat up straight, and his back joints creaked and popped in protest. What had happened to him? He used to be the strong one, the one people looked up to. He'd trained armies. Helped win a war. Fought foe after foe and won. But he was losing the battle within his own mind.

The moment he saw those bodies move toward him, King Piester, dead yet walking, something shifted in him that he knew he wouldn't recover from. This was not the life he wanted. Killing men and having them come back to haunt him.

He was a coward, he knew, but he slipped away from the fight and wandered back to hide in the underground castle. He'd figure out the logistics of his resignation later. Let Aura know that he was not worthy of leading or protecting anyone. He couldn't even protect himself.

The castle was empty, except for him. He wandered

the halls at night and got used to life by himself. When Emily showed up, though, he knew he couldn't stay. Eventually, people would return, and life would have to regain a level of normalcy he was no longer capable of.

He wanted to find a quiet piece of land close to where he was born, farm, and live in peace for whatever time left he was allotted. He would turn away any visitors and, one day, if he was lucky enough to get old, he would lay in his fields and die. Return to the earth and make his contribution to whatever plants or animals found use for his body.

When Emily came through his door, his first thought was complete and utter dread. What if she was there to arrest him? Would Queen Aura see his desertion as treason? Would he die, not among the woods and nature, but by a rope around his neck, feet kicking for purchase they would never find?

One fear was replaced by another. No, he was not going to be executed, not now at least. But more fighting? He had no more fight left in him. Even the task of finding King Theaus seemed insurmountable to the point of impossible.

He'd made a decision.

He would leave. There was no one here to rule. No citizens who needed him. He would slip away like he had before. Maybe it would even be assumed that he was dead. Then no one would come looking for him. Amaline would be sad, he was sure, but she too would move on with her life. She could remember him the way he wished her to, strong and capable. There was no need to taint his image with the truth of who he was.

Aura would find someone else to lead the people of Grustmiener. Or maybe after the war, there would be no kingdoms anymore. Maybe the world would be open and filled with peace. He liked that thought. He decided not to entertain the notion of them losing. Of what that could mean.

He went into the storerooms and took some supplies. Food that would otherwise go bad, and a sturdy bag, which was slick and waterproof. He grabbed a cape made of the same material and several tools that would help him get started on working the land. The rain would make the ground soft, and he hoped that would make it easier to clear a small area of trees and build a home for himself.

After some back and forth consideration, he decided to take one of the horses from the stables. When he entered the structure, only a single mule was there, foot deep in mud. The animal called loudly for him, and a pain ran through his chest. No people meant no workers. No workers meant no one had fed this beast for...he didn't know how long.

He threw some grain to the grateful animal who took large mouthfuls. He filled a smaller bag with more feed and wiped down a molded saddle. It did not look used, much less like it was going to be missed. The mule, too, seemed forgotten for some reason. She was small and tried to bite him when he went to put the bridle on.

"I just fed you," Omire growled.

The mule responded by sinking her teeth into his upper arm. After some wrestling and promises of more food, she finally settled down and allowed herself to be saddled and supplies added to her back. Omire decided he would walk and lead her. She had to be weak with lack of food, and he wasn't sure how far they were traveling. With another mouthful of grain, she followed obediently into the deluge.

They walked for three days before the land leveled off and the rain turned into a light drizzle. Omire figured they had to be close to the Vertronum boarder. There were no signs that this parcel of land had been previously owned, and he decided to claim it for himself.

For his first order of business, he built a small shelter for the mule, whom he decided to call Happy, hoping it would brighten her mood. It seemed to have a limited effect.

With a roof over her head protecting her from the rain, Happy's mood did seem to improve a bit. She only tried to bite Omire twice that day, which he took as an encouraging step forward in their relationship.

The work was quiet and tiring, both of which he welcomed. He'd opened the wound on his arm, the crude stitches he'd sewn himself. He let it bleed and ache, a reminder of the betrayal he couldn't escape.

On the sixth night, his structure had a roof, and he was able to get out of the rain. He fell asleep listening to it tickle the branches and leaves above him.

In the morning, he'd taken Happy out to gather more supplies and decide on a perimeter to his new home. The rain had stopped, though the ground still squished beneath her hooves. Omire struggled to get through some muddy parts, but they move through without any incident. He was just about to attach a bundle of leaves and twigs to a rope tied around her back when he heard a snap behind him.

Instinct took over.

Happy's ears stood straight up for the first time since he'd met her. She stared straight ahead, indicating to him where the noise had originated from. Omire listened hard, but he could make out no more noises. Happy on the other hand stood rooted in place then swiveled her head so fast, she cracked Omire on the cheek with it.

He was about to raise his hand to rub the sore spot when movement caught his eye in the direction she was looking. In a fluid movement so rehearsed he didn't have to think about it, he withdrew his sword and held it at the ready.

In seconds, King Theaus was upon him.

Happy sprang back several steps and let out a squeal as the two men's swords crashed together. Omire felt the tightness in his muscles from working the land, but it felt as if it was a separate thing. That new part of him, the new future he was creating for himself was separate from this Omire. The side of himself that fought, that lifted a sword up and down with precision was not the man he was anymore. This older version was appearing for the last time. He would fight this battle and be done. No matter what happened, this part of him would be dead forever.

"We do not need to fight," Omire said.

"I know what side you are on," King Theaus grunted between blows. "You will never cease. Your side is set to destroy me and my people."

"That is not true. I have no battle with you, not anymore."

"Well, that is convenient, is it not? You are the appointed King of Grustmiener, having stolen the crown with the help of that terrible woman the west calls queen, and no you no longer want to fight? It is too late for that."

"Capture. Mercy." Omire was finding it more difficult to speak. The old version of him was fading, taking the newer one along with it.

"Lies," King Theaus said through clenched teeth.

"Where is your army?" Omire asked, hoping to distract him or to buy himself more time.

Strange, how he was so willing to throw his life away mere days ago and now he fought for it with each ounce of strength he had left.

"I do not need an army. I am king."

The swords clashed and clanged as the rain started up again. The hilt felt slippery in Omire's grip, and he used both hands to keep it steady. King Theaus also seemed to be struggling. It was clear both men were exhausted. Now it was just a question of who would last longer.

Omire felt a strong shove on his shoulder and a sharp pain in his chest. He was knocked to the ground and was unable to spring back to his feet. He rolled over in time to see Happy, that glorious, ornery mare flashing teeth and hooves, dancing on the body of a man crumpled beneath her.

A wheezing noise started coming out of Omire's chest, and he struggled to sit up. Looking down, he discovered the source of his previous pain. Happy was the one that knocked him down, but King Theaus was the one that drove the sword into his chest. He watched as the blood pulsed out of him with each pump of his heart. It was a mortal wound, he knew.

He found it funny that in trying to avoid any more fighting, he managed to complete the one task that was asked of him. Lady Grustmiener and Queen Aura were all who remained. Whichever one was successful in the battle over the other would rule all four kingdoms. It was even possible that he'd secured his own legacy.

Someone was sure to stumble upon these two bodies. Would it be assumed that it was King Theaus who was building the hide-out? That Omire traveled with the mule to find and then defeat him? It was a nice thought.

As death neared, his fear oozed out of him along with the blood. What had he been so frightened of? Of dying? Dying was not hard. He was comfortable upon the earth. The rain had stopped, and he could just make out the roof of his structure. His vision was right. He had found a piece of land, claimed it for his own, and would die upon it. It was a shame that it happened so soon.

Happy smelled the sitting man. It was a different scent then she was used to of his. She didn't like it and turned to leave, choosing not to pick up her feet as she walked over the other man. She returned to her temporary structure and ate the rest of the grain before making the journey back to the castle grounds, now empty and without a ruler.

Chapter 51

Old and New

Deserae clutched Aura so firmly, it was difficult to breathe. Aura heard low gasps in her ear each time Heza shifted, flew faster, slower, higher, or lower. Really, anytime the dragon didn't remain perfectly still—which was never—the poor woman made some sort of noise. Luckily their journey was a short one.

This world was so strange and foreign to Aura. Some things were familiar, the trees and even some of the dwellings, but everything else was mind-boggling. Dark shapes moved swiftly on black surfaces. Levi had called them cars, and evidently, they held people in them somehow.

She wondered how he lived in this place. It seemed so complicated. There were a million directions to go, and it looked like people went every which way. She wondered how the rulers of this land kept everyone safe and accounted for. She thought her kingdom was large, but compared to this, it seemed like hers was merely the size of the palm of her hand.

Levi flew reassuringly next to her with Toli. The man had a far-away look in his eyes. He'd informed them that he had the ability to alter or erase memories. It enabled them to fly lower since he could change what people saw when they looked up. She wasn't sure exactly how it worked, but she was glad he was with them.

"Where should we land?" Amaline called. The woman seated behind her on the griffin looked green and kept her eyes shut.

"I think Central Park is our best bet," Levi yelled. "It will give us a bit of coverage. I don't think Toli is going to be able to hide us forever."

Aura looked back at the man who was turning a frightening purple color with his intense concentration. She didn't know what this park was but hoped it was big enough to hide the large dragons and griffins. Something told her that this place wouldn't welcome them, and she'd be heartbroken if something happened to them now after all they'd been through.

They'd been traveling for about twenty minutes when Aura spotted large, strangely shaped mountains in the distance. The closer they got and the more curious she became for they didn't look random like the mountains she was used to but had steep, perfect angles. She realized they were buildings of some sort yet they seemed to tower over the landscape. It amazed and frightened her how these buildings touched the sky. They were at least five times taller than the top tower at Esotera. Maybe these ones were held up by the clouds surrounding them? Or magic? There was no other way they could stand that tall on their own. She felt very small and far away from home.

Levi pointed to a green mass below them. "There!"

They landed, and Aura's feet had just touched the ground when she heard a yell. It was clear they were visible now, Toli wasn't able to protect them any longer. She stiffened and placed her hand on her sword as she turned.

"Aura, oh my gosh I found you." Emily threw her arms around her then peeled off with a yell when she spotted Milskar.

"What are you doing here?" he scolded through clenched teeth. He didn't return her hug.

"Are you serious? You're in trouble. You're in trouble, and I was the only one able to warn you. I assembled anyone who would come and brought them here. We're fighting. This is my home. Everywhere is my home, frankly, and I won't let that woman take any more of it from me." She spoke in clear and measured words as if she'd been practicing this speech for hours. Maybe she had.

Milskar softened and kissed her on the cheek before introducing her to their new travel companions. Emily called out, and hundreds of people walked out from behind bushes, trees, and rocks surrounding them. She introduced Hai and Edda, letting Calanthe have the honors with Quan.

They walked toward each other and Aura was sure they were going to embrace, but they each reached out their hands and grasped each other's upper arms. It looked painful but must not have been for they were smiling.

"You had orders to stay," Calanthe said, looking Quan full in the face.

"You must have known I would ignore them."

Calanthe smiled broadly. She never ceased to confound Aura. Just when she thought she had a handle on the woman, Calanthe did something so unexpected, Aura wondered if she knew her at all.

There were hundreds of faces surrounding them, some Aura recognized, and others she didn't. Were they fighters from her world or this one? One man moved forward and embraced a still-green Deserae. It was a warm hug but appeared to upset the man named Toli. Aura wondered how they all knew each other, though this was certainly not the time for such matters.

"We need to find Lady Grustmiener," Aura said, bringing the little reunions back to reality. She spoke in a low tone so only those around her could hear. She looked around at the throngs of people filtering around her. Her heart swelled and tightened in appreciation and fear.

"And the other fighters," Emily reminded them, pulling Aura from her wandering thoughts.

"What shall we do with the animals?" Aura asked.

"I think we should leave them here," Toli said. "I can't keep blocking them. There are too many people here. I could maybe do some clean up after all this is over, but it's too risky. As soon as something starts, cops are going to be all over this place."

"Cops?" Amaline asked.

"Law enforcement," Toli said. Receiving blank stares, he added, "peace keepers?"

They nodded, but Aura wasn't totally sure what he meant. Maybe that was how the rulers knew what was going on. They had armies of their own not just for fighting battles, but for preventing them. It was something she'd have to think about when they got home.

She thought over what he said before speaking. "No. They are coming with us."

"Aura," Levi said. "You heard him. He can't protect them."

"I am not leaving them." She reached out a hand and placed it on Heza's in the spot she liked to be rubbed between her shoulder and wings. The dragon shut her weary eyes and leaned into her touch. "If we get into real trouble, we may need them."

"And if *they* get into trouble?" Levi asked.

Aura turned to address them. "If this fight is going in such a way where you become the targets, I want you to leave. Leave and come back to this place. You will be safe here, and we will come for you when the fighting is over." Her words were met with growls of protest, but with no other way of communicating, Aura turned away from them.

"They aren't going to leave you."

Aura hadn't noticed them at first. The excitement of seeing Emily and being introduced to new faces made these ones lost in the crowd somehow. She felt like someone had punched her in the gut and turned to Emily, anger and confusion building in her.

Emily shrugged. "They insisted."

"They aren't going to go," Kiya repeated. Standing next to her, looking younger then Aura remembered, were the other kids. Jada ran forward and embraced them, and they each began talking excitedly about what had happened since they'd been apart. That is, all of them but Galina. She stared straight at Aura, challenging her to tell them to hide, to leave, to not participate.

They lost something, too, Aura told herself. *They are also fighting to protect their homes.* She nodded her head and received a slight dip in response.

Chapter 52

The Battle Continues Again

Whistles, noises, and loud voices bombarded Lady Grustmiener's ears. The lights of the kingdom around her flashed and added to the commotion. She wondered how people lived here. How they were able to think straight with everything happening at once. She longed to control it, but she also longed to leave it as soon as she could.

More people arrived that were on her side. She didn't know any of them, but those that stood around her greeted the new people warmly and talked in too low of voices for her to hear.

They stationed themselves around her though, so clearly, they were willing to take up her cause. She would be glad to be rid of this fighting. To be done with this clawing to the top of power and be able to finally revel in the joy of ruling. She would sit atop the world and have others do her bidding without resistance. She would speak, and people would listen. It would be a glorious time.

"Hey," a man in a dark outfit and hat with a golden symbol on it yelled at them.

He placed an object in his mouth that emitted a loud noise. It hurt her ears, but she fought the urge to cover them, a move she felt would make her look weak. The small girl, Julia, moved forward to speak to the man, but someone pushed her away.

"You gonna arrest this crazy lady?" a horse-like creature asked loudly. The man paid it no mind. *What a strange place this was*, she thought again.

"You need to move along," the man said to their group again.

In an instant, everything seemed to shift. Those around her moved in closer, pushing her back a step while those on the other side of their circle crowded in. The man in the dark outfit called out, and more men and women in dark outfits rushed in. They held objects in their hands that Lady Grustmiener didn't recognize but caused the people and creatures on both sides to yell and protest.

"Oh, so you are just going to taze anyone?" one of the creatures' handlers asked.

"We have a right to be here," a bird creature said.

"You need to move along. Clear this street," the man said.

More yelling happened, and someone pushed someone else. Fear crept into Lady Grustmiener's chest. This wasn't how the battle was supposed to go. She didn't know who these men and women in dark clothes were. Witches and wizards maybe? They were the only people she knew who wore similar-colored matching outfits. Had she underestimated this place? She would have bet her life that as soon as she defeated Cecily the rest of this world would bow to her, and she could walk away with little to no bloodshed. Sure, there would be those who would resist, there always were, but soon they would realize it was futile and submit to her.

Now she was wondering if betting her life was a mistake. Why didn't she have power over these people? She was shouting too, yelling for those around her to stop and lay down their arms and listen to her, but they didn't. They continued as if she hadn't spoken at all. The air felt thick here as if it pushed anything she said down into the ground where no one could hear it.

"What is going on?" she bellowed to Julia. However small, she felt a connection to the girl and knew if anyone could explain what was going on or how to help, it would be her.

"We need to get out of here," Julia yelled back.

The girl took her hand and pulled her a few steps from the crowd, but another hand reached out and grabbed her on the shoulder.

"I need you to stay here a minute." It was the voice of the man in the dark outfit. Lady Grustmiener turned to face him, Julia already trying to explain something and that they had to go, but the man didn't release her shoulder.

"Unhand me," Lady Grustmiener said.

"Look, I've been dealing with you weirdoes all day," the man said, his grip even tighter.

Rage replaced the fear in her. She threw her hands up, knocking the man's fingers off of her. In one fluid motion, she drew her sword and held it straight out at the man.

The world went silent for a split second before it exploded yet again in noise.

"Put it down!" one of the women said.

"Hands up!" another called.

"Drop it."

"On the ground."

"Lady Grustmiener, no." Julia's voice and eyes were filled with terror.

Lady Grustmiener had had enough. She brought the sword down, the man falling along with it.

"What the—" someone yelled. Screams reverberated around her now and people ran in various directions. Even some of those that had traveled with her fled, but others moved in closer to her, putting themselves between her and the people in dark clothes, who seemed to multiply in the seconds it took the man to fall and die.

"Hands up!"

"Move, all of you move the hell out of the way!"

"We need to go." Again, it was Julia's soft voice that cut through the confusion and reached her. The girl was begging and tugging on her sleeve, desperately trying to get her to leave, but she would have none of it. This place was hers. The ground, the people, the animals, even the men and women in the matching outfits yelling at her.

Something whizzed through the air and stuck into the front of her. It had sharp barbs that cut into her chest. It was painful, but from the expression on the woman who'd released the contraption, it was clear it was supposed to hurt more. Lady Grustmiener reached up and pulled the objects off of her, taking two small pieces of skin along with it.

"You dare try to harm me?" she bellowed.

Now they were listening to her. Now everyone around her was listening. It was as if the volume of the kingdom had turned down, faces turned in rapt attention. Something flashed out of the corner of her eye, and she saw a picture of herself on one of the large screens. It startled her. How did they get a copy of her? What witchcraft did these people have?

She turned her attention back to those standing in front of her. If the copy of her was able to cause her harm, it would have done it already. "Lay down your arms and bow to me. I am now your ruler. Doyenne Cecily is dead." She let the words hang in the air, but no look of recognition was received.

The woman who had shot the barbs at her stepped forward. "Miss?"

"My name is Lady Grustmiener, ruler of the Four Corners and your land as well."

"Right," the woman said slowly, her hands raised. "Lady Grustmiener, it is? You are scaring a lot of people. I am going to need you to come with me so we can work this out."

"You do not order me, I order you. You lay down your weapons. Your feeble attempts to slay me will be unsuccessful. I cannot be defeated."

The grip on her sleeve tightened, but she paid it no attention. Something greater had pulled her eye. Down the road, maybe a half mile, several large forms moved toward her. Far away screams could be heard. The kingdom was crumbling in panic. She needed to get control over it soon, or it would get increasingly difficult to do so. She called again for those around her to lay down their arms, but they, too, heard the commotion and turned around.

"Holy mother of God," a man said.

It was so soft Lady Grustmiener barely heard him. The lights to her left flashed again, but now instead of a face that looked like hers staring back on the brightly colored square, a dragon appeared. It was large and purple in color with Queen Aura astride it.

Chapter 53

Risen

Julia desperately tried to get Lady Grustmiener to follow her. Follow her where, she didn't know, but she needed to get the woman out of here. After she killed the police officer, mayhem crashed in around her. The other officers were screaming and one pulled out a taser, but it had no effect on Lady Grustmiener. Now they were drawing their guns, but there were so many people around, Julia was frightened something terrible would happen if they started shooting.

They needed to leave. She somehow needed to convince her that they could leave the battle, that it would continue without her, and they could move on to the next place. Maybe she could get her alone, kill her herself, but not here. If she tried, not only did she think she'd fail on the first attempt, but she was worried someone would try to pull her off or the cops would shoot her.

Julia realized that she may not live through this battle. It dawned on her when she was trapped in the car in the Lincoln tunnel on their way here. There was a slim chance she'd survive this, but if she was going to go, she was taking Lady Grustmiener down with her. But she wasn't willing to sacrifice her life without that. It was a two-for-one deal or no deal at all.

Shouts were now coming from farther down the street. She'd never heard a city so loud and so quiet at the same time. No horns blared, the TV screens were on closed caption now. The only sounds were yelling. Some in anger, some in fear, some in confusion, but they were all human sounds. That's when she heard the rumble. She didn't recognize it at first, the small shifting under her feet, the sound, heavy even this far away. When she turned and saw what was on the big TV screen next to her—Heza and Aura—Julia's heart sank and sang at the same moment.

They were here, they had come to rescue her and, in doing so, had placed themselves in incredible danger. Whether Julia made it or not, there was no way they were all going to get out alive.

Lady Grustmiener saw them as well. She now stared fixedly down the street. Julia knew there was no way she was going to get her to leave now. Julia glanced back up at the screen.

The news cameras were fixed on the newcomers, though the text at the bottom was still curiously inquiring if this had to do with *MagiCon*. Speculation about what new movie this was promoting or how they made such realistic and movable creatures were scrolling with increasing speed.

The camera panned, and Julia's breath caught. No. No, it couldn't be real. He was dead. She'd seen him die.

There, sitting atop a great golden griffin, sat Levi. He stared straight ahead, not acknowledging the people screaming and clamoring to get close. There must have been some force field around them because while people reached their hands out, none came into contact with them.

Julia was torn. Should she run to them? Dispel any pretense that she may be on Lady Grustmiener's side, or stay where she was and hope an opportunity would arise? Maybe this was the time? Maybe she should make her move now while attentions were elsewhere. She could possibly do it.

The man standing next to her had his arms raised above his head, hands shielding his eyes to help him see what was approaching better. His shirt was lifted just an inch, but it was enough for Julia to see the revolver tucked into his pants. Her mind was made up before she even realized it.

She reached forward and pulled the gun from the man's waistband and turned the weapon to Lady Grustmiener's back. The man turned to protest, but Lady Grustmiener hadn't noticed what had happened. Julia lifted it and aimed the muzzle up and pulled the trigger.

Click.

The noise was the loudest thing Julia had ever heard.

She pulled the trigger again, hand shaking and heart racing. Click. Click. Click. She saw the golden outlines of the cartridges as the cylinder rotated. It was loaded, she could see it was loaded, but nothing happened. Where they empty? Already fired? The man reached forward and wrestled the gun from her. The movement must have caught the attention of the officers, because they began yelling at the man now.

"Drop the gun!"

"Hands in the air!"

They pulled their weapons out as well. Julia covered her ears and shut her eyes. This was not supposed to happen this way. She was going to get shot and die, and it would be meaningless. She would have made no difference in the world other than making this terrible thing happen. She was never one-hundred percent sure about God, but began praying anyway, hoping, begging, for help.

Nothing happened. No loud bangs, nothing. She opened her eyes and saw the fear in the officers' faces. Each was pulling the trigger on their pistol, but nothing was happening. A few pulled their slides back and forth, ejecting a cartridge and loading a new one, but that one didn't work either.

The cogs in Julia's brain turned slowly. The taser didn't work. Guns didn't work. Cell phones didn't work. There must have been something with their magic that messed with things in her world. She felt naked without the safety of items that she always thought could help protect her. She'd never wanted to hold a gun before, but pulling that trigger, she wanted it to work. She intended to kill Lady Grustmiener. The fact that it didn't left her angry and confused. She touched her waist and felt the small dagger she'd stashed there. She pulled it out and wheeled to face Lady Grustmiener, but she was already gone, disappearing into the fray.

Chapter 54

Levi tried to take deep, measured breaths. It was strange. He'd never been to New York before. His book tour was scheduled to end here, and he'd planned to stay several extra days to take in the city sites. Times Square was at the top of the list. If you'd asked him a few years ago, he never would have imagined making it here, much less on top of a griffin.

There were mixed reactions around them. Some people clapped while others screamed. Parents placed children on their shoulders while others buried their heads, frightened at what they saw. Levi wanted to call for them to run. To escape this place and save themselves. He tried. He tried telling them how dangerous it was and to leave, but they merely laughed and waved.

They must have thought his group was on parade. He turned to Aura. "They won't leave. They think this is a show. That it isn't real."

Her eyes were clear and focused. He'd never seen her more determined. "We will protect them," she said.

"We will fight this battle for them. When we are done, they will be safe for the rest of their days."

Levi nodded, but he wondered how they would be safe now, right now.

In the distance, a large crowd of people stood. They were a mix of police and people in costume. He scanned the crowd but didn't recognize any faces. It was hard for him to concentrate on searching while he also tried to form a bubble around his group, keeping those on the sidewalks away. It was working. He saw people try to push forward and be thwarted, but as soon as the fighting began, he'd be unable to keep it up. Toli had given up trying to keep them invisible as well. When they entered the street by the park he'd done a good job, but the farther they moved, the more people there were and the more impossible it had become.

"I can't do it anymore," he called to them. Slowly people acknowledged their presence until they had a small, but growing, crowd following them.

The screens in the square were filled with images of himself and Aura. She looked fierce and beautiful. Heza, too, had a look about her that Levi had never seen. The cameras flashed from his face to Amaline's, Calanthe's, Emily's, Deserae's, and the rest of their group. They made a formidable sight, whether you knew they were real or not.

And that's when he saw her. In the distance, standing in the middle of the sidewalk and waving her arms, Julia stood.

Relief poured over him like a hot shower. His senses heightened, and his focus became solely on reaching her.

"There," he yelled and pointed his finger. He gestured back but wasn't sure if Julia saw him. As they got closer, he realized she wasn't raising her hands, they were stationary above her head. He scanned the crowd, and his heart sank as he saw the cops, weapons drawn and pointed at her. "No! Gilbert, go!"

He broke formation and charged forward. Aura yelled, but the move had been made. He heard everyone following behind him. The officers were fumbling with their weapons, then turned, transfixed on the figures approaching them. At that moment, more screams were heard, but they weren't the happy, attention seeking one as before. These were filled with real fear.

He leaned back, and Gilbert slowed. Aura caught up with him, looking wildly around at what may have stopped him.

"Oh my God," Emily said. It was quiet, like an exhale of words. Levi turned and saw another group of people coming at them in an intersecting direction. They moved in a strangely halting manner. Something wasn't quite right about them, but he couldn't immediately figure it out. A beam of sunlight hit the front of the group, highlighting the boy who was leading them.

"Isn't that…" Levi let the words roll into this air, unable to finish the thought.

"It's Luther," Emily finished. Her breathing was ragged and panicked. Milskar was on the ground leading the dragon she was on. He turned to place a re-assuring hand on her leg. "No, no, we need to get out of here," she said. "This is bad. This is terribly bad. We need to get out of here and get these people out of here."

Her eyes rolled like a wild animal's. She had worked so hard on making it back to them. On not allowing the fear to creep into every action she did, and now it looked as if she had just escaped. Like she'd just burst into Aura office demanding their surrender all that time ago. Levi wanted to throw his arms around her and tell her it would be okay, but he didn't know that. He didn't know what it was going to be and saying the lie would only pain them both. He looked straight at her and tried to catch her eye, but she wouldn't stay still.

The screams rose, and Levi turned to see the scrolling marquis on every lit surface surrounding them.

In big block letters, repeating over and over it said: *MagiCon officials confirmed. Visitors are not approved performers. Origins unknown. Subjects armed and possibly dangerous. City on lock down. MagiCon officials confirmed.*

It felt like the world slowed.

Levi sucked in a breath as an arrow flew by his head, sinking deep into the chest of Amaline.

Chapter 55

A New Army

They moved quietly through a side street, though Luther could hear the commotion up ahead. An older woman stepped out into the alley but shrank back in fear when she saw them. Luther stood in front, followed by about two-hundred bodies, some living, some not. It was not a large army, definitely not as large as he wanted it to be, but it would do. He had a single mission. Those he brought were merely to form a distraction to help him reach his goal.

They passed a TV repair shop and on each of the screens in the window images flashed of Times Square. He saw Lady Grustmiener then the woman Emily who'd been held captive at the same time as him, followed by the red-haired woman. His jaw set and he marched forward with renewed purpose.

The street was large, and he worried they may not find them right away. He stopped to address those he traveled with. "When we step out, there is going to be a lot going on. We must stay focused. It will be loud, some may try to stop your progress, but we must not let them. We are on a mission for our survival. We must defeat the ruler of Esotera and the former ruler of Grustmiener. Their deaths will secure our future." Yells and woops emanated around him. In his mind, he willed the dead to march on, placing the image of the two women inside them. Letting them know their sole purpose was to track them down and kill them. Nothing was to stop them. They were not to engage with anyone unless that person tried to stop them, then they were to use any means necessary to continue their mission.

"There!" Achan called. Luther turned just as a large dragon passed feet from them. Lieal raised his bow and let an arrow fly through the air. Luther yelled, and his small clan rushed forward, spilling into the street.

Dragons and griffins took to the air, taking their riders with them. Those on the ground picked up their weapons and tried to defend themselves, but it was clear they weren't expecting an attack from the side. Their focus had been straight ahead, Luther turned and saw another collection of people standing there. Nothing was particularly magical looking about them, some were even in cheap costumes, but the way they charged toward the commotion made it clear they were interested in joining the fight.

Police spilled into the street, trying to direct cars and people away from the fight breaking out. The confusion sent people running their way and several were cut down by one side or the other. It was nearly impossible to know what side anyone was on. Luther allowed his mind to wander in tendrils, finding their way to the fallen bodies. They soon rose and followed the others marching up Seventh Avenue.

Luther stood with his back against a building, observing those around him and searching faces for the ones he sought. He once tried to look through one of the dead's eyes to see farther up the street, but the sensation was so unpleasant, he decided not to do that again and took to scanning the horizon.

A large man and Lieal were locked in battle. Luther thought he recognized the man, but couldn't put a name to the face. He was sure he must have seen him on the battle field of Esotera. Shouts above made the men pause in time to see a griffin land and deposit its rider. Luther saw Emily try to fight through the crowd. The man yelled but was pushed back and swallowed up by the crowd. Luther watched as he tried to fight his way back and Emily fought her way forward. Lieal smile wickedly, holding his sword behind his back.

Luther thought it was strange that no one else approached Lieal. There were fighters scattered around them, but Emily seemed to be the only one focused on him. The anger in her face was palpable. Luther understood. He hated these people as well. Hated that he had to work with them to be successful, but needed them he did, so he put his distaste aside. It was clear Emily was on a mission of revenge and Lieal was the closest one to enact that on.

He was transfixed by their fight. Emily seemed to claw at Lieal as they fought, teeth bared. Her counterpart was calm, moving his sword back and forth in a bored manner. He'd slashed his sword, cutting her arm deeply but instead of giving up, Emily screamed in a primal way and moved swiftly, causing a gash to form on the side of Lieal's face. His eyes widened in surprise before narrowing in concentration. The blood poured from his open cheek. Luther reflexively put his hand to his own face, unable to fathom the pain the man must have been feeling.

Lieal acted as if nothing had happened other than an

annoying scratch. He moved forward and the clash of their swords, along with the cries of the other man reverberated around Luther. He was about to step forward, to take Emily from behind and end their battle once and for all, but it was unnecessary. In two moves Lieal had her pinned. Their figures fell and were swallowed up by the other fighters.

Luther stood on his toes, trying to get a better vantage point, when Lieal rose. His face and right chest muscle were bleeding freely, but he stood. Emily did not. Luther reached his thoughts out and pulled her toward him. She moved slowly, as the dead usually did. A deep red stain covered the front of her dress. Her left thigh showed through a large split in the fabric, revealing white bone. When she placed weight on it, the leg buckled slightly before enabling her to shuffle forward. It frustrated him when the dead were cut this way. It made their movement more cumbersome, and as a result, less useful to him. Her eyes were milky white and stared into nothing. He repeated the request to her that he had to the others and she turned left and headed uptown.

The truth had set into the pedestrians around them. This was not a show. These people were not part of some parade. This was somehow, unimaginably, real. This battle was happening. People were dying. Creatures were flying through the air. The danger was all around them.

They fled in panicked droves, and Luther found he had to slip back into the alley to avoid being trampled. He still felt those moving under his command, though. He knew they continued on with their mission. With his back against the buildings once again, he moved along the walls back out into the street, walking in a side-step. He turned back just in time to see the man reach Lieal. The guttural scream reached his ears even though he'd moved about a hundred yards away. Lieal raised his weapon, but already weakened, he was no match for the man's fury.

The sword slashed back and forth, up and down. The fact that Lieal was still standing was only due to those pressing in on him, holding him up. Even from Luther's vantage point, even without having to feel the air around him, Luther could tell Lieal was dead, but still, the other man brought his sword up and down. Blood splashed on the man's face, coating it in red. Someone moved, and Lieal finally fell. Luther didn't bother calling out to him. He was of no more use.

Chapter 56

Alive

Aura couldn't get the image out of her head. Heza had taken to the skies moments after the arrow passed by her head. Passed by her head and hit Amaline. Hit Amaline and, and…

She couldn't finish the thought. But she couldn't clear the picture of Amaline falling off her dragon and being swept underfoot either. Or the cry Aura heard that, for a moment, she thought came from deep within her own soul, but realized it was Levi letting out the most pained sound Aura had ever heard. The mourning period was short as both Heza, Gilbert, and the other creatures launched themselves skyward. They'd gone into action like they had many times before. Too many times before.

Below she caught Julia's hopeful eye. Heza swooped down as yells below mixed to a swell. In the distance, Aura saw Luther and noticed Emily battling another man. The fight was brief, the two fell down and were swallowed up by the crowd. Aura's eyes were transfixed on the place, but only the man rose. Moments later Milskar rushed forward and killed him. A figure rose from the crowd and walked toward Luther at a halting pace. Aura's stomach turned, and she had to look away.

Heza touched back down, and Aura dismounted, taking the dragon's face in her hands. "You need to keep yourself safe, but help where you can. Watch though, I don't want anyone to die unnecessarily." The dragon looked at her knowingly before taking back to the air.

Aura knew Heza could open her mouth a spew a fire so hot the battle would be over in an instant, but her people were mixed in too tightly to risk it. Those she cared about and cared for. It wasn't worth risking all their lives. Aura would find and destroy Lady Grustmiener once and for all. Peace would become their new normal, but not if she gathered new enemies along the way.

Wings beat loudly next to her, and when she turned, Levi stood by her side, Gilbert already flying away. She nodded to him and moved toward where she spotted Julia. They pushed through the crowd. Aura reached her hand back, and Levi grabbed it without hesitation. His grip was strong, and each time she squeezed harder, he returned the pressure. The crowd thinned enough, and they stood side by side for a moment before he let go. Her hand felt cold and exposed without his.

Julia rushed toward them, throwing her arms around Levi's neck, exclaiming how he was alive, before wrapping Aura in a hug as well. "I knew you'd find me. I knew you'd come here," she sobbed.

"We would never leave one of our own behind," Aura said, running her fingers through the girl's dark hair.

Julia sobbed harder for a moment before taking a deep breath and pulling back. "I lost track of her, of Lady Grustmiener. She was right beside me, but once the cops drew their guns, she vanished," Julia said.

Levi looked around them. "It doesn't look like anyone was shot."

"The guns don't work. Nor the tasers or cell phones. I think the magic is messing with them."

"Toli warned us of that," Levi said, turning to Aura. She didn't know what it meant but hoped it was a small victory for them.

"Show us where the last place you saw her was," Aura said. "Maybe we can retrace her steps from there."

They moved several paces away before Julia stopped. "Here, I turned around, and she was gone."

As the words left her mouth, Levi cried out in pain. Someone had crashed into him, sending him straight to the hard ground. The street was different colors of gray and black beneath her feet, both equally hard. Levi's head made a terrible cracking sound, but he rolled and got quickly to his feet, drawing his sword. He turned and slashed at his attacker, dropping him in one action. Panting he turned to face Aura. Pain surrounded the irises of his eyes, but she wondered if it was from his head or something else. She was about to open her mouth to make sure he was all right, when the crowd swelled and moved toward her. Levi was pulled one direction while she was pushed another. She reached out her hand and grasped Julia's wrist as she stumbled back. When she looked up, Levi was gone.

ᲔᲠᲔᲒ

Levi's feet shuffled, carried by those around him. He tried to keep his head down, hoping no one would notice him until he could figure out what his next game plan should be. Though, honestly, all he wanted to do was lay down. Lay down and give up. Seeing Amaline with that arrow through her chest, the surprised expression caught on her face as she fell, tore something so deep inside Levi. He wasn't sure if it would ever mend.

He heard Aura calling for him, but he wanted to protect her, too. If Lady Grustmiener saw he was still alive, the element of surprise would be lost. He didn't want to endanger anyone else. This was between the two of them. He was tired of other people dying because of it.

Levi was jostled back and forth and tried to hide his sword by keeping his right arm tight against his side. He snuck glances at those around him and had no idea who these people were. Had they come with Emily? Or the kid Emily called Luther? Lady Grustmiener? Or were they simply tourists, caught in the wrong place at the wrong time? He noticed the uniform to his right, an officer with his arms out trying to herd the group to where he thought safety may lie. Levi wondered if it resided anywhere in this place.

As they passed a small alleyway, Levi slipped into the shadows, allowing the group to pass him by. He took several deep, shaky breaths trying to calm his mind. In all these thousands of people, he needed to find her. Needed to find Lady Grustmiener and destroy her. Anything that happened after he could deal with. Amaline. He could deal with that later. He stepped back into the street when his world fell apart again. He felt like his chest had caved in on itself.

With a hobbled walk, Emily moved slowly through the masses. Her lifeless eyes stared straight ahead, blood covering the front of her blue cotton dress. Goosebumps broke out over him, and he started shivering involuntarily. He tried to push her away, push her to safety. He knew she was dead. Levi had seen this before, seen what this Luther person could do. He recognized that Emily wasn't Emily anymore, but he still wanted to protect her. To keep at least her body safe.

He pushed his mind to her, tried to move a bubble to surround her, but he felt his powers move through her as if she was made of air. She stumbled on, oblivious to him or his attempts at protection. Looking both ways, he stepped out and strode to her, taking the front of her dress and pulling her toward him and back into the darkened alley.

Her irises shone milk white, almost disappearing into the whites of her eye. Her pupils were a light blue color, pin-pricks and unfocused.

"Emily, Emily please," he begged.

She shuddered and threw her arms up with surprising strength, breaking his grip on her.

She moved toward him and grasped at his neck. He pushed her back, causing her to stumble and a sickening crack to emanate from her leg. The bone, once exposed, now bent straight through her skin at an awkward angle. She walked forward, causing it to protrude even more. Levi shuddered, trying to imagine the pain, but Emily paid it no mind. She reached for him again. He lifted his sword.

"I am so sorry." He wielded it from one side to the other and shut his eyes. He heard her head and body crash to the ground in two separate noises, but he didn't look. He turned around and marched back into the street, her blood staining his trembling hands.

Chapter 57

Once and For All

People poured in and out of the roads in equal measure. Lady Grustmiener was unsure of who was there to fight and who got caught up in the action, but numerous were engaged in sword and hand to hand fighting. She recognized one figure a few yards from her.

Achan was engaged with a man who held a stick above his head, blocking his blows. He ultimately proved too strong for the man though. After Achan's third strike with his sword, the man's stick cracked loudly and littered the grown with shards of splintered wood. The next blow dropped the man where he stood. The woman standing next to him cried out and rushed forward. She knelt and cradled the man's head and screamed at Achan. He didn't wait for her to rise, bringing his sword down where she stood. She crumpled and lay unmoving on top of the fallen man.

She watched Achan move through the crowd, striking down people in his wake. Screams were heard all around and loud, whirling noises in the distance. More of the people in dark clothing spilled into the street. Some had strange layers on and large, black objects pressed against their shoulders. Lady Grustmiener assumed they were weapons by the way the users held them, but if they did anything of consequence, she couldn't figure out what it was.

She thought she'd glimpsed a face in the distance, but it was impossible. There was no way he was alive. She must have imagined it. There were so many different faces around her, they were blending into one another. She searched for a swatch of red hair, but so far was unable to spot Queen Aura in the masses.

Standing off to the side, back pressed against a wall, she did see someone familiar. Luther inched along, eyes scanning the distance. She felt a smile forming on her face. She was pleased the boy had come here. Now that she saw him, she also noticed the dead walking among those spilling into the road.

The dragons were calling from above, deep bellows of anger and frustration. She looked up and saw the purple one circling the crowd, releasing small puffs of smoke and fire. The animal was in distress, but for some reason wasn't attacking. This must have been because of Queen Aura. She must have told them not to attack. What a foolish woman.

She could have ended this battle promptly by having the animals set everything below them in flames, but they flew uselessly instead. The griffins were put to some use, flying low and scattering people, but they, too, didn't attack.

It was during one of these swoops that Queen Aura appeared. She was engaged in battle with a man. Was he from this world or hers? He fought but was greatly overmatched. The fight was over quickly. Aura wiped the blood from her sword and turned, freezing in place. Her eyes hardened, locking on Lady Grustmiener's.

The queen moved forward, and Lady Grustmiener matched her stride. They met on the raised portion of the road.

"It was foolish for you to come here," Lady Grustmiener said.

"You are the foolish one."

She laughed. "You no longer rule. Your title is meaningless. I killed Levi. I killed Doyenne Cecily. I rule anything your eyes may land on. Lay down your sword, and I will spare your people. I will order everyone to stop fighting, and they will listen because they have to."

"Have they been listening so far?" Queen Aura said, her sword gripped tightly by her side.

Neither woman raised their weapon, waiting for the other to make the first move.

Lady Grustmiener considered the other woman. There was a beauty to her. Her red hair felt too much, as if it was vying for attention unnecessarily, but she had a confidence about her that was appealing, nonetheless. They could be powerful together. She could have a role in Lady Grustmiener's world if she would submit. If she would pick life over death.

"We could be great together," Lady Grustmiener said.

It was Aura's turn to laugh. "Do you not understand? You do not get to live. You do not get to destroy anything else. Your power is done."

"Done, my power is just starting. Nothing can stop me now. You think you can? You think you can defeat me?"

"Why not? I am a better fighter than you. I have a larger army. You came here woefully unprepared. You think killing one woman can give you rule?" Aura asked.

"Not just one woman. One woman and one man. I have killed Levi. I have killed those who had power. I have that power now."

"Only he is not dead."

As if on cue, a movement out of the corner of her eye diverted her attention. There, impossibly, stood Levi. It could not be. This had to be a trick. Maybe the witches and wizards in the dark clothes had done it. She scanned the horizon and noticed the witches from the north were here as well. Fighters charged them, but were pushed away and fell, motionless, by the raising of a hand.

In an instant, everything seemed to be falling apart around her. She screamed in frustration. She was so close, so close to realizing her dreams and taking her rightful place, and this boy—this terrible, frustrating, resilient boy was standing in her way again.

"I killed you!" she bellowed.

Levi walked slowly to her, eyes flashing between her and Aura. "You did."

"What kind of dark magic is this?" She backed away. Maybe this was a dream. Maybe none of this was real, and she was still laying in the forest in Grustmiener, broken and with nothing. Maybe the events of the last several years hadn't happened yet, and this was a glimpse at the future. A future she was still able to change. She closed her eyes, but the scene was still the same when she opened them.

"You are the only dark magic," Queen Aura said.

A rustle to her right signaled the arrival of the golden griffin. He looked just like he had in her dreams, onyx eyes with a deep burning fire within them. He opened his mouth wide, and she was expecting to be swallowed whole, but the creature merely let out a terrible sound. Calls above from the other flying animals returned similar noises. Where they planning on staging a separate attack on her?

She'd been so transfixed watching the griffin, it startled her when her back hit a solid object. She reached one of her hands back and felt the cool, smooth surface, but didn't turn around to see what she'd come into contact with. Levi and Aura had advanced on her and now stood mere feet away. They stood looking at one another, no party sure what the next move should be or willing to be the first to make it.

"Do you surrender? Do you call off your people and this futile war?" Aura asked her.

"Surrender? And become a prisoner of your kingdom? Never. This battle will never be over. There will always be those who will rebel against your rule. You will never have peace."

"You are wrong," Levi said. "People long for peace. We strive for it. We mess up, we create problems, sure, but no one wants to live in fear. We have a chance to stop that, once and for all. We have a chance to enable people to live side by side. To live without fear. People long for peace," he repeated.

She laughed and lowered her voice. "People long for power."

"Not anymore," Aura said. "People will have what they need. People long for power when they think they do not have any. I will return power to them. They will have power over their own lives."

"You are a foolish young woman."

"No, but you are an evil one."

It was time. She had worked so hard, had fought day after day to regain her rightful place in the world, and this child was not going to take it from her. She knew she was defeated, knew that there was no hope of escape, but she could at least take Queen Aura with her.

Lady Grustmiener stared straight at Levi. She knew how to destroy him. She pushed off the wall, sword held straight in front of her, and charged into Queen Aura, their screams mingling together.

Chapter 58

Friends and Enemies

Julia watched in horror as person after person fell, bleeding into the streets and on the sidewalk. A tank rumbled down the street, though the abandoned cars made the going slow. People ran in every direction, and several times she got knocked down.

Men and women in SWAT gear with rifles darted between cars, weapons raised and fingers on the trigger. *They don't know*, Julia thought. *They have no idea their weapons are useless.* She wanted to call them, tell them to go home and hide, that they could only be in danger being here, but her voice didn't seem to work anymore. To her added horror, she saw people running with news cameras and microphones. Julia wondered how many more people would die. And how many of them would be people she cared about.

With a swell in her chest, she spotted Deserae and Toli. They stood with several other people in an arc, the group fighting as they pressed forward. Julia wanted to run to them, to throw her arms around them and thank them for coming. She locked eyes with Deserae for the briefest of moments before the other woman released a fire ball that knocked several people back. Julia would thank them later.

As she ran down the street, she came upon Kiya and Tab. Their reunion was brief as the fighting continued. Tab was strong, pushing people out of the way and swinging his sword when people tried to engage them. Kiya was muttering a stream of words, Julia assumed she was repeating what the griffins and dragons were saying, but everything was so loud, she couldn't hear what was said.

Julia held on to Kiya's left hand as the other gripped a small dagger. They didn't look threatening, heck, they were so small, Julia wondered if anyone would even notice them, but suddenly Kiya was pulled from her grasp. A man plunged a knife deep in Kiya's chest. Julia screamed, but the sound was swallowed up by the noise in the city. Tab turned and raised his own weapon, but the man was too quick, removing the weapon and charging Tab. They fell and rolled out of site under the feet of fleeing, terrified people.

Backing away, Julia fought the urge to turn and run. Kiya. Sweet Kiya, who's only power was to talk to animals. Who didn't want to fight, who didn't want to hurt anything, to be killed so brutally. So needlessly. And Tab. She scanned the crowd, but he didn't re-appear. She tripped over a body and scuttled back on her hands and feet but was kicked by several people. The pain felt good, felt real. A tangible thing to hold on to when everything else was falling apart. She wanted to lay on the street and be trampled. That's when a hand reached out and lifted her.

"Come with me," the boy said. Julia stood and followed him without hesitation.

They ducked behind a dumpster. The smell was wretched and brought Julia back to the present. The boy pulled Julia down, so they were hidden from those on the street.

"I saw you with her. I need you to get me close," the boy said.

"Who? Who are you?" She was confused and scared and tired. When was the last time she'd slept? Or eaten? Or been able to take a single deep breath?

"My name is Luther," he said. "I need to find Lady Grustmiener. I saw you with her, did you travel with her?" Julia nodded. "Good. I need you to take me to her."

"I lost her," she said. "I turned around, and she was gone."

"Shit," Luther said quietly. He peaked his head out before sitting back next to her. "We have to find her. I need to find her."

"Are you with her?" Julia didn't know who to trust anymore, or if there was even anyone left in the world to trust.

"In a way. I was. Are you?"

They paused and stared at one another. It was clear this person was hiding something from her, but what was it? She'd never seen him before, but his mannerisms seemed more of her world than the other. But he knew of Lady Grustmiener, recognized her. For the moment, whether the end results were the same, what they sought was in alignment.

"Let's go," Julia said. "Together we'll have better luck."

Luther smiled and helped her to her feet. She was shaky, but he held her hand firmly. She tried not to think about Kiya and Tab and followed him back into the mass of people. The throng seemed to have doubled since they'd stepped away. There was fighting everywhere.

Twice, people slammed into them, before Julia was able to get her wits about her enough to form a protective bubble around them. Luther looked at her and smiled, evidently knowing that she'd done something to help them.

Every few feet they stopped and looked around. Julia saw flashes of red everywhere, but she was never able to pin-point if any of them were Aura. The dragons and griffins swooped in and out of the crowds, scattering and sometimes picking people up. A body landed inches in front of them, dropped from high enough to kill the person on impact. She hoped the creatures were able to determine which side everyone was on, she sure couldn't.

A terrible noise came from down the block echoed by the animals in the air. For a moment, Julia looked back to ask Kiya what they were saying, and her death hit her all over again. She stopped and felt the tug as Luther was pulled back.

"What is it?" he asked, scanning the crowd, wondering if she had spotted something.

"The noise. It seems like it is coming from the ground."

"What do you think is making it?"

She pointed up ahead. "A griffin, I think, up that way."

A form brushed by her, making her skin grow so cold she shuttered. It didn't make sense. Julia's protection held. She could see people bouncing off of it, but somehow this man passed right through. She reached a hand out and the man turned, his eyes white and teeth bared at her. The man's right arm was missing, and blood pooled down his side, splashing on the street as he moved.

Julia screamed as the man pushed her to the ground, but just as abruptly as the attack began, the man rose and moved wordlessly away. Luther bent down and cradled her head with his hands.

"I'm so sorry. It thought you were trying to stop it."

"Stop, what? What was that?" She rose and looked around them. It wasn't obvious at first, but she noticed other man and women with the same glassy eyes. Most had terrible wounds. Wounds that should have killed them. She swung back and looked at Luther.

"They are with me," he said calmly. "They aren't going to hurt you. They are only going to hurt two people and anyone who gets in the way of that mission."

She felt the vomit bubble up in her throat. "What two people?"

He hesitated. "Are you with her, really with her, Lady Grustmiener?"

She shook her head. "No. No, I was spying."

"Good. I am coming to kill her."

Relief washed over Julia. Between all of them, all those fighting for her demise, one of them would have to be successful. There was no way they could all fail. His words chugged slowly through her mind before resting in place and setting off a light of recognition.

"Who is the other person?" Julia asked slowly.

"Queen Aura."

Chapter 59

The Dead and the Dying

The world slowed in front of Levi, as if it moved through thicker air than before. The sounds, too, he noted, were muted. Even Gilbert's screams of rage and the returned sounds from above seemed to float away into nothingness.

The only thing that moved quickly was Lady Grustmiener.

She was watching him. Her dark eyes fixed on his, and he braced, expecting her charge. He should have formed a shield. Should have lifted the sidewalk up somehow to move Aura out of the way. He had plenty of time to prepare, they'd been talking. Talking? He'd let her casually speak to them, and he did nothing. Several times he looked over to Aura, and she appeared calm as well. It was over. There was no need for more bloodshed.

When Lady Grustmiener rocked forward, Levi was sure, certain in fact, that she was coming to him. But she didn't. She moved straight forward with her sword out. Straight to Aura. He was too slow. He realized it the instant the woman moved. There was no way he'd make it in time. He tried to protect her, but he knew he was too late.

Aura screamed, startled also. Was this how she was going to make her end? A futile mistake on his part? How was he going to live with himself to know that he'd been responsible? That he'd promised to save her and could do nothing of the sort.

The sword was straight and true as it plunged straight into his chest.

His.

Milskar.

Levi didn't see him approach. Hadn't seen him crouched just out of sight. Didn't know that the man saw what they didn't see. Just as Lady Grustmiener made her move, he did as well, throwing himself in front of his queen. His beloved ruler. Aura screamed with shock and fear as they descended upon her.

A second later Gilbert had knocked Aura back as he drove his beak into Lady Grustmiener's throat. Milskar's sword pierced Lady Grustmiener's body as Levi plunged his own deep in between her shoulder blades. Levi pulled back his weapon, taking her lifeless form along with it. He extracted his sword, letting her crumple to the street. Gilbert swiftly grabbed her with his claws and took to the sky with her lifeless body, blood covering his beak and face.

Aura crawled forward and held the sword that still resided in Milskar.

"You are going to be all right," she said to him.

He smiled, revealing red-tinted teeth. Levi stumbled and fell to the ground in front of them.

"Tell them," Milskar gurgled. "Tell them." His eyes widened and relaxed, his incomplete sentence still forming on his lips.

Aura fell forward on him, sobbing into his shirt. Her red hair covered his face, and Levi was glad he didn't have to look at those cold, dead eyes. He placed his hand on Milskar's leg and felt a twitch below him. Aura must have felt is as well, because she sprang back. Levi pulled out the sword still stuck in his chest, though he knew that it wouldn't help. The man was dead. There was no saving him now.

His eyes, once dark brown, were turning a milky white. Recognition slowly spread through Levi's bones.

"Aura, get away from him. Move, now!" he yelled. She stared at him in terror and hurt. She tried to stand, but fell back to the ground, her legs evidently too shaky to hold her. She was covered in blood. Had she been hit too? Was any of the dark liquid hers?

"Levi." Tears spilled down her face as she stared at him.

"Get away, go!" He still held both swords when Milskar stood. Aura let out a choked scream.

"Aura, run!"

Levi was confused. He didn't think he'd uttered the words, but who else could be warning them? He looked around at the horrors surrounding them. People were screaming and running. Others were locked in battle. And the dead. The dead were descending upon them. He could pick them out as they moved through. Again, he tried to push them back, to form a wall, but they moved through it as if they were made of air. He now knew what they were here for.

The voice called again for Aura to run and Levi saw Luther picking his way around cars, people, and officers. Steps behind him, Julia followed. Levi watched as she pulled on Luther's clothing, tried to drop objects in front of him, but he pushed her off and stepped over any obstacles she tried to thwart him with. He lost sight of her for one terrifying moment before he realized she had picked up a sword.

"Julia, no!" Levi called back to her. Aura screamed as Milskar reached her. Levi rushed forward, pushing him off of her, his weapons clattering to the ground. "Cut off their heads, Aura, cut off his head." He held Milskar back, but the man had been so strong, so much bigger than him, he needed both hands to hold him back and was unable to finish him off himself.

"Levi, I—I—" Aura stuttered. She held her sword, but made no move to attack him.

"It isn't him anymore. Aura?" In a fluid motion, the blade swung through, dropping Milskar to the ground. She fell into Levi's arms.

"What is going on? This should be over. No one should be fighting anymore," Aura said. "It is over."

"It isn't. Luther."

As the words left his mouth, three more bodies descended upon them. One woman's eye was missing, revealing a gaping hole in her head. Levi kicked her back and picked up his sword, stopping the woman before she was able to move closer to them. Aura took care of the other two. Confusion on her face but determination as well. He stood in front of her, which somehow made him a target for the dead. Five more came out from the crowds. He walked out to meet them, hoping to draw them away from Aura.

They were strong. Impossibly strong. It didn't even make sense how any of them were moving. One man had a knife sticking out of his belly, his organs spilling out, but still, he moved. Still, he tried to kill Levi. He heard Julia call again and saw Luther moving closer, but he was unable to do anything. He tried to block him, tried to push him away, but his mind was so busy fighting, he didn't have the energy to divert. He considered laying down and allowing the dead to take him. Maybe it would be slow enough that he could protect Aura, give her a fighting chance. He watched through outstretched arms and chomping teeth as Julia caught up with Luther. More bodies pressed in, and he could see no more.

⋐⋑

Julia ran as hard and as fast as she could. She had to warn them. She knew as soon as she did, Luther would see her as a threat and possibly turn on her. The risk was worth it.

Across the street, she spotted Desi. It was as if the fighting had taken a pause, a breath, as the two women locked eyes. Desi nodded and smiled, and Julia returned both gestures. When the battle was over, they'd talk and possibly embrace. They would try to speak at the same time, hesitate, and laugh. Julia would tell Desi that she was sorry for leaving and in return, Desi would say she was proud of her and knew it was the right decision.

The premonition was so clear in Julia's mind that the fighter coming up behind Desi and killing her didn't immediately register.

"No," Julia whispered.

It was too much, all too much. She shut her eyes against her surroundings. Toli. She needed Toli. He'd erase her memories and the image of Deserae's shocked face as the blood poured from her neck. He'd make it all go away.

As he pulled her forward, Toli stumbled out of the crowd. He walked right by Julia, his milk-colored eyes unfocused. She shrank back.

"Don't worry, you're with me. They won't hurt you," Luther assured her. As if fear of attach was the thing Julia recoiled from.

Up ahead, she watched as Lady Grustmiener leapt forward to kill Aura. Saw Milskar take the blade and Gilbert, and Levi destroy her for it. Luther whooped in triumph and turned back to beam at her.

Desi. Toli. And now Milskar. She needed this to be over. There had to be something she could do.

He still held her hand, pulling her forward. Julia allowed him to touch her only so she could have his protection while she worked. She tried to move the dead, tried to counteract whatever power Luther had on them, but she was unable. Her magic had no effect on them. She tried other things, one time even dropping a set of traffic lights in front of them, but he nimbly leapt over them, pulling her along. She could wait no longer.

"Aura! Run!" she screamed. Luther froze and looked at her. She broke his grip and darted behind a car. For a moment, it appeared that he was considering coming after her, but decided against it and pressed on. Julia leapt to her feet and followed.

Possibly sensing the urgency or pushed on harder by Luther, the dead were appearing from everywhere. Julia crashed into two, sending them sprawling to the ground. One was unable to get back up, its leg snapped clear off. She shuttered at the sight but kept moving.

Up ahead, Levi had disappeared under a mound of the dead. Aura backed up, terror evident even from yards away. Julia pushed harder and reached out to grab Luther by the collar. They'd both been running so fast, the sudden jostling pitched them both forward, and they tumbled into the street. Julia scrambled up and thanked the heavens a sword lay inches from her.

"So, you are going to stop me?" Luther seethed. "I bet you haven't stopped anyone in your whole life."

Julia thought back to her training. To the mishaps. To the laughter and the feelings of stupidity. She flung her energy up, lifting Luther off his feet. She'd miscalculated, and he landed back down, a loud cracking sound, but he was still standing. His left foot bent at an awkward angle, his ankle appeared broken, but he stood all the same and even smiled.

"Worthless, I see," he said.

She screamed and rushed him, sword held out like Tab had taught her. Tab, who had fought so bravely and now was somewhere else. Possibly marching with those lifeless white eyes. Luther caught her in the face first, his fist making firm contact. The pain burst through her, blinding her right eye momentarily, but the action also caused Luther to shift precariously on his broken ankle. It buckled under the weight and dropped him to one knee.

"No one is worthless," Julia said. "As long as a person has a purpose and a will, they are worth everything." She brought the sword down, the strength of the dead and all whom she loved behind it.

Chapter 60

Taking Stock

Everything stopped, as soon as Julia plunged her sword into Luther's chest, as if she'd flipped a switch. To Aura's left, Levi had been enveloped by a group of fighters that had that same terrible look that Milskar did. Aura had moved forward to help him, but another set came at her. It was clear they were dead. That they were *supposed* to be dead, but they moved with purpose toward her anyway. She held her sword up, took a deep breath, and waited for them to come to her when she saw Julia kill the boy. The bodies dropped at once.

Aura scrambled over them to the place where she saw Levi get swallowed up by them. She threw body after body to the side, finally revealing him. His eyes showed relief and confusion.

"Julia," Aura said, her chest bursting with pride and gratitude. "Julia stopped them. She saved us all."

Levi smiled up at her. "Little Julia Jones."

Aura helped him up and embraced him so hard he let out a sharp breath of pain, but she didn't care. She needed to feel him, needed to know that he was alive and whole and that she was alive and whole. They clung to each other for, Aura didn't know how long. Levi loosened his grip and took her head in his hands. They were caked in blood and were rough against her cheek as he bent down and kissed her.

Warmth radiated through her. She ran her fingers through his hair and kissed him back hard. They were alive. They had both impossibly made it. She pulled away, worried she never would if they continued any longer.

Julia marched up to them, and they embraced her, the three of them clinging to one another and crying. The noises around them changed as well. Aura looked up to see fighters laying their weapons down while other cheered. She saw large versions of her face plastered over the buildings. She wasn't sure how they got there, but she was beaming.

The images scrolled and she saw a large, green woman on fire. Her outstretched arm held a torch, but flames licked down it and covered her crown. A dragon flew past her, but Aura was unable to make out who it was.

Bodies littered the street, and people stepped around them to maneuver. The dead had dropped where they once stood, no longer posing a threat. Aura searched the faces but didn't find any she recognized. She walked a few more steps before a golden form made her pause.

Serenity lay on her side, which did not rise and fall with breath. The pain of losing her father reared up within Aura. Soon, she wouldn't have any connections left to him. The thought made her feel hollow inside.

She reached down and ran her fingers through the mare's pale mane, now stained with blood. Aura saw past her injuries to the beautiful creature she was. She kissed her one last time on her gray velvet nose and thanked her silently for their years together. Down the road, she saw the white fur of Alcippe move through the crowd, and a small bit of peace came back to her.

Aura heard noises behind her and looked up to see the witches surround them. She pulled herself away and embraced Filia.

"Thank you," Aura said, her voice still thick with grief. "Thank you for your help."

"The fighting is over. The road to peace is still a long one ahead of us, but this is the first day of the rest of the world."

Aura nodded and watched the hooded women leave. She wondered where they would return to. Her land? The north? Perhaps somewhere here? It didn't matter. They were free to travel wherever they wanted. They were all free.

A dark shadow loomed over her as Heza landed. The dragon had a large gash over her eye but appeared otherwise unhurt. Aura kissed her on the nose. She scanned the horizon and counted four more creatures in the air. Gilbert was nowhere to be seen. She'd have to ask Kiya where he went.

One by one, members of her army picked their way through the crowd to them. The residents of the kingdom of New York seemed to sense the fighting was over, and they moved hesitantly out from behind barriers and hiding places. They clung to one another and cried. Those in the dark uniforms surrounded them, but they didn't appear to want to engage and allowed Calanthe and Edda through their ranks.

Aura hugged each of them. "Where are the rest?" Aura asked. Milskar's image flashed across her mind, but she pushed it away.

"I do not know if there are any left," Calanthe said.

Aura noticed both women had tears in their eyes.

"Hai," Edda started. "Hai did not survive. I saw her fall and get up again, but I saw her fall. I do not understand."

"There was someone controlling the dead, but he is dead now. We do not need to fear him," Levi assured her.

"I lost sight of Milskar," Calanthe said. "He was coming to find you, and I was behind him, but we got separated." She searched the crowd. "Have you seen him?"

Aura felt the tears in her eyes as she nodded. "He saved my life," she said. "Saved it at the expense of his own. He took Lady Grustmiener with him though. He helped kill her."

"If he had to go," Calanthe said firmly, but her eyes swam with tears. "That is how he would have wished it to be, saving you, my queen."

Aura embraced them once again. Levi stood next to her, favoring one leg, and shook Calanthe's hand.

"Emily," he said softly. "Emily didn't make it either."

"Or Kiya," Julia whispered. "I think Tab as well."

Aura's chest tightened painfully. She understood there would be a great cost, knew that some may pay with their lives, but she didn't expect so many.

"What do we do now?" Aura asked.

Levi leaned down and kissed her. "If I had a dollar for every time someone asked me that."

Chapter 61

Aftermath

The minutes and hours after the battle were a whirlwind. News crews shoved cameras and microphones in Levi's and Aura's faces as the police herded them into squad cars. Aura sent the creatures into the sky and told them to return home. Levi doubted they were going to, but they took off, evading any possible capture.

The residents of the city stood transfixed with the scene around them. Children cried for their parents, partners yelled for their counterparts. Some stood motionless, rooted in place by shock. Sirens were heard everywhere. Every single TV screen in Times Square showed images of their faces.

Then another face Levi recognized popped up on the screen. Someone was interviewing Kailly. She fielded questions about *Saving Esotera* and if she knew if any of it was real. Reports were coming in from all over the country, all over the world in fact, of the magical coming out of hiding.

It was overwhelming. The reporters were yelling at them as well as the officers tried to hold them back.

"Levi, Levi Roberts, who is this?"

"Is this Aura?

"Did you really go to Esotera?"

Levi shielded his eyes and gripped Aura firmly as questions were called out to them. They were placed in the back of a car, and it sped away instantly. He whirled and saw Calanthe, Galina, and Julia being placed in cars as well. He wondered how he was going to explain this, if he could explain it. Aura gripped his hand tightly but sat speechless next to him. That was all right, they'd have their whole lives to talk. They had their whole lives now for whatever they wanted.

At the precinct, they tried to separate him and Aura, but he refused. When someone came forward to try to pull him away, the man jump backed as if he had been shocked. They fearfully allowed them to sit in a room together with the promise that Levi would not harm them.

The interview took hours, but still, Aura didn't speak. Several times she was addressed directly by a detective, but Levi spoke for her. Confirming reports from world leaders were evidently coming in. Yes, they knew about the magical land. They knew the possibility that their secret would be revealed. It was even speculated that some of the leaders may be hybrids themselves. Conspiracy theories were running rampant.

On the second day, Levi's parents showed up. He held on to them so strongly it took Aura soft touch to break him away. He introduced them to each other and heard her speak her first words in over thirty-six hours.

"It is a pleasure and an honor to meet the people who raised Levi."

They weren't able to stay for long but promised they had gotten a hotel in the area and would come back every day. Information trickled to them in small pieces. The state attorney's office was debating on pressing charges. Insurance companies were contemplating suing. *Saving Esotera* was sold out of every store that carried it.

Any requests for updates on the others held by the police went without answer. Levi tried to calm himself. They were safe. Nothing would get to them, and it would all be figured out. At night, he and Aura took turns waking each other from nightmares. Every time he closed his eyes, he saw the dead in the darkness behind his lids. Emily came to him and Milskar. Sometimes even Nikolas, blaming him for his parents' death.

Aura struggled out loud with the choices she'd made. Was it right to come to this world? To bring so much fighting and death? Levi tried to reassure her, that the decision to come here was the only one, but he wasn't sure if his words had much effect on her.

He looked deeply into her eyes and hoped she could see the way he saw her. How good and pure and true she was. How she loved her people and how their pain was her pain. How she would do anything to protect them. He leaned forward and kissed her. She tasted lightly of honey and something slightly metallic.

She pulled back and looked straight into his eyes. Tears pooled and fell down her face. She made no attempt to wipe them away.

"Adam," she said.

He shut his eyes for a moment, trying to block out the pain. She reached forward and grabbed his hand.

"Emily," he whispered and looked at her.

She looked broken and fierce and beautiful. "Milskar."

Levi swallowed hard. "Amaline."

"Kiya."

"Tab," Levi said.

Tears poured from her. He saw her chest rise as she took a breath to steady herself. "Theirra."

"Theirra," he echoed.

"Do you think we will ever see them again?" Her question was childish and pure.

He nodded. "I do, but not now. Now we need to make sure we don't forget their names. That the world doesn't forget their names."

"But it hurts so bad," she choked out.

He felt like his heart was breaking and ripping from his chest. He took a step toward her, his nose close enough to touch hers. "It does. It may feel like you won't be able to live, that you won't be able to carry on, but you must, *we* must. This is what they worked for, *died* for. We need to help put the pieces back together."

She nodded. As painful as it was, Levi knew it was true. They had lost so much. Each time he blinked, he saw Amaline's face as the arrow hit her. Emily's eyes, glassed over and crazed. Milskar diving in front of Aura, saving her. Levi would never forget and would make sure no one else did for as long as he had the gift of life.

After ten days, a man came and unlocked their cell door. "You both are free to go." He stood aside but didn't make eye contact with either of them. They followed him out, stopping in the lobby. "I can't return your weapons," the man said with no apology in his voice.

"We don't need them anymore," Levi responded.

It felt about as freeing as being out of the cell to say those words.

They stepped into the street into throngs of reporters. They began to push through, but a soft voice stopped him. He turned and saw Julia beaming at him. Galina, Quan, Calanthe, and Jada stood behind her, tired smiles on their faces as well. Galina had a large bandage covering one of her eyes and Jada was on crutches, but they were there.

Levi and Aura rushed forward and embraced them. Hands touched faces, lips met cheeks, arms encircled. They had made it. They had lost so much, yet gained so much in return. The cameras pressed in, but they ignored them.

"And now?" Julia asked.

"We go home," Aura said, pulling on Levi's hand.

"Home, where's that?" he asked her.

"I have no idea," she said and took his hand in hers. "But wherever it is, we go together."

Chapter 62

A New World

The world didn't become one perfect and harmonious place overnight. There was no magic that could do that. But in pieces, things knitted themselves back together.

A strange thing had happened though, the portals remained opened. No longer was their existence hidden from unknowing eyes and minds. They opened like doors to other worlds, which in a way, they were. Maps would need to change, but that would come in time. For now, people went through them and were amazed to see what was on the other side. The peace treaties and division of power was a formality. The whole world had changed. Old notions of rulers and territory were questioned, and no one knew the answers just yet. What they did know was that this beautiful woman named Aura was queen of it all.

That was enough for now.

Aura returned to Esotera along with Edda and Calanthe. She needed to see what was left, who was left. Levi would follow. For now, he was needed here to field questions and help figure out where the world would go from here.

Lady Grustmiener's body, pried from Gilbert's claws, was dropped into the vast ocean without fanfare. Levi rode high into the sky on Heza and did it himself. He was taking no chances this time.

Gilbert had taken a liking to him and stayed behind while the other magical creatures followed Aura. Levi worried that it wouldn't be safe here for him, but then he reminded himself that Gilbert was about five-hundred pounds, could fly, had claws, and…well, was a griffin. Though for all the beast's toughness, it was clear he adored the attention of on-lookers and posed for cameras and behind Levi during his interviews. As popular as Levi was becoming, Gilbert was the real star of the show.

Levi also helped identify the bodies of those who died in the battle. Each time he passed a face he recognized, it was like the whole thing became real all over again. He was glad Aura wasn't present for this, but selfishly wished for her desperately. He spoke to each of them. Thanked them for his sacrifice, promised to not let them be forgotten. He repeated their names each night before he went to bed.

On the third day, Levi, Julia, and Galina sat at a table picking at some food. They'd been doing interviews all morning with various news stations and were slouched with exhaustion. Over the din, a voice called Galina's name barely above a whisper. Like a startled horse, her head shot up and in the direction of the sound.

A woman stood holding the hands of two small girls. Galina rushed into their arms as the three sobbed and melted into one another. Galina pulled away for just a moment to lock eyes with Levi and Julia. She nodded, and they nodded back. She had made her decision. She would stay with her family.

The witches also left them, though Levi wasn't sure when or where they would go. Maybe return to the frozen north, or find more hospitable accommodations on his side. Whatever they chose, he never heard from them again. Rumors swirled that great magic and healing was coming from various parts of the world, but the accounts could never be confirmed. Whether it was them or not, Levi didn't know. But he hoped that they were able to live out the rest of their lives in peace and comfort. They'd earned that much.

The damage to New York was estimated in the millions, but one night the city went to sleep and in the morning found it as close to brand new as one could hope for. It was clear there were some people out there with incredible magical powers. Their actions in the veil of night helped more than any PR Levi could have done to have the world accept them.

The Statue of Liberty, while charred in places, stood as the same beacon of hope she always had. People gathered along the river to marvel at her. It appeared nothing could make her fall.

After two weeks, Levi felt it was time to re-join Aura. He invited Julia to come with him, and she eagerly agreed. If anyone had a right to choose where they lived, it was her, and he was pleased that she chose them. The rebuilding would be long and painful, but he knew they could do it. People flooded into both sides, taking full advantage of the openness. They may even need to reconsider naming this place, Earth seemed so much bigger now than it previously had.

As people came back and forth between the two worlds, a curious thing became apparent. The time differences had ceased. Whatever magic had held the worlds separate, no longer felt the need. Levi wondered whose time would take over. Would people live longer, like in Aura's world, or pass more quickly like in his?

He hoped the former was true. He wanted to live as long as possible. He wanted to see everything this new world had to offer.

Epilogue

Ninety-Six Years Later:

The lazy afternoon sun illuminated the fall trees around him. Levi closed his eyes and let the warmth wash over his face. Fall had always been his favorite time of year and, all things being equal, he was glad to be alive to see it at least one more time.

A scream snapped him out of his happy daze. He scanned the grass below him before his eyes found the source. His great-great-granddaughter squealed with laughter as she was chased by her father and their pet eron. To each side of him, clustered in pockets around the hill, were his descendants. He couldn't quite remember exactly where he was. Esotera? San Francisco? Omaner during their beautiful, but brief, thawing period? It didn't matter. He was happy, though if he had to be perfectly honest, there was one thing that would have made it even better.

As if on cue, a flash of red even more vibrant than the leaves, caught his attention out of the corner of his eye. He looked over, afraid to hope for what it meant. There she was.

He hadn't seen his wife in almost five years—five years! It was a relief, like he'd been holding his breath this whole time and didn't even know it. Five years. Sometimes it felt like it had been an eternity. When those we love leave us, each day can feel like a hundred life-times.

Aura moved closer to him with a radiant smile on her face. She looked just like she had when they met all those years ago. Oh, to remember that meeting! Him in his apartment, her bursting in, and the adventures the next years took them on. He placed his hand on his knee and used the leverage to get up. His body had become so tired since she'd died, and the effort made him pause to catch his breath. She raised her hand out toward him, and he hoped as he reached for it that he would find it solid and warm.

A movement to his right made him hesitate for just a moment, though. He looked behind himself. He couldn't help it. There his son sat with his wife. Levi knew he was leaving the Earth in good hands. Turning back, he noticed several more people stood, as young and whole and beau-tiful as Aura in front of him.

Breaking away from Milskar, Emily ran forward and hugged him. She did not speak. There would be plenty of time for that. Kolas shook his hand, and Theirra, looking more alive in death than she ever had in life, beamed at him. As he focused, others came into view. His parents. Resbuca. Amaline. His daughter they had lost when she was very young.

With effort, he pulled his gaze away. Aura was now right in front of him. He looked at their hands, suddenly intertwined, and noticed how young and unblemished they were. Her grip was firm and filled his whole being with light. He moved forward a bit and noted that the typical aches and pains had vanished. His body was youthful and strong again.

The journey of his life played like a movie in front of him, but he paid it no attention. It was his life. He knew what happened. But at the end of it, at the end of all of it, was Aura. No matter the obstacle, whether it was worlds, or time, war, or death, they would always find one another. She was there, and he was home.

And frankly, there was no greater magic in the world, in any world, than that.

The End

About the Author

Kristin Durfee grew up outside of Philadelphia where an initial struggle with reading blossomed into a love and passion for the written word.

She has also been a writer since a very young age, writing short stories and poems, though now is focusing on longer works. She is currently working on her next novel for Young Adults.

Durfee currently resides outside of Orlando, FL, and when not enjoying the theme parks or Florida sun, she spends most of her time with her husband, son, and their quirky dogs. She is a member of the Florida Writers Association.

www.ingramcontent.com/pod-product-compliance
Lightning Source LLC
Chambersburg PA
CBHW061013120726
47910CB00006B/1912